Deer Season

...when hunters become prey

Jack A. Rogers

CEDAR HILL PUBLISHING

Deer Season ~ when hunters become prey

Copyright © 2005 Jack A. Rogers All Rights Reserved

No part of this book may be copied, duplicated, transmitted, or stored in a retrieval system by any means, electronic or mechanical, without the written permission of the copyright owner.

First Edition Spring 2005

Editing by Pat LoBrutto

Cover design by Rebecca Hayes

Formatting and book design by Rebecca Hayes

Published in the United States by
Cedar Hill Publishing
P.O. Box 905
Snowflake, Arizona 85937
www.cedarhillpublishing.com

ISBN 1-933324-09-0

Library of Congress Control Number 2005925081

Prologue

A long howl pierced the chilly late October air.
Frantically, John Pearson looked around the thick evergreen forest, gasping for breath. Blood pounded in his ears. He had been running since daybreak. He was near exhaustion. A network of ropey vines and gnarled limbs grabbed at his legs and ankles as he tried to get down a steep incline. He fell and cart-wheeled, end over end, until he slammed into a rotting stump of a fallen oak, the precious air knocked out of his lungs.
John Pearson clutched his chest and tried catching his breath. A green cathedral ceiling of pine boughs arched high over his head, obscuring a clouded sky. A six-inch gash on his thigh oozed bright crimson and smeared a dark stain through the thick fabric on his blue jeans. He winced in pain as his hands tenderly nursed the aching wound.
Another bloodcurdling cry came from atop the rise behind him.
His glassy eyes panned the forest.
He saw nothing.
He struggled just to stand upright and stumbled off with his arms stretched out in front. A tangled web of thorny undergrowth flayed at his legs and torso. The sharp needles of the evergreen forest poked and stabbed at his

face and eyes. Hundreds of bloody pinpricks and tiny scratches covered the exposed portions of his skin.

Suddenly, the forest gave way to a clearing of mixed tall grasses and brown milkweed. Dark clouds like giant ore freighters rolled straight out of Lake Superior some ten miles to the north. A light but cold mist began to fall.

An object on the horizon shimmered in the distance like a desert vision. Eventually, he recognized it as a building, a rectangular structure of some sort, slightly off to his left and toward the top of a small hill.

Immediately his spirits rose. He felt a sense of relief, if only briefly. He hadn't seen anyone since Valerie, and now she was dead. He could hardly get himself to believe what had happened to her. He could not erase the vision from his mind, his once lovely wife, her long wavy blonde hair matted with fresh blood.

He heard the distinct crackle of wood from deep in the forest. Hackles raised on the back of his neck.

They were coming.

He glanced up and measured the distance to the rectangular structure. He had no other choice than to take to the open field and hope he could reach his goal before...before they reached him.

John Pearson ran. The wound in his thigh throbbed. Misty air poured in and out of his lungs in huge gulps.

He could hear them behind him.

His eyes focused on the building, which grew larger with each of his labored strides. Suddenly he recognized its distinctive shape and dull red color. Rusted iron wheels imbedded deep in the hard clay held the thing firmly in place. It appeared to be an old, abandoned railroad caboose.

It made no sense. He wondered how it had gotten there.

The impact sent him reeling into the air, crushing his spine and snapping the vertebrae in his neck with a vicious crack. He was already dead by the time his body returned to the earth mere seconds later.

    A lone boot with the bloody stump of his foot still inside marked the spot where John Pearson landed. A cold autumn mist mingled with the blood on the boot's leather surface.

4

Chapter One

"Impatience can kill ya!"
Anonymous

    Jimmy Roland slipped his bulky arms through the narrow sleeves of a bright, neon-orange windbreaker. The flimsy grease-stained jacket bore the proud emblem of the United Auto Workers emblazoned across the back; a canary yellow circle inside a blue circle, with small human stick figures locked hand-to-hand that ran along the outside circumference, and the letters "U.A.W." in big bold, blue capital letters right smack dab in the middle.
    Jimmy was a union man
    So were his Daddy and his Granddad before him. His Granddad even claimed to be a part of the original sit down strike that started the unionization movement against General Motors back in 1937, at the old Fisher Body Plant Number One in Flint, Michigan. Granddad always bragged about how Grandma and all the other workers' wives would come over to the plant, surrounded by company bulls, and sneak food and other essentials to their striker husbands inside. Without the bravery and support of their spouses, Granddad and his brother union revolutionaries might have starved to death in their noble cause. As it was, Granddad claimed he lost almost twenty-five pounds over those forty lonely days. Knowing the feisty nature of his

Granddad, Jimmy suspected he and Grandma just might have figured out a way to get together at least once or twice for more than just a lunch or supper.

Things had changed over the past sixty-plus years, and not necessarily for the better.

Dad and Granddad died years ago. The power of the union, along with its membership, ebbed and flowed like the uncertain ocean tide over the years. The city of Flint had changed too. Once prosperous, the rusty factory town with its proud history now harbored a multitude of abandoned, boarded-up manufacturing plants and a population but two-thirds its size just thirty years before. Back in the eighties, when things were real bad and a lot of folks were losing their jobs to foreign competition, there was an old saying going around as people moved on to better places or new jobs: "Last one outa town, make sure you turn off the lights."

Jimmy Roland, however, decided to hang around and he managed to survive, somehow. With over twenty-five years of union membership, Jimmy had actually worked maybe some fifteen or sixteen years, at most, in several of the auto plants scattered around Flint. The rest of the time, he was either laid-off or on strike for the usual stuff worth striking for, mostly higher pay and more medical benefits,

His calloused fingers fumbled with a stuck zipper on his windbreaker.

"You're not wearing that jacket to work, are you?"

Brenda gave him the exasperated look reserved exclusively for her husband. They had had this conversation, if you could call it a conversation, many times before.

"Yeah. Why?" he mumbled, still stymied by the stubborn zipper.

"'Cause it's dirty. I haven't washed it in probably over a month, and you got some fresh grease stains on the front that I haven't had time to work on yet."

Still in her long flannel nightgown, she came over to him from the kitchen sink where she was cleaning up what remained of the eggs and bacon and toast left over from breakfast. She slapped his hands away from the zipper and had the thing working in three or four seconds. Her fingers were still long and slender, but the rest of her had put on twenty or thirty extra pounds since high school. She ran the zipper up to about the middle of his broad chest. A couple of oily stains showed prominently across the front, where Jimmy's jelly belly lay hidden underneath. She shook her head in disapproval.

"It's okay," he said.

"No it's not. People'll think I'm not much of a wife, letting you go off to work in dirty clothes." She took her hand and rearranged several out-of-place hairs on Jimmy's forehead. It was an act of love, one she had been doing unconsciously for almost a quarter of a century for her sloppy husband.

"It's okay," he repeated.

She sighed. Brenda had been married to Jimmy twenty-five years come next May, and she wasn't about to change the stubborn oaf in the next thirty seconds. She wore her hair in a disheveled ponytail, porcupine ends sticking out in all directions. Strands of gray spackled her head, with occasional glints of brunette and auburn; she was overdue for a visit to the beauty salon.

"Just put it in the wash when you get home from work tonight," she ordered. She placed a quick kiss on his rubbery lips. She smelled of butter and bacon grease.

"Okay."

Jimmy started walking out the back door into the garage.

"You forgot your lunch."

He stopped, turned around, and grabbed a black aluminum lunch pail from her. The lunch pail looked exactly like the dented mailbox on the street out in front of their house.

"Thanks. See ya later."

He pecked her on the side of her cheek.

"And don't forget to deposit your paycheck," she reminded him. "We got all kinds of automatic payments coming out of the checking account and there's hardly any money in there now."

"So what's new," he remarked with a wry smile. Hardly a week went by without some sort of financial crisis in their life. Jimmy's weekly paycheck always went entirely for bills, it seemed. They survived from paycheck to paycheck, like most union folks. As a result, they didn't even have a savings account at the credit union any more, except for Brenda's small Christmas Club account.

Brenda worried about that occasionally, whether or not they'd have enough money to retire on someday. They'd have to depend on a pension from General Motors at some point, along with any social security they'd get from the government. It was the same for many Midwesterners working in blue-collar towns like Flint and Lansing and Detroit.

"Well, just make sure you stop at the bank after work and deposit that check. Now go on." She gave her husband a friendly little swat across his butt as he walked out the door.

* * *

Jimmy went into the garage, closing the door and Brenda behind him. As his eyes adjusted to the darkness, all he could see were the shiny hulks of two vehicles in the shadows. His fingers fumbled against the wall as he searched for the automatic garage door button.

The doublewide garage door ascended upward, clattering and clanking all the way. The noisy door reminded him that the chain needed some fresh grease, a job he'd been putting off for some time despite Brenda's constant admonitions. Jimmy's eyes winced as the sudden sunlight emerged on the other side.

The distinct odors of oil and sawdust filled the otherwise stuffy garage. A busy array of hammers, files, screwdrivers, wrenches, saws, planes, drills, pliers, chisels, electric cords and a menagerie of other tools hung from hooks neatly anchored along the plywood-paneled walls. Several large wooden tool chests, an eight-foot band saw, and a drill press crowded the wall opposite the garage door, making little room for the parked vehicles.

Jimmy squeezed his tummy, still crowded with Brenda's eggs and bacon, through the narrow space between his pickup truck and her car. He was careful not to scratch against his wife's pride and joy, a two-year old Pontiac Grand Prix with everything on it. She'd have a cat-fit if he accidentally left the slightest mark or scratch on *her* car. He climbed into the truck and slipped the key into the ignition and the pickup purred to life. Carefully, he backed out of the garage.

Once outside, he turned off the engine and got out. "Forty-Two Degrees," he recalled the weatherman saying. Seemed a bit colder than that. He snatched a pack of Marlboro's out of his jacket pocket and lit a cigarette. Brenda didn't like, didn't allow him to smoke in the house. That included the garage. He inhaled deeply, sucking in the cigarette smoke along with a lungful of the chilly November air all at once. At least it hadn't snowed yet. He expected the first snowfall of the season anytime now. Hell, Jimmy remembered one unexpected Halloween blizzard where the snow ended up waist deep in the front yard, making it impossible for the neighborhood kids to trick-or-treat.

"Not this year," he muttered to himself. "At least, not 'til after deer season."

He sauntered over to the side of the garage on the outside of the house to check on all the "toys," as he and Brenda liked to refer to them, that he had stored there.

Two matching silver Ski-doo snowmobiles were sandwiched together behind a twenty-foot motorboat along with a John Deere riding lawn mower beside it. A faded chocolate tarpaulin covered all the junk and provided some protection from the outdoor elements as well. Parked out front on a gravel apron next to the driveway was a battered WindStar motor home, the ol' "R.V." as he called it. Jimmy had picked up the R.V. several years ago for a "song and a dance", as he liked to boast, from some poor bastard who had been permanently laid-off from the Buick plant on the east end of town. Such economic opportunities presented themselves only too often in Flint. He checked over the toys, like he did every morning, making sure, first of all, they were still there, and secondly, they hadn't been vandalized at some time during the night. In Jimmy's blue-collar part of town, one couldn't be too careful about such things.

The neighborhood harbored a number of unsupervised, light-fingered teenagers who always seemed to be getting into a fair share of trouble. Most of them were on a first name basis with local patrol officers in the city of Flint. They seemed to possess an inborn communistic attitude, which Karl Marx would have appreciated, that whatever belonged to someone else, also belonged to them. As a result, things often wound up missing from people's houses or garages all too often. The stuff sometimes ended up getting wrecked in the process or, more than likely, never returned. The objects of their larceny ranged from curiously irresistible mailboxes to unattended cars.

If it wasn't nailed down, it was at risk of being stolen.

Jimmy inspected the heavy galvanized-steel chain that ran through the axles of all the vehicles, and then wrapped several times around the trailer holding the motorboat securely in place. The objects were shackled together like the unwilling travelers on a slave ship bound for a life of hard labor in the New World. Each link, over an inch thick and forged from tempered steel, would deter the most earnest of would-be thieves. Anyway, he had enough insurance to replace any of his toys if they ever got stolen or damaged. Jimmy couldn't afford to buy any life insurance, but he couldn't afford not to buy the best homeowner's insurance policy on the block.

As he rounded the corner of the R.V., examining it for any signs of damage, he happened, quite by accident, to brush a bit to close to the neighbor's chain-link fence. Their dog, standing nearby in the yard and staying inconspicuous on purpose, let out a menacing bark. Jimmy hadn't seen it.

"Son of a bitch!" he yelled, the hairs standing on the back of his neck and his heart pumping like a diesel train engine. Once he recovered, he got mad. "Get outa here, you mangy bastard." He raised a menacing fist toward the canine.

The dog, a short-haired mutt of indeterminate breeding and weighing about forty pounds, stopped barking but held his ground a few paces inside the yard, far enough away from Jimmy to avoid any contact.

Jimmy didn't like dogs, nor did he care for those who harbored them. He and the neighbors had had their share of altercations over the years as well. Jimmy was always finding dog poop in his own front yard and didn't like it one bit. He blamed the neighbors living closest to him with dogs, whether or not they were the one's responsible for the sorry mess. He figured if it wasn't their dog that committed the dirty deed, then it had to be one of their friends. Guilt by association.

Jimmy finished his inspection of the R.V., keeping a sharp eye on his canine adversary the whole time. He puffed nervously on his Marlboro, taking in seven or eight big drags, and then flicked the smoldering butt in the direction of his growling nemesis. In a flash of sparks, it hit the animal's inky black nose dead center. The dog flinched only slightly.

Jimmy went back to the pickup truck, plopped his fat ass into the cushy fake leather seat, started the engine, placed the gearshift in reverse, and backed down the short driveway. The cozy little red brick, one-story house came into full view through the windshield. Once in the street, he turned and headed off toward Saginaw Street after first waving goodbye to Brenda, who stood in the large living-room picture window in her flannel nightgown, waving back at him.

* * *

Jimmy Roland possessed the look of someone not very anxious to go to work that day, frankly, an expression he had plastered across his face most of the time. He wore an old blue baseball cap that covered his peppered and thinning hair. The square jaw of his youth had since given way to baggy jowls, hanging along either side of his always-rosy cheeks. A brief stint, playing goaltender for his high school hockey team, resulted in two small scars on the sides of his chin.

Jimmy had on his usual work ensemble consisting of blue jeans, a flannel shirt, and a pair of faded gym shoes he had bought at the indoor mall a couple of years ago, the last time Brenda had managed to drag him shopping. For that matter, Jimmy wore the same kind of clothes on Saturdays and Sundays and on his days off, except when he went to church. If he was lucky, that meant only Easter and Christmas, unless someone died or got married. Then Brenda forced him to get dressed up in his good pair of leather shoes and brown pants. He hadn't worn a shirt with a tie since, hell, maybe since his younger brother got married ten or twelve years ago.

Jimmy drove due south on Saginaw Street while his mind wandered. Deer season occupied Jimmy's mind.

Several minutes later, Jimmy approached the stoplight at the corner of Saginaw and Bristol Road. He noticed a long line of traffic in the right-hand lane. Already late for work and increasingly nervous, Jimmy jostled in his seat, his impatience growing with every tick of the clock.

"C'mon, let's go." he yelled aloud. He drummed his fingers impatiently on the steering wheel.

After several agonizing minutes, only two cars remained in front of him; a blue Ford in the lead with a woman driving and two kids jumping around in the back seat, and a beat-up Dodge Intrepid behind her. The light turned green, but the reluctant Ford didn't budge.

"Damnit!" He leaned on the horn. The driver of the Dodge in front of him gave Jimmy a dirty look through his rearview mirror. The woman driving the Ford, however, seemed completely oblivious.

Jimmy had had enough. He jerked his steering wheel hard to the right and stepped on the gas. His pickup roared forward, spitting up bits of rocks and debris on the Dodge. He pulled up next to the Ford and stared at the startled woman, who looked up at him with big, saucer-sized eyes.

Jimmy saw a narrow gap in the oncoming traffic and floored the gas pedal, deliberately cutting the Ford off. Somehow he made it, although another car coming up directly behind him had to slow down in order to avoid rear-ending him. It honked in displeasure.

"Yeah…Yeah…." Jimmy remarked aloud again, ignoring the noisy overture. At least he was moving at the speed limit again. Feeling the heavy breakfast churn around in his suddenly upset stomach, he accepted the fact that he would be late. His blood pressure began to ease.

The driver of the Dodge Intrepid had other plans, however. He caught up to Jimmy about a half mile later, swerved in front of Jimmy, and slammed on the brakes, causing Jimmy to do the same.

"Shit!" Jimmy exclaimed, caught off guard by the near collision.

The Dodge slowed to a turtle's pace of about fifteen miles an hour.

Jimmy recognized the car right away. Although he felt an initial pang of guilt, the feeling quickly dispersed the longer he proceeded at a snail's pace against his will. Several of the cars piling up behind Jimmy began honking their horns. Jimmy followed suit. The driver of the Dodge ignored their loud entreats and eased off the gas even further, adding further insult to their misery. Finally, an opportunity presented itself. Jimmy's truck lurched into the left-hand lane and accelerated. He pulled up next to the recalcitrant Intrepid and rolled down the window on the passenger side.

"Asshole!" Jimmy yelled loud enough so most folks living along the Canadian border some sixty miles away probably could hear.

The other driver, a curly, redheaded bastard wearing a dirty Grateful Dead t-shirt, flashed a sarcastic grin and then saluted Jimmy with his middle finger raised. Jimmy ignored him, stomped on the accelerator, and left the long line of traffic in his rearview mirror in the dust. His belly ached.

* * *

The swirling red, white, and blue emergency lights on sheriff Ollie Svenson's big Buick cruiser and the other three other police cars lit up the narrow dirt road like a carnival midway. It was a dark, cloudy morning just a little after daybreak and the sheriff could barely see one of his deputies standing next to a blue Ford sedan almost completely hidden by a clump of evergreen bushes and parked off the side of the roadway. The deputy was talking to a couple of Michigan State Troopers dressed in their traditional crisp blue and gold uniforms. The sheriff opened the door to the cruiser and got out. He left the engine running and went over toward the small congregation of police officers.

"Morning, sheriff." Don Walker, one of the troopers, tipped the black leather brim on his cap with his left hand as the sheriff approached.

"Yah. Good mornin' to you too, Officer Valker." The sheriff spoke with a slight Norwegian accent, one still common to many residents living in the small towns and villages located in the Upper Peninsula of Michigan. His cheeks seemed rosier than usual. A thick frost covered most of the vegetation in the area with a milky-white coating of icy crystals.

"How's things been in the big city of Newberry, Ollie?"

"Oh…things been pretty quiet…as usual," the sheriff replied. "Not much happens in town. Most days is just like the one before. We like it that way, for sure. Folks in these parts are generally law abiding…most of the time. Better than a buncha murders like they get down in Detroit. We mostly get some drunks and speeders every now and then. That's about it."

Trooper Walker nodded and smiled. "Sheriff, this is trooper Grant Stevens." The two men shook hands across from one another. "Trooper Stevens is normally assigned to the far Western half of the U.P., but he wasn't far from this area on patrol when we got the call from your Deputy."

"A good day to you too, Trooper Stevens."

"My pleasure," Trooper Stevens replied.

The sheriff was dressed in his usual uniform, consisting of a pair of scuffed brown shoes with brown pants, a brown shirt and a brown winter jacket, which he wore completely unzipped despite a definite chill in the air. He had a slight potbelly, which made him feel self-conscious around the state troopers. Perched on the top of his head was a brown Smoky the Bear hat with a shiny silver badge pinned on the front that officially proclaimed him as, "Sheriff, Luce County, Michigan."

He glanced over at the blue Ford sedan and then turned his attention to his deputy who had been silent since his arrival. "Freddy, why doncha you tell me where you found the body."

Freddy Haizer, a young buck deputy, just a couple of years out of high school, looked nervous. Up until that morning, the most serious crime he had ever been involved in was a domestic dispute between Bobby Hays and his wife Clara over on the east side of Newberry. Ol' Bobby had gotten tanked up one evening over at the Mindy's Place, a local watering hole just off the main highway. Apparently, Bobby was getting a little too frisky with another woman patron when Clara walked in unexpectedly. Pretty soon a fight broke out between the three of them. The bartender called the sheriff's office and Freddy Haizer showed up eventually to break up the altercation. As it turned out, Bobby Hays ended up the only casualty of the day with a six inch gash on his forehead complements of Clara, who ended up hitting her cheating husband with an empty beer bottle.

Freddy swallowed and started telling his story. "Well, sheriff, like I was telling the troopers here, I was just out patrolling highway 83 about seven o'clock this morning when, all of a sudden, a goddamn deer comes out running from the woods and slams into my patrol car."

"No need to use profanity, son." Sheriff Svenson gave his young deputy a stern look. The two older, more experienced troopers found it difficult not to smile.

The deputy continued. "Yes, sir. Anyway, I hear this big old clunk, so I immediately stop the car to see what's going on. The deer, in the meantime, runs up this here dirt road. So I'm thinking I hit the thing pretty hard and it may be injured. I park my cruiser and go looking for it. About twenty or so feet up the road, I find the wrecked Ford over there with nobody in it, windows all knocked out, just like you see it now. I kind of remembered we got a notice three or four weeks ago back in the office to be on the lookout for a missing couple driving a blue Ford sedan. So I decide to investigate."

Freddy shifted the weight on his lanky frame from one leg to the other. "First, I looked things over...don't see very much on the outside of the vehicle. Then I go in the car and manage to open the glove box and pull out the registration. Says the vehicle belongs to a John and Valerie Pearson down in Kalamazoo somewhere. I didn't recognize their names right off the bat as that missing couple but, sure enough, turns out to be their car. Anyway, there ain't nothing else in the car so I check around the outside in case there's somebody hurt nearby. That's when I found her purse...and some clothing...and then the bones."

"We're pretty sure they're human," Trooper Walker chimed in. "State D.C.I. will do some tests to determine for sure after we're done here at the scene. Can't really tell what she might of died of...assuming the remains are actually her's and not someone else's."

"Inside the purse, I found the usual kind of stuff you find in a woman's purse, including money and a wallet with all sorts of identification," deputy Haizer added. "Here's her driver's license." He handed the thick, plastic-coated I.D. card over to sheriff Svenson.

The sheriff took the card in his calloused fingers and examined the photograph of a middle-aged, blonde woman, staring straight into the camera lens with a blank expression on her otherwise attractive face. Besides containing such information as the woman's height, weight, social security number, and date of birth, the license further indicated her name, Valerie S. Pearson, and a Kalamazoo, Michigan home street address. Unconsciously, he nodded without saying a word.

He handed the license back to his deputy and walked over to the Ford. "What in tarnation do you think happened to the car?" The sheriff asked.

"Beats the hell out of us," Trooper Walker chimed in. "All the windows are busted out...there's a dent on every square inch on the exterior...looks like the damn thing's been through one hell of a hail storm or someone took a sledge hammer and pounded the shit out of it."

Sheriff Svenson considered objecting to Trooper Walker's course language, but then thought otherwise. "Where'd you find the body, Freddy?"

The deputy shifted back to his other leg. "About a hundred yards west of here, just up the path that-a-ways." He nodded in the direction where the dirt road narrowed down in width and disappeared into a clump of sumac trees on either side. "The troopers got the place marked off. But like I said, there ain't much of a body left…other than a pile of bones and a bunch of ripped up clothing. Looks like she must've died a couple of weeks ago, at least. The critters got to her bad, ate most of her up over the past couple of weeks probably. No telling how she really died."

The sheriff's nose crinkled up at the unpleasant image of scavengers eating on the dead body of the woman. He headed up the dirt road without saying more. Deputy Haizer stepped lively to catch up to the sheriff while the troopers stayed behind.

"See you later sheriff," Trooper Walker said. "We'll make some calls and make sure the boys from D.C.I. get notified."

"Suit yourself," the sheriff said, not bothering to glance back at them. He had been down over in Escanaba, visiting his mother in the Lutheran nursing home, when he got Freddy's call. As a result, his deputy and the state patrol had completed most of the work that needed to be done on the case.

When they got out of earshot of the troopers, sheriff Svenson let his deputy get right next to him. "Don't like them troopers nosing 'round my county much," he remarked in a low voice so that only Freddy could hear him.

"Yes, sir. I knew you wouldn't," Freddy said just trying to keep pace with the sheriff's big strides. "I didn't have much choice though…you being out of town and all."

"That's okay, Freddy. No use thinking it's your fault; I know you better than that. I just don't like outsiders stickin' their noses in my business, that's all." His cheeks flushed with the remark. "Did you see any signs of the husband, Freddy…Mr. Pearson?"

"No, sheriff, we didn't find nothing else. The troopers sorta think the husband may have killed his wife and left her body and then run off. They was going to issue an A.P.B. for him later this morning after their investigation."

Sheriff Svenson considered his deputy's analysis. "Funny he'd leave the car that way, abandoned and all tore up," he said. "I wonder how he planned getting out of these woods without having a car of some sort? And why not take her money with him?"

Freddy shrugged his shoulders. "Guess they didn't think of that."

The two men stopped at a grassy knoll cordoned off by a waist-high ribbon of bright yellow tape tied to some stakes hastily driven into the ground. The two men stepped over the boundary.

"I found the purse first…right about here," Freddy said. "Thinking something may be wrong, I decided to look around. I found the remains just over there." He pointed to another spot marked by a slender stake painted bright, neon orange.

The sheriff was already headed in that direction. When he arrived at the spot, he went down on his haunches and removed his Smoky the Bear hat off the top of his head. He held circular brim by the outer edges, passing it through his fingers like the steering wheel of an automobile, as he studied the site.

Bones were scattered about the area: a partial ribcage, thighbones and femurs, and the massive pelvis. The rest of the skeleton, along with the skull, was spread over an area roughly six by nine feet.

"No sign of the other body, huh?"

"Nope. This is all we found," Freddy answered. "You think maybe someone other than her husband killed her, sheriff?"

Sheriff Svenson picked up several of the nearby bones and carefully examined them. Each one of them had a number of indentations and scratches evident on their surface.

"I'm not so sure of that, Freddy. See these marks here on the bones?"

Freddy bent over to take a look. "Sure, sheriff. I told you the critters around here made pretty short work of the body. All the bones have teeth marks like that, all over 'em. She must've died or been killed, the body left here, and the remains got eaten up by scavengers."

"Yah, for sure, Freddy…that's possible," Ollie said. "But maybe whatever caused them marks is what killed her in the first place."

Freddy's eyes grew the size of saucers. "You mean like a bear…or something like that?"

The sheriff's fingers ran over the polished surface on one of the bones. A horrible and familiar memory emerged in his mind. He then put a specimen from the pile safely in the inside pocket of his jacket and replaced the rest of the bones back where he found them.

"Yah, Freddy…something like a bear." He stood up and looked off into the surrounding forest. "Well, let's see if we can figure out what happened to this lady's husband if we can."

The young deputy noticed his mentor slip the bone fragment into his pocket. He had always been taught never to disturb a crime scene. He wondered what the sheriff was doing, taking one of the bones with him, but decided to keep quiet for the time being.

Chapter Two

*Oh, you can't scare me, I'm sticking to the union,
I'm sticking to the union, I'm sticking to the union.
Oh, you can't scare me, I'm sticking to the union,
I'm sticking to the union 'til the day I die.*
The Union Maid – Woody Guthrie

The plant clock read 8:22 as Jimmy punched his time card for the regular day shift. He placed it in a metal slot right above his name on a wall with several hundred other identical slots and names. He'd probably hear from Pete Davis, his line foreman, sometime during the day. This made it the fourth time since the first of October he clocked in late. Maybe Barney Noble could smooth things over before some disciplinary action took place. That's one of the things union stewards were supposed to do.

He synchronized the time on the plant clock with the Detroit Lions logo wristwatch won at a union meeting raffle last football season. His watch showed 8:20.

"Be just like management to screw us and set the time clock fast," he grumbled.

He grabbed his lunch pail and sauntered over to a Coke machine and deposited three quarters. The familiar red and silver can tumbled out the bottom. He pulled the tab and took a couple of swallows before heading down the line, can in hand. He belched loudly several times.

It took Jimmy almost five minutes to cover the entire distance on foot through the massive General Motors V-8 Engine Plant. On his way, he encountered several other assembly lines, some of them manned by actual human beings; most automated by clever robotic machinery, performing a variety of mundane work functions. Machines easily outnumbered humans in the concrete and metal environment.

Clatter, thump, boom.
Clatter, thump, boom.

He passed a massive forge, puking out engine block after identical engine block onto a greasy conveyor belt. Another machine, with awesome steel lobster claws, reached in and grabbed the contents, welded something to the undersides with sparks flying, then released them back onto the conveyor belt.

Clatter, thump, boom.
Clatter, thump, boom.

Gradually, the monotonous sound subsided as he traveled, only to be replaced by some other loud noise produced by another manufacturing process.

In the dusty memories of his mind, Jimmy recalled his first impressions on the line over twenty-five years ago, as a new union employee fresh out of high school. The constant din of metal-pounding-on-metal terrified him those first several weeks. He was scared shitless. Dante could not have envisioned a more hellish inferno.

In those days, the old timers enjoyed referring to new guys on the line as "bugs," because they'd walk around with big wide eyes and flinch at the slightest provocation. Often the old guys would toy with the new bloods by giving them frivolous assignments close to dangerous conditions, just to see how they'd react under the pressure. On more than one occasion, a "bug" quit the job right there on the spot. Some of them even peed in their pants. The old timers laughed at those stories for years afterwards.

Jimmy did neither, but that doesn't mean he wasn't scared. He just got used to the inhospitable conditions faster than some others. What choice did he have? He'd been bred for this kind of life. Jimmy's vocational compass pointed in only one stubborn direction, and he could do nothing to bend the course.

Jimmy's plant manufactured V-8 engines and various components used in a variety of cars General Motors produced. Five lines ran sixteen hours a day, six days a week, and two shifts a day. On Sundays, they didn't make engines. Instead, the assembly machines received the required regular maintenance from a reduced staff. Much like worker ants serving their queens, they attended to the machine's every need. The goal was the same; increased production, survival of the colony.

A quality inspector on the fuel injector line, Jimmy had earned the position for only one reason, seniority. Seniority had long ago replaced hard work and energy as a means of improving one's job. All the good line positions, the high paying ones, went to the workers with the most seniority. The fact that you might be young or ambitious or willing to work your tail off meant nothing. You had to wait your turn. You had to let the system bludgeon that eagerness out of you and allow yourself to become old and set in your ways and, of course, dependant on the Union which encouraged such a lame-brained system.

Jimmy's work day was far more interesting and varied than the typical line job of doing one routine, boring, operation over and over and over again, day in and day out, month after month, year after year. As quality inspector, he checked the entire process to insure the fuel injection components coming off the line had been assembled properly and had half a chance of working once added to the entire engine assembly. His very first job fresh out of Roosevelt High School, at the massive old Buick complex east of town now lying idle, involved painting the numbers on odometers, a task now automated and performed by mindless robots. For sixteen months, he labored eight to ten hours a day, doing one simple, mind-numbing task; a great assignment designed to damper the spirit and enthusiasm of a new, young employee.

A concert of greetings and good-natured ribbings from his fellow compatriots and union members for his usual lateness followed Jimmy down the line. Eighteen workers, including five women, manned the final fuel injector assembly station, working first shift. Tight knit, the group suffered little turnover, the jobs being highly sought after because of favorable working conditions. The line was fairly quiet and there wasn't much dust and dirt that seemed a natural and ever-present part of the assembly process. Most of them had twenty or more years of service with the company and either knew someone in management or had a friend in the union with some pull.

Jimmy cleared over sixty grand a year and made an easy ten or twenty thousand more when overtime became available. G.M didn't like hiring part-time workers, preferring to work the dickens out of the available staff when demand required extra work. The guys and gals on the line benefited the most from this policy, by making lots of money, while local union officials recognized the policy for what it really was, a means of controlling and dampening future union membership growth. General Motors was winning the bloody war. In 1978, seven big facilities in Flint employed over seventy-seven thousand workers; only some twenty-five thousand or so remained. Jimmy never thought of himself as being among a dying breed.

He hung his union baseball cap along with the bright orange windbreaker in a half-locker located on the west wall of the plant, right next to a lunch break area that was about the size of a small children's outdoor playground and littered with a dozen or so empty aluminum picnic tables.

He put Brenda's lunch pail in the locker, grabbed his heavy leather tool belt, and placed it around his chubby waist so it kind of hung somewhere halfway between his love handles and his buttocks. His hand ruffled through his itchy scalp as he closed the door and reset the combination lock with a twist of the tumbler dial to the left.

" Jimmy!" Barney Noble, the union steward, slapped him on the back before he had a chance to even turn around. Barney worked over on the next line, but as a local union representative, he spent time with the workers at several assigned stations. "We found some problem units second shift screwed up last night you need to check out. There's a buncha them waiting for you."

"Sure," Jimmy said.

"Hey, didja see that Red Wings game last night? Went into overtime and Detroit managed to score a goal about five minutes into it. Kicked ass man."

"Yeah," Jimmy replied while taking a sip from his Coke. "I was channel surfing back and forth between them and the football game, but I managed to catch the ending. Maybe the Wings will finally make another run for the Cup."

"Fat chance with Colorado playing like it is."

They both grimaced about Detroit's chances to win the elusive Stanley Cup again, professional hockey's most treasured prize. The Wings had dashed the hopes of its hungry fans in past years when they had been predicted to win.

"Say Barnsie. Do me a favor, will ya?

"Yeah…sure Jimmy. What?"

"I punched in late a couple of times this month, and…. well, you know. Pete'll have a conniption as usual. He may even want to write me up or something." The line foreman, Pete Davis, got bent out of shape when employees came in late. Enough written warnings in your personnel file could get you time off with no pay, even lose your job if the problem didn't get fixed.

"Okay, Jimmy. Let me see what I can do." Barney started to walk away when he remembered something. "By the way, today's your last day right? Vacation next week?"

Jimmy flashed a long, toothy grin. "That's right. Eight o'clock tomorrow morning, me and the boys are outa here. Deer hunting season."

"You and half the goddamn plant." Barney grimaced.

No other holiday or event, not Christmas or Easter, not even the Forth of July, had the disastrous effect on autoworker productivity in the state of Michigan as the first several weeks of deer hunting season. In past years, some car manufactures were forced to close down whole assembly lines because of the popularity of deer hunting. Motels and campgrounds in small upstate towns and villages filled to capacity during the annual shooting extravaganza. An economic boom, of sorts, occurred each year in those treasured locations lucky enough to attract their share of the annual hunter migration. The crazed hunters spent inordinate amounts of money on food, bullets, and booze…and women. Hookers from as far away as Chicago and Cleveland traveled to northern Michigan for the opportunity to rake in scads of money, plying their way from room to room, trailer to trailer. An ambitious girl, regardless of her looks, could make several thousand dollars in one night, catering to the lonesome needs of their antler-driven clientele.

In terms of carnage, both deer and hunters incurred significant depletion of their ranks by the time the season ended. Several hundred thousand deer would meet their maker, often carrying several loads of misaimed buckshot, until eventually succumbing to their wounds and slowly bleeding to death. Scores of hunters experienced a similar accidental fate, either getting shot by a drunken companion, or suffering a fatal myocardial infarction due to the unaccustomed exercise or excessive alcoholic consumption. Now and then, a hunter would freeze to death; often their fates and bodies would not be discovered until the following spring thaw, unless some other furry woodland creature happened upon them and ate the remains.

For all the effort and expense, the state's food supply during the late fall season became awash in deer meat, deer sausage, deer jerky, and other questionable deer by-products. Meat lockers and processors made a mint, cutting up the deer remnants into edible sized portions for storage or transportation back home to the family. The residential refrigerators and freezers of the successful hunter were often stuffed with several hundred pounds of deer carcass for several months, much to the chagrin of the hunter's wives who quite typically despised the taste of the gamy animal to begin with, didn't know how to cook it properly, and would never allow a single chunk of the meat to cross the lips of any child under the age of eighteen. After all, no decent mother would allow her offspring to eat parts of Bambi or his mother.

Despite such minor inconveniences, deer hunting represented a right of male passage of sorts, and a chance to commune with your fellow, knuckle-dragging Homo sapiens. The season provided the opportunity to enjoy a full week of endless gambling and card playing, conducted in musty campers and cheap hotel rooms, filled with the thick smoke of cheap cigars, with nary a spouse in sight to remind a poor fellow he needed to change his underwear.

Quite simply, deer hunting provided the greatest single excuse for a weeklong, knockdown, drag-out, male-bonding, drunken, outdoors extravaganza.

The perfect male vacation.

Jimmy's grin never left his face. "Yeah, got the ol' WindStar ready last night. Packed up a bunch of food and beer and getting my guns and clothes ready tonight."

"Where ya headed?"

"Going up to the U.P. First time up there. Around Grayling's where we usually hunted last couple of seasons. One of the guys heard about a place where they put some corn out in late summer, early fall. Tends to attract the deer and keep 'em in one place. Hear you can get a lot more deer up around Superior."

"Who's all going with ya?"

"There's four of us going; me, Tony Gianinni," Jimmy nodded in the direction of a tall, skinny coworker on the line with his back to them, "Tom Karrski over at the Platform Plant, and my brother from Port Huron, Sam."

"The Dago and the Polock's going with you, huh? Haven't seen the meathead in ages, since he transferred over there…what…two, three years ago?"

"Yeah, he's doing pretty good. Had an operation on his ticker a couple of months ago, one of them balloon jobs. I guess he's okay; his doctor said he could go."

Barney Noble didn't hunt or fish or do much of anything outdoors, a rarity in union ranks. He enjoyed an entirely different kind of quarry, the female kind. He had a reputation for being a "ladies man" and was always hitting on the females who worked on the line. Actually, deer season thinned the ranks of the male population in the plant for a while, making for less competition. As far as he was concerned, that made his chances all the better.

"Well, you fellas have a good time. Don't be gettin' shot accidentally now."

"Will do."

Barney headed over toward Denise Williams, a forty-something year old woman who consistently wore jeans several sizes too small, working about fifty yards further up the line. She'd been the latest target of his advances. Jimmy walked over to Tony Gianinni.

"Hey, you skinny son-of-a-bitch."

Tony Gianinni spun around and removed a pair of thick safety glasses everyone in the plant was required to wear. He was dark, swarthy looking, and wearing a big old pair of brown, steel pointed safety shoes that anchored him to the floor. The heavy shoes seemed to be all that kept his one hundred and thirty-two pound, six-foot, one-inch frame from flying off the earth into orbit. The combination of the two men standing next to one another resembled Laurel and Hardy.

"Jimmy! Glad to see you could finally make it into work today. The old lady keeping you up too late at night?"

They had been friends since high school. Even then, Jimmy had always outweighed his Italian compadre by fifty or more pounds, despite Tony's five-inch advantage in height. Tony even served as best man at Jimmy's wedding some twenty-plus years ago, although he had never married himself. He was the confirmed bachelor of the group and seemed to prefer living in a small trailer on the north side of town in quiet seclusion. This despite the fact he came from a large Italian Catholic family with many brothers and sisters and aunts and uncles and cousins living nearby. He had the reputation for being a loner, although when it came to fishing or hunting, he was Jimmy's best friend and eager companion.

"God damn slow traffic…made me late again," Jimmy remarked.

"So's the R.V. ready to go?"

"Bet your ass. Stocked with about ten cases of ice cold brew and a couple of fifths of Jack Daniels too."

Tony held up his hand and Jimmy gave it a meaty slap.

"Heard we might expect some snow up there sometime over the weekend," Tony said, stuffing his shirttail back into the narrow waistband of his pants.

Jimmy frowned. "Hope not, but that's exactly why I want to get on the road early. My brother's coming over from Port Huron first thing tomorrow morning. If we get started by eight or nine o'clock, we can be up in the U.P. by mid-afternoon, if we're lucky."

The plan called for them to stay nights in a small, woodsy motel located smack dab in the middle of Luce County, reputed to have the highest population of deer in the state of Michigan. During the daylight hours, Jimmy's old WindStar mobile home would transport them around the county, carrying their food and booze and ammo, in addition to providing them with temporary shelter while they were out hunting. Four men could hardly fit inside with all the stuff, but when it turned cold or the weather got bad outside, it was a comfortable place to be.

"Don't forget your goddamn huntin' license this time," Jimmy ordered. Tony forgot to bring his last year and ended up not being able to hunt the entire trip. In the upside down world of male-only deer hunters, one could commit no greater blunder.

"Yeah, yeah." Tony shook his head.

"I'd better get started working," Jimmy said, downing the last sweet drops of Coke and then throwing the can, basketball style, into a fifty-five gallon drum barrel half-filled with trash.

"See you later Jimmy."

Tony readjusted a pair of plastic safety goggles on his nose and returned to using a compressed air hose to clean various component parts prior to them being inserted into the injector housing. Jimmy headed over to the inspection area. The injector line, resembling the flexible metal track on an army tank, only much longer, moved along beside Jimmy at about the same speed of his leisurely stride. The line had started moving at exactly 8:15 that morning and wouldn't stop its relentless movement until 10:30 that night, barring an unanticipated emergency or accident. A deep, constant drone of heavy machinery and generators permeated the air, making the whole place seem as if it had been swallowed into the restless belly of some gigantic creature. The human parasites who worked on the line labored on, completely oblivious to their plight.

Fifty or sixty disassembled injector assemblies waited for Jimmy, stacked in a careless pile on two huge tables made of tempered steel, each over ten feet in length and weighing over two hundred pounds apiece.

"Shit!" Jimmy muttered upon his arrival, seeing the mess. Second shift had screwed him again. Every day this week, they had left him a pile of assemblies, which meant not only conducting the time-consuming inspection itself, but also writing up all the required paperwork that went along with the task.

He loosened the tool belt surrounding his swollen waist and tossed it with careless disregard on one of the tables. A Phillips screwdriver came spilling out, rolled off the table, and fell through a crack in the metal grate floor. Jimmy had lost a lot of tools that way over the years.

"Damn," he remarked, peering down into the unfathomable hole. "Gonna be one of them mornings,"

* * *

Jonathan Briggs, a somewhat nerdy meteorologist working for the national weather service in Traverse City, Michigan, reviewed the nine o'clock barometric and satellite readings streaming off the fax machine from the national office. Recent data indicated an intensifying low-pressure area near southwestern Manitoba province in Canada along with a change in the jet stream over the northern U.S. plain states. Those guys down in Atlanta were pretty prompt in passing on such information to the local offices.

He took a sip of decaffeinated coffee from a cup that had the face and shape of a cross-eyed Daffy Duck, a birthday present his six-year-old son had given him last July. Several of his son's kindergarten crayon artworks hung from the walls of his work cubicle. Mrs. Briggs insisted that Jonathan only drink decaf because of some trendy magazine article, describing the health horrors of regular coffee consumption. Jonathan was one of those rare husbands who never contravened his wife, the same way he had never disobeyed his mommy when he was much younger. The term, "henpecked," best described Jonathan Briggs.

He placed the cup down on a map of North America, inadvertently covering up the states of Maine, Vermont, and New Hampshire, along with a fair share of the North Atlantic Ocean in the process. He poured over the new information, slack-jawed, like a numbskull plumber who had just put the wrong fitting onto a pipe.

"Hey, Darrell! Come over here and take a look at this," he yelled to his fellow companion, sitting over in the next-door neighbor cubicle.

Darrell minimized the card game he was playing on his computer screen, so that he could finish it later, and went over to Jonathan's desk.

"What you got?"

"Look at this."

Jonathan handed him a series of pressure, wind, and temperature maps taken in sequence over the past twelve hours.

"Humph." Darrell ruffled through the papers a second time.

Jonathan grabbed Daffy and took a sip out of the duck's open cranium. "Looks like we may have a storm brewing up North."

Darrell's mouth twisted like a piece of licorice, while mulling over the prospect. "Lotta deer hunters headed up this way. A little bit of snow will make it easier to track the buggers."

"What's say we update the forecast? Say…one, two inches here 'round Traverse City. Two to four in the U.P."

"Yeah, that'd work."

Jonathan continued. "Low pressure should track a little south of Lake Superior…maybe sometime tomorrow afternoon…and then be out of the area by early evening."

"Well you better update all the forecasts. We got a doozie of a weekend coming up with lots of folks from downstate hitting the highways. Let's get the word out early as we can, before a hundred thousand deer hunters start driving on a bunch of slick roads and end up in every ditch along the expressway from here down to Detroit. Give 'em some time to get either chains or snow tires put on their vans, R.V.'s, and pickup trucks."

"I'll issue a snow advisory bulletin beginning at seven tomorrow morning, so all the local T.V. and radio stations can start broadcasting."

"That should work," Darrell said.

"Most of them hunters are used to a little snow. Shouldn't be a big problem, even though it's the first of the season," Jonathan replied with absolute certainty, based upon all his formidable meteorological and prognostication skills. He sipped a little more coffee from Daffy's brain while Darrell went back to playing his card game on his computer.

* * *

A magnifying glass revealed a number of serrated scrapings and distinctive punctures along the bone presumably belonging to the late Mrs. Valerie Pearson. Sheriff Svenson compared the specimen to several other bone fragments he kept safely locked away in his center desk drawer in his office back in Newberry.

They all contained the identical marks to one another.

The sheriff sat back in his chair and considered the ramifications of his discovery.

Scattered on the desktop in front of him, besides the various bone specimens, were a raft of newspaper clippings and articles. The edges on some of the newspapers had turned yellow and brittle with age. Some of the more recent articles contained stories about unsolved cases and reports about people who had mysteriously disappeared while living or vacationing in the Upper Peninsula of Michigan.

Over the past twenty-five years, since the sheriff began keeping personal statistics on the subject, over fifty cases involving missing persons remained unsolved. And although the number of cases seemed large at first blush, he thought an equal number of individuals are probably reported lost in just one month in most major metropolitan areas of the country.

Still, sheriff Svenson had a feeling.

The telephone rang.

Ollie picked up the receiver. "Sheriff's office. Ollie Svenson speaking." His Norwegian accent curled around his last name as he spoke.

The sheriff half expected to hear the squeaky little voice of his roly-poly wife on the other end. She usually called him around lunchtime everyday if for no other reason just to talk with him. Instead, it was Michigan State Trooper Don Walker. He informed the sheriff that preliminary autopsy results performed by State D.C.I. indicated the remains his deputy had found that morning in fact belonged to Valerie Pearson, as they had all suspected. An exact cause of death could not be determined because of the poor condition of the few remains found. Some kind of severe trauma, however, leading to her death was a definite possibility. The missing husband, John Pearson, would remain a prime suspect whom state police authorities would like to question. As a result, an All Points Bulletin had been issued in regard to his whereabouts.

"Thank you for the information, Officer Valker," the sheriff said.

The trooper went on to inform sheriff Svenson that since the Pearsons' were from downstate Michigan and the husband was now missing, the entire matter fell under the jurisdiction of the State Patrol. Although the sheriff's assistance and that of his deputy was appreciated in discovering the remains of Mrs. Pearson, their continued role in the investigation would no longer be required on a regular basis. Trooper Walker waited several seconds for the sheriff to respond.

The sheriff's lips twisted together in disgust. Finally, he said, "Thanks again for the results, Officer Valker. I'd appreciate any update in the case that comes up."

The trooper gave his assurance to Ollie that he would.

The sheriff hung up the phone and went back to examining the bones with the magnifying glass.

"Son of a bitch," he muttered under his breath. He pronounced each word clearly and slowly. Sheriff Ollie Svenson rarely resorted to the use of profanity.

* * *

Ten o'clock, although not an official time for a scheduled break, turned out to be one on the fuel injector line. Theoretically, breaks were not allowed on any assembly line. The relentless manufacturing process was non-stop for sixteen hours a day, requiring constant work to be performed. The line stopped only for emergencies, such as an equipment failure, or for some careless, unfortunate human being who might have gotten himself snared into the gears of a man-eating machine and was in the process of being torn to shreds. Any person could stop the line if they perceived a dangerous condition of any sort by pushing one of the large, bright red buttons located about every ten yards along the half-mile automated line. The "Safety Buttons" looked just like the red and white circular targets found on a rifle range. Most automobile assembly lines in the United States worked in similar fashion.

It used to be quite common for production to come to a complete stop many times during the day, particularly in earlier years, when the union possessed much more power. Line stoppages were often used as a way to get back at the company or to sabotage heavy production schedules. Back then, a disgruntled worker might decide to stop the line, and hence halt the production of an entire plant facility, just because he needed to take a long crap and didn't want work piling up while he sat on the can reading the Detroit News sports section.

Line stoppages had dropped substantially over the years, except around contract negotiations between the company and the union. Then the incidents of line stoppages increased, as critical deadlines approached. These stoppages were, of course, due to the increased safety concerns of the union workers, at least that was the "official" reason reported to management. Despite the loss of tens of thousands of union jobs and the influx of European and Asian automakers into the United States, some union members continued to fight their decades-old losing cause in much the same way they had thirty or forty years earlier. Such lame-brained tactics might have worked back then.

Jimmy finished up working on one of the fuel injector assemblies left over from the second shift, documented the problem on the appropriate company forms, and then sent the unit down the line for final assembly. He had made a fair dent in the size of the pile, but there were at least twenty-five others he hadn't even touched. He noticed several of his coworkers gathering around one of the picnic tables for a mid-morning break.

"Hey Roland! C'mon over." One of them yelled. "Lyle and 'The Chief' are watching the line."

Since the line did not stop and production continued, at least two people stayed working on the line, just to make sure that nobody got into any trouble. They all took turns during the week, so that their friends could take a morning and an afternoon break. Jimmy usually took Wednesdays.

He put a generous dab of some company-provided, vile-smelling cleaning lotion on his filthy hands, rubbed the stuff through his fingers, and wiped the greasy residue on a tattered towel he had liberated from a local bowling alley. He grabbed an old porcelain coffee mug from under one of the tables and went over to the communal coffee pot. The chocolate colored liquid tasted strong and scalding hot. Jimmy threw down a couple of swallows without a flinch. He had long ago burned out his taste buds; the boiling hot brew now seemed normal to him.

An open box of glazed and chocolate-covered donuts, rested on the picnic table, free for the taking. Jimmy grabbed one and popped the whole thing in his mouth, his cheeks expanding like a squirrel gathering autumn nuts.

Denise Williams, sucking on the end of a Newport cigarette, watched him gobble the donut with disgust. "You pig!" she remarked loudly on purpose, so all the others gathered around the table would hear her. A couple of them chuckled.

Jimmy grabbed his crotch and gave his privates a good, hard tug. "I got your breakfast right here, Lips. Right here." Several of them laughed aloud at his crude gesture.

"Sorry," Denise retorted with a coy grin. A plume of cigarette smoke coursed out her nostrils. "I was hoping more for a Big Mac."

"Well then you're in for a big surprise. I ordered you up a Whopper instead."

A chorus of hoots and howls went up around the picnic table. The group thrived on this kind of friendly but crude banter.

"You tell her, Rodman." Someone said.

A lot of the guys on the line called Jimmy, "The Rodman." Most everyone who worked in the plant had some sort of nickname. "Bones," "Shorty," "Chief," "Mousey." All of them worked on the injector line. Usually, a nickname given to someone had something to do with a distinguishing, always unflattering, physical characteristic or flaw. Some nicknames were kinder than others, some downright cruel.

Everyone on the line referred to Denise Williams as "Lips." Denise fancied dressing up most of the time like a country singer who wore a pair of blue jeans two sizes smaller than they should be. She also had a penchant for wearing shirts or blouses that left a lot of cleavage hanging out. Hans Groeters nicknamed "the dumb Croat," once looked a her and said, "Them jeans are so tight, they must be rubbing her pussy lips raw." He spoke with a slight eastern European accent that made it sound all the funnier. The moniker stuck, "Pussy Lips." Out of some crazy, male chauvinistic respect for Denise's feelings, however, the boys shortened it to just, "Lips," at least when she got within earshot.

Jimmy received the nickname, "The Rodman", under similar circumstances. Up until the late eighties, the company provided large locker room areas for the workers along with communal showers in several of the plants. One day, while Jimmy was taking a shower, someone noticed his uncircumcised penis. "Jesus, take a look a Jimmy's cock. Surprised you don't ever trip over the end of that rod, man." The guys liked it, even though Jimmy never did; it embarrassed him. That made it all the better as far as all his fellow comrades were concerned. The more a name bothered someone, the longer it hung around.

Things could have been worse for Jimmy, though. Poor Hank Eversman, better known as "Shorty," worked second shift. He too bore a nickname based on the size of his privates.

This process of cruel teasing had the disguised purpose of leveling the playing field. Everyone who worked in the plant, no matter what their social or economic status, got treated with the same mutual disdain and disrespect as anyone else. Whether you were a general foreman in charge of an entire assembly line or a brand new "bug" sweeping up floors, you got treated the same. The union pounded that concept into your thick skull from the time of your initiation, for as long as you worked on the line. You might be rich; you might think you were good looking; but none of those things mattered inside the plant.

You had to be there, just like everyone else, "workin' for the man."

As Tony Gianinni liked to say, summing the whole thing up with his own homespun Dago philosophy; "Their shit don't smell any better than mine."

Jimmy chewed on his mouthful of donut and then swallowed the gooey gob in one big knot. An unusually quiet group huddled around the picnic table that morning.

"Anybody bring the newspaper today?" he asked.

"I think it's in the crapper," Frank Simmons answered, knowing full well he had left it in there five minutes earlier.

"Thanks, Frank." Jimmy said.

"You're welcome."

Frank Simmons bordered on being a smart ass most of the time. No one liked him very much, but he had over thirty years seniority and a brother-in-law at union headquarters down in Detroit. As a result, he'd probably retire before he would ever consider leaving the injector line. As much of a democracy they liked to think they had, the people working on the line had very little say or choice about who got to work with them.

Besides Frank, Lips, and Jimmy, there were several others sitting at the table: Tony Gianinni, of course, who always took his breaks with Jimmy; Bobby Ray Lauder, a redneck hillbilly transplanted from Kentucky; and two black guys who performed all the maintenance on the line, Moses Freemont and Elroy Stevenson. Moses led a small congregation of Christian evangelists on Sunday mornings, earning him the title of "The Preacher." Of course, Jimmy and Tony always sat next to one another. At times, they were as inseparable as twin brothers.

Jimmy opened a new pack of Marlboro's, took one cigarette out, lit and inhaled the smoke deep into his lungs. A trail of blue smoke emerged from his nostrils like the exhaust from a city bus.

"Hey, Preacher." Jimmy decided to liven things up a bit. "I need you to pray for Tony Gianinni and me this weekend." Jimmy shot his Italian friend a mischievous wink.

"Jimmy, I pray for you two white boys all the time. But I don't think it's working very much."

That raised a few chuckles around the table and got everyone's attention.

Jimmy persisted. "Nope...nope. This time I'm real serious."

"I'm always willing to ask the Lord's help for someone," Moses answered. "But what you exactly wanting him to do for you?"

"Well...you see Preacher, me and Tony, along with a couple of other fellas, are heading up to the U.P. this next week. Deer huntin' season, you know. It's gonna be a real long trip, of course. We'll be gone for some time, away from our wives and kids."

"So you wanting me to pray the Lord keeps you boys safe until you get home?"

"If you want to add that in, that's okay," Jimmy said. "But I was kinda hoping you'd ask him to provide us with a couple of big fat bucks we can blow to smithereens, and then we can bring 'em home with us and hang their trophy heads on our family room walls when we get back."

Another chorus of laughter went up.

The Preacher shook his head. "You're gonna burn in hell, Jimmy Roland. You're gonna burn in the fires of hell, you keep on messing with the Lord."

Jimmy got to laughing so hard himself, he could hardly reply. "Well if I do end up in hell, Preacher, I hope ol' Satan lets me smoke some of that fresh venison."

The crowd roared. Preacher gave up.

"Huntin' deer ain't nothin' like huntin' turkey down south," Bobby Ray Lauder chimed in with his thick country drawl. He had a pasty complexion, the color of cooked macaroni.

"What you taking about, you crazy hillbilly?" Tony asked.

Bobby Ray knew he had hit a sensitive nerve and loved Tony's knee jerk reaction. "Huntin' turkey takes brains and skill, not like shootin' a big ol' fat ass deer that's been corn fed in some cow pasture to fattin' him up, so's he's easy to plug."

"You're full-o-shit." Jimmy jumped in.

"'Taint so. Turkey's a damn smart animal. You got to stalk 'em real careful like. If'n he hears you comin', he'll run away quicker than the devil, hide in a bramble patch somewheres, an' you ain't never gonna find 'em." He let the message sink in. "Deer, on the other hand, gotta big ol' ass on it a feller can't hardly miss, unless he's blind…or a dumb fuck."

"Watch your language," the Preacher warned. Folks on the line tolerated most cuss words, except the word, "fuck," especially if a lady was present, for which Denise half qualified. You could gamble and use the word, as was too often the case, but you usually got a bigger reaction than you might expect. "Fuck" was to be used only in the most extreme of circumstances, such as indicating one's extreme anger or displeasure about something, or when referring to the company or management.

Tony and Jimmy felt obligated to defend their Michigan, time-honored tradition with an intelligent, well thought-out and persuasive verbal argument.

"You are dumber than a Kentucky fence post," Jimmy retorted.

"Dumb shit." Tony added.

Bobby Ray's lips parted in a gap-toothed smile about as wide as a four-lane highway. He enjoyed torturing Yankees, feeling a personal loyalty to the south even though he had left there more than two decades ago.

"Huh-oh," Elroy Stevenson said. "Here comes trouble."

He bobbed his head in the direction of the line where Pete Davis, the line foreman, headed their way.

"Fuck," someone said. No one challenged the remark.

The unpopular foreman strutted through the assembly area, stopping every now and then to pick up an errant piece of trash on the floor or to inspect a piece of noisy machinery. His stiff back seemed to be made out of the same inflexible material as his navy blue pants and matching shirt, heavily pressed and well starched. Jimmy claimed he had a two-by-four stuck up his ass. He always had a metal clipboard tucked under his arm that contained the work orders and schedules for that day's production.

"Mr. Davis", as he preferred himself to be called, but rarely so respected by the folks working the line, was a company man through and through.

Moses and Elroy got up and left at the first sight of him. They had had their share of confrontations with Pete Davis over the years and tried to avoid the man whenever possible.

Pete Davis tended to show up during their break times. He thought it his personal mission to make sure the breaks didn't stretch out too long and every one got back to work as soon as possible.

The rest of them waited for him to swagger on over.

"Mornin' Pete," one of them said.

"Mornin' fellas." He glanced at Denise without making a correction. He knew that pissed her off. She let it go, knowing the rest of them were thinking, "Asshole," just as much as her.

"We got a safety briefing scheduled first thing Monday morning. Don't anyone forget." Pete's eyes bore in on Jimmy as if to emphasize the point.

They all nodded.

"I'm on vacation." Jimmy said, a blue haze of smoke tumbling out of his mouth and nose as he spoke.

"Me too." Tony added.

"Me three." Frank Simmons waved his hand in the air like a third grader trying to get the teacher's attention because he had to go pee.

Pete sighed with his usual frustration. He raised his right leg, placing his foot on the edge of the picnic table seat, and leaned forward on his elbows.

"That's right...deer season. I guess the three of you are headed up north next week."

"Yup," said Jimmy and Tony in unison.

"I ain't a part of them two. Just taking three days off to be with the Missus," Frank remarked, wanting to make sure he distanced himself from what he thought to be two of the bigger troublemakers on the line. Little did he realize that Pete Davis liked him even less.

Pete ignored Frank on purpose and continued. "Well, do me a favor and remind anyone who is going to be here about Monday's meeting."

The only thing louder than the group's silence was the incessant hum of machinery.

Pete took his foot off the seat and adjusted his pants around his middle.

"Anything else going on today I need to know about?"

"Yeah. My last paycheck wasn't big enough. How 'bout staking me an extra hundred bucks 'til next payday," Denise wisecracked. A couple of them snickered under their breath.

Pete cracked a smile on just one side of his face. "Sorry. Can't help you there, Lips. Sounds to me like a union problem." He always tried to get in a dig at the union every time he could. That was one of the reasons they didn't like him.

"I'll be down the line or in my office if anything comes up today. Let's get back to work," he ordered. He noticed the open box of donuts, lying on the table, and helped himself to one without even asking. "See you later," he said, munching on the donut as he turned and headed down the line.

    They sat there for about a half a minute in silent protest to Pete's verbal instructions, but then, one by one, they dragged themselves up and went back to work with Tony leading the way. Jimmy tossed the butt of his burning cigarette on the cold cement floor and crushed it under his foot. He yawned and stretched his ample frame before lumbering back to the pile of injector units waiting for his attention.

Chapter Three

"Work is the curse of the drinking class."
Oscar Wilde

"C'mon Freddy, let's take a ride."

The young, lanky deputy needed no further prodding to get out of the office even though the weather outside seemed about to turn nasty in typical November fashion. "Sure, sheriff. Where we going?"

"I just want to take a better look see around where you found them bones this morning," Ollie Svenson replied while securing the leather belt to his gun and holster around his flabby middle. He snatched his brown jacket and Smokey the Bear hat off the coat rack and tossed the keys to his four-year old Buick cruiser over to his deputy who caught them in mid-flight.

"I thought them two state troopers had taken over the investigation?" Freddy asked.

The sheriff looked none too happy. "Well…there's still the matter of the missing husband, ain't there?"

"Yeah."

"And by the looks of that gray sky outside, we might be in for the first snowstorm of the season. Snow just might be covering the ground 'til next spring, so this may be our last chance to see if there's any clues hanging around regarding what happened to that lady's husband."

The deputy grabbed his hat and coat and hurried out the door, trailing just behind the sheriff.

Some thirty minutes later, after an uneventful trip to the northern limits of Luce County on narrow two lane highways, Freddy eased the cruiser down the familiar dirt road. He passed on by the abandoned blue Ford sedan, now tagged by state police for eventual towing, and parked closer to the spot where he had found the remains of Valerie Pearson. He turned off the engine and they got out of the car together. Although the area was still cordoned off by official looking state police investigation tape, there was no sign of any state troopers or investigative staff around.

"They must be all on a real long lunch break," the sheriff snickered softly.

"What?" Freddy asked.

Not intending his remark to be heard, the sheriff walked briskly to where the bones were found. The area had been completely swept clean, the bones already removed by investigative authorities from the state's Department of Criminal Investigation. A north wind rustled through the season's crop of plump pinecones and scented pine needles high in the evergreen trees over their heads. The air felt damp and cold, like it often did just before a winter storm.

Hands perched on his hips and legs spread apart, the sheriff scanned the ground and surrounding forest, trying to make sense of what may have occurred at the scene.

"What happened to all the bones, sheriff?"

It took Ollie a couple of seconds to clear his mind of thoughts before answering the deputy's question. "Oh, I'm sure them troopers picked everything up by now they thought important, Freddy. That's okay. They don't know what they're looking for anyway. We got more important things to figure out."

"More important things, sheriff?"

"Yah, for sure," Ollie said. "It don't make much sense to me why the husband would murder his wife and then just leave the car and all her money behind. And how about that Ford getting all banged up. Who do you suppose did that?"

Freddy let the sheriff's observations percolate awhile in his youthful brain. "So you think someone else other then Mr. Pearson killed his wife?"

"Yah, for sure. And maybe him too."

"This morning, sheriff, you seemed to think that maybe a wild animal or something may have been responsible. What'd you mean by that?"

The sheriff had been walking slowly around the area with his attention focused on the ground. Something caught his eye just then and he hunched over to get a better look at it.

"Whatcha looking at, sheriff?"

"See these markings here on the ground, Freddy?"

The deputy leaned over from the waist and looked where the sheriff was pointing. "Looks like a bunch of holes in the ground...like someone took a screwdriver and poked the tip all over the place."

The sheriff smiled. "Right, Freddy. Them holes you see is all around where you found Mrs. Pearson's remains and all around the Ford too. If you look in some of the other places nearby, you don't find many holes. Now take a closer look at one of them holes."

Freddy did as instructed. He got down on his knees and moved his head down close to the ground.

"What do you see, Freddy?"

"I'll be darn," Freddy responded. "Looks like...a bunch of smaller marks next to each hole...animal tracks of some sort. What do you think they are, sheriff?"

"I'm not exactly sure, but it looks like they were made by...a claw or a paw or...something like that. Those tracks lead off into the woods over there and get further spread apart from one another as if they might have been running...or chasing something."

The deputy continued examining the tracks. "Sure don't look like tracks made by any kind of animal around these parts."

"I'm not so sure about that," the sheriff said. "And I'm pretty sure there's more than just one of them. Looks like three or four of them at least."

"Maybe we should follow those tracks, sheriff? Could be they'd lead us to where the husband took off."

"These tracks is over three weeks old, Freddy. Lucky if we could follow them more than a quarter mile or so." The sheriff looked up into the clouded sky. "Besides, I think we got a storm brewing up. All these tracks are gonna get covered up with a foot of snow here pretty quick now."

Just then the two men heard the sharp snap of a branch off in the distant forest. Their heads raised like anxious deer caught in the headlights of a speeding car.

"Who's there, by golly?" The sheriff yelled. "This is the police! C'mon out where we can see you!"

The sheriff's order was soon followed with a commotion of more branches breaking and the sound of heavy footfalls receding back into the forest.

"C'mon, Freddy." Ollie took off towards the sound with surprising speed for a middle-aged man of his size.

Freddy followed suit, letting the sheriff lead the way. He soon found himself being whipped constantly by a host of thorny vines and tree branches, the result of the sheriff's speedy wake in front of him through the thick underbrush. He tried to keep up as best he could.

They ran for several minutes until they arrived at the approximate location where the sounds had come from. Freddy suddenly noticed the sheriff had drawn his gun; he did the same.

An eerie silence surrounded them, although they could hear the occasional crackle of breaking twigs and branches off in the distance, as whatever they were chasing drew further away. A strong, musty animal scent lingered in the still air.

Freddy's nostrils flared, tasting the odor. "What do you think it was, sheriff? A big buck or something?" He glanced over at Ollie, who was bent over studying something on the ground. The deputy joined him at his side.

A series of tracks appeared on the soft soil, just like the ones they had been examining around the site where Mrs. Pearson's bones were discovered, only these were fresh. The tracks looked like divots, which had been hacked into the ground by pitching wedge or nine iron, with a single hole at the front part of the print as if made by a sharp object of some sort. Neither the sheriff nor Freddy recognized the tracks belonging to any animal they had ever seen. The tracks were big, about the size of Freddy's hand with his fingers splayed open wide.

"Holy smoke!" The young deputy's eyes were open wide, lustrous marbles surrounded in white.

"Yah, Freddy." The sheriff agreed. "That's for sure."

Something howled in the distance just as fresh flakes of snow started to filter down from the clouds. The icy flakes landed on Ollie's rosy cheeks and melted like butter on hot corn.

"What do we do now sheriff? Should we go after 'em?"

Ollie sighed in resignation, staring off into the distant forest. "Storm's coming up, Freddy. We better get back to the office. Too late to catch 'em now," he said. "Besides, I'm not exactly sure what we'd find out there in the woods."

The expression on Ollie Svenson's face made Freddy nervous. He'd never seen the look of fear in the sheriff's eyes before.

* * *

At about three-thirty, toward the end of the day shift, Tony was finishing up some final lathe work required on several base injector units. Like his pal Jimmy, he wanted the workday to end and his long awaited vacation to start. His gawky, thin frame moved about the cold cement floor of the plant with a definite fluidity as he worked around the heavy machinery. Tony had a gift with machines, whether it be working with saws or drills or presses or lathes. He could finish most jobs in half the time it took others to do. Around machines, he knew what he was doing and had great confidence in his work. In some ways, Tony preferred the company of machines. Besides Jimmy and Tom Karrski, he had few other friends.

He completed the project, sending the refurbished units down the line, and went over to Jimmy at the next workstation over from his.

"So are we all set for the trip?" Tony asked, anxious for the shift to end and start their deer hunting enterprise.

"Yeah. Most everything's packed. I loaded up the camper last night."

Tony nodded. "Good. I got most of my stuff ready and can bring it over any time, tonight or tomorrow morning."

Jimmy thought a second or two. "Awww…just bring it over tomorrow morning. I gotta do a couple of things around the house before taking off for a full week. Besides, I probably gotta take care of the old lady sometime too, if you know what I mean."

Tony understood perfectly well even though he wasn't married.

"A man's work is never done." He gave Jimmy a clever wink. "By the way, Jimmy, are you heading over the Smokehouse for a beer after work?"

"Does a bear shit in the woods?" Jimmy replied.

They both went to finishing up whatever work remained until the second shift started arriving. Jimmy's replacement, a pudgy little guy by the name of Joe Dourghty, showed up right on time, four o'clock. Jimmy was wiping some cleaning lotion off his hands for the last time. He wouldn't have to smell any more of that rancid stuff for at least another week.

"Hey Jimmy," Joe said, removing an almost identical tool belt to Jimmy's and placing it down on the now-empty workbench.

"Thanks for the screw job, Dourghty," Jimmy replied, still a little pissed off.

"What are you talking about?"

"All those goddamn assemblies you jokers left last night. Took me almost all morning to get through them all."

Joe shrugged his shoulders. "Don't blame me. Number three bore machine started spitting out bad assemblies around eight last night. Hell, by the time we discovered the problem, it had screwed up about a hundred of 'em." I fixed forty of them myself, right before quitting time. If you got a problem, take it up with maintenance."

"Shit, they don't know what the hell they're doing half the time."

"Tell me about it," Joe agreed.

They were friends again now that Jimmy vented his anger.

"So who's taking your place on the line next week?" Joe already knew about Jimmy's vacation and hunting trip.

"Denise Williams will fill in. She's okay."

"Crap. She don't know jack-squat."

Everyone hated vacation replacements. They were expected not only to fill in for the person on vacation, but they usually had to do their own job as well, meaning both suffered. The company, however, was not about to spend more money on hiring and paying for extra staff, nor would they allow additional overtime. Corporate bottom line profitability prohibited such luxuries. So things got screwed up or delayed until whomever was missing returned back to work. Quality suffered; the American consumer ended up paying for it.

A loud whistle wailed, indicating the change of shifts.

"See you later, Joe."

"Hope you bag a big one, Jimmy." Joe settled in for his next eight hours of drudgery.

Jimmy grabbed his stuff and threw it in his locker. Five minutes later, he punched out on the time clock for the last time until he returned from vacation. He joined a crowded river of his coworkers, streaming out the plant much like a chorus of salmon spawning upstream. They traveled with the same mechanical precision as the moving assembly line beside them.

His pace picked up once he hit the union parking lot. Upwind from the plant, the November air smelled fresh and sweet. He got in his pickup and immediately lit a cigarette and then waited in a long line of other cars and trucks, inching toward the narrow one-lane exit out of the parking lot. He began to feel a little bit of giddiness in anticipation of his week ahead. The brim of his UAW baseball cap shaded his eyes from the bright sun, already hanging low in the western horizon. Finally, he made it out into the street and peeled the tires once he hit the black asphalt pavement.

Five or six minutes later, after first stopping off at his local Credit Union branch and depositing his paycheck as Brenda had reminded him to do earlier that morning, he pulled into the parking lot of the Smokehouse Lounge. A colorful array of cars and pickups and S.U.V.'s, every single one of them American made, were parked every which way, in a kind of planned disorder, in the gravel parking lot. The aging neon sign above the faded yellow brick building had a green martini glass with an red straw sticking out of it and five colored bubbles floating above, only two of which were lit up and working. The

Smokehouse Lounge was a favorite after-work watering hole, especially for union folks from all over Flint. It was always crowded from four to six in the afternoon and ten to midnight, at the end of regular plant work shifts.

The place was as rough as its clientele. When anyone went inside, no mater what time of day or night, they noticed two things right away; the well-worn jukebox on the wall next to the men's room that *only* played country music, and a thick cloud of smoky haze suspended about five feet off a beer-sodden linoleum floor. The place reeked of smoke and beer and fried food.

Jimmy punched through the swinging front door and headed directly for his usual table, where several of his regular drinking buddies already had a twenty-four-ounce glass of his favorite draft beer waiting for him. The scene had been repeated day after day, more or less the same way for the past twenty-five years of Jimmy's union life, with only the occasional change of characters. Jimmy had two constants in his life he could always depend upon: his wife, Brenda...and beer. Both had contributed equally to the growth and current status of his prodigious gut.

"Jimmy!" Several loudmouthed patrons sitting at the bar yelled above the din of the other tables. He gave them a friendly wave.

He went straight to his table and for the beer, grabbed the glass, and swallowed about a third of the contents before coming up for air. He wiped the leftover foam from his upper lip on the sleeve of his orange windbreaker.

"Hot damn, that's good," he said, belching afterwards.

There were four of them around a battered table that rocked back and forth on its unbalanced legs. They were all leaning forward on their elbows, like conspirators planning their next bank robbery. Jimmy lit another cigarette, throwing the match into an ashtray choked full with an assortment of mangled butts and burnt matchsticks.

"What do you call a Chinaman with just one testicle?" Jimmy asked the group with a devilish grin.

No one came up with an answer.

"One hung low."

Laughter.

"What's the difference between a rooster and a blonde?

No answer again.

"A rooster says 'Cock-a-doodle-do', while a blonde says, 'Any-cock'll-do.'"

They roared in unison.

An old Willie Nelson song moaned in the background.

Tony Gianinni had arrived first, Tom Karrski drove over from the Platform Plant out south of town, and Bill Briggs, who retired from the A.C. Delco plant last year, got there right before Jimmy arrived.

"Wish I was heading up north with you guys next week," said Briggs. A silver-gray Santa Claus beard and wide handlebar mustache hid his thin pink lips from view. His beer disappeared in huge gulps down his hairy mouth hole. "Can't get around like I use to though."

They all looked at him with a curious expression. Briggs had never been invited to go along with them. They sort of figured he was talking in general terms, just wishing he had been asked to go up deer hunting with anyone. He'd had a hip replacement operation a couple of months ago down at the University Hospital in Ann Arbor and was still hobbling around with a cane.

"Maybe we'll bag a seven pointer for you," Tony said.

Briggs swirled the beer left in his glass, his mind wandering to prior hunts as a younger man and mourning the passage of his youth.

"Hey Meatball, you all packed?" Jimmy asked, puffing his cigarette.

Tom Karrski had the look of a crusty lumberjack, right down to the red flannel shirt and ruddy brown boots. A knit cap covered his curly blond hair. "Ready to go," he answered, thumbs up. His eyes were glassy and red, the result of several shots of bourbon he had consumed earlier in the day. Tom's eyes were always bloodshot.

"Bring your stuff over tomorrow morning before we leave at nine. Otherwise, it ain't gonna get there."

"Will do," Tom said. "Don't forget to bring a television, by the way. Maybe we can catch the Lions game on Sunday."

"Already taken care of my man. Jimmy thinks of every thing." He tapped the side of his head with his index finger.

"Hey...watch it buster." Tina, the only waitress in the place, scolded some guy sitting at the bar who had snapped her rear end with a rubber band. She came over to the table and turned her attention to Jimmy and the boys. "You guys want some more beer?"

"Sure, I'll get another round," Tony offered.

Briggs and Karrski nodded their approval of the notion.

"Naw, I'd better head on home," said Jimmy.

"Suit yourself," Tina bubbled. "Three drafts comin' up." She scurried over toward the bar with a handful of drink orders.

Jimmy downed what little beer remained and pounded the empty glass down on the table. "Who do I owe for this?" He asked.

"It's on me," Tony said.

Jimmy reached into his back wallet, pulled out a five-dollar bill and tossed it in the middle of the table, wet with spilled beer and moisture dripping off the glasses. "Give that to Tina then." He pushed the chair back with his legs and stood. "See you guys later."

"So long, Jimmy."

* * *

Jimmy pulled out of the driveway of the Smokehouse Lounge a little after six o'clock. The twenty-four ounce schooner of beer he had consumed inside, drinking with his fellow union buddies, still sloshed around in his belly. The last flickering rays of sunshine reflected in the review mirror as he headed toward home. Brenda would be putting the finishing touches on their supper right about then.

His pickup truck could practically drive on autopilot, if it had one, since he traveled the exact same route every day for the past twenty or so years. On the short trip home, he always listened to the same radio station, 102.5 FM, the oldies station. The only thing different each day was the songs they might be playing. Jimmy knew most of the lyrics to every "oldie" by heart.

The truck rounded a curve, taking it onto Bristol Road, a straight shot with few traffic lights for the next ten minutes. Jimmy rolled down the driver's side window about halfway and lit his last Marlboro for a while, since Brenda wouldn't allow him to smoke in the house. He dragged in a few satisfying puffs as the truck approached sprawling Woodlawn Cemetery, the city's largest, on the right hand side of the road. He glanced at all the chalk colored grave markers, glowing in the sunset beyond a mile long, wrought iron fence that fronted the graveyard.

Jimmy's Dad and Granddad were buried over in the Veterans of Foreign Wars section, where all the markers were aligned perfectly, like a battalion of dead soldiers marching through the green grass. Granddad fought in the World War, "Double ya, Double ya, Two," as he liked to put it; Dad in Korea. Somehow, they managed to be interred together in the same cemetery, separated by a mere fifty yards and about a hundred other corpses. As much as their lives took a similar path, however, their deaths ended up the complete opposite.

Granddad died the way people were supposed to die; at home, asleep in his own bed, at the ripe old age of eighty-three. He just conked out one night and never woke up.

Pretty sweet, Jimmy thought. *Not a bad way to go.*

Dad, on the other hand, died the way too many folks died nowadays, succumbing to the ravaging effects of brain cancer and the lethal doses of radiation and chemicals used to kill the cancer. He was sixty-seven.

Jimmy averted his eyes from the cemetery and all the passing grave markers, trying not to think about Granddad and Dad and death. It didn't work. He couldn't shake the image of his Dad in those last, horrible days.

Granddad died in peace.

Dad had suffered.

Dad withered.

Dad was murdered. Not just by the cancer, but also by the doctors and the wicked treatments they administered.

Jimmy and Dad never talked about it much. They didn't discuss things like being sick and medicine and doctors. It wasn't right. Stuff like that was personal. If Dad wouldn't even tell his own son about the amount of his monthly pension check from the plant, or how much money he had sitting in his bank checking account, how could they be expected to talk about important stuff like dying and death?

They discussed it once, though, and Jimmy would never forget.

Dad was about six weeks into his radiation treatments, trying to kill whatever remained of the tumor the doctor hacked from of his brain through a six-inch, crescent shaped gash on his forehead. Jimmy never could figure out why Dad had to endure all those painful treatments if the cancer had already been cut out of his head. Maybe it was like one of those stubborn dandelions, flourishing along the edges of Woodlawn Cemetery, he thought. You could easily pull up the yellow flower and jagged green leaves, but getting at the root was another matter. If you didn't kill the root, the damn dandelion just kept coming back.

Jimmy hadn't expected his Dad to talk about it, ever. But one day, his old man decided to elaborate for some reason.

"The radiation's the scary part," Dad said, with wide saucer eyes that reminded Jimmy of Casper the ghost. "They took me into this room and strapped me down to the bed."

Jimmy thought they called it a "gurney", but he wasn't sure.

Dad continued. "Then a nurse comes in and draws this thin line with a pencil on my forehead from here to here." He indicated a line with a shaky index finger that ran from his right temple to the center of his eyebrows. "That's the target, where they put the radiation. Then the nurse gets the hell out of there and closes a big door behind her, leaving me all alone. That damn door is made of metal and is about this thick." Dad held his callused hands about two and a half feet apart from one another.

"I lay there, absolutely still, not flinching a muscle. I don't want something else getting burned that don't need to get burned. Then in a couple of minutes, that radiation machine starts buzzing, so I know it's turned on. It follows right down that line the nurse drew on my forehead."

Then came the scary part for Jimmy.

"Son," Dad said. "I can't really feel anything while it's happening, but I know it's working cause that machine keeps on buzzing. I know it sounds funny, but toward the tail end of the treatment, I can smell something burning in my nose. Now, there's no smoke or anything like that. But I swear to God, I can smell the burning inside my head. Then in a couple of days, I know I'm gonna be to be real sick for sure."

Jimmy concentrated on what exactly burnt away inside his Dad's skull besides what remained of the tumor. He imagined memories and feelings and intelligence, and all those things that your brain does without you even realizing it, getting destroyed by accident. What all did Dad lose every time that radiation machine buzzed across that thin pencil line?

Dad never talked about the treatments again. Dad never mentioned what the radiation machine actually looked like, any details about the room, or described any of his doctors or nurses. Jimmy had to fill in the blanks, and he did.

All Jimmy could picture in his mind were those old black and white Flash Gordon movies made back in the 1930's he used to watch on T.V. as a kid, where Flash was always being tortured by Ming the Merciless, using some terrible, god-awful machine. Jimmy envisioned Dad strapped on a black leather gurney, just like Flash, with a huge ray gun about three stories tall, pointing right at his frigging head. Standing behind a thick Plexiglas window was a doctor, looking just like Ming the Merciless, and a nurse, who looked exactly like Dale Arden, Flash Gordon's girlfriend. The doctor, with Ming's bald head and evil eyes, would turn the ray gun on full blast with dramatic fanfare, and sparks would start flying from an instrument panel filled with all kinds of switches and electronic gadgets. Then, from the very tip of the ray gun, a big old bolt of electricity would come shooting out right into Dad's forehead, causing his body to writhe in agony on that leather gurney. He could see nurse Dale's face, aghast in horror, and Ming's diabolic grin, through the thick Plexiglas window

The only difference; Flash always got away. Dad didn't.

It was a terrible, childish image, but one Jimmy couldn't shake. That's what Jimmy saw when he drove past Woodlawn Cemetery every day, thinking about his

Dad and how he died. Because of that, Jimmy was afraid of doctors and hospitals and dying. Going to the doctor for Jimmy was worse than pulling teeth and the reason why he never went.

Gradually, the graveyard faded in the rearview mirror while the beer still sloshed around in Jimmy's stomach. He flipped what remained of the cigarette out the window and stepped on the accelerator so that the truck would speed up, trying to outrun the images in his mind and return home to Brenda, as fast as he could.

* * *

Later that same night, Tom Karrski pulled out of the Smokehouse Lounge parking lot and drove his Pontiac GrandAm south toward the little countryside village of Fenton where he and his wife, Ginger, lived in a small two-bedroom frame house in the center of town. On his way home, he stopped at one of his favorite places, The Last Stop Liquor Store, perched just off Old Mill highway on the outskirts of town.

He tumbled out of the low slung two-door sedan, his head spinning slightly from the bourbon and three twenty-four ounce glasses of beer he had managed to quaff down during the past two hours. His brown eyes winced at the winking neon Budweiser Beer sign in the window as he entered through the heavy fortified front door of the Liquor Store.

He went straight to the third aisle on the left, where most of the hard liquors were displayed. In the middle of the aisle, several dozen fifths of Jim Beam were stacked on the top shelf right next to the crystal colored bottles of vodka and gin. He grabbed the necks on four bottles of the cheap bourbon, two in each hand, and clambered up toward the register back up front.

As he placed the precious cargo on the counter, the clerk recognized him right off. "Say, Tommy...how's things going?"

Tom wrestled with his wallet, stuck in the back pocket of his jeans. "I'm okay, Norm. How 'bout you?"

The clerk studied Tom's ruddy face, his slightly bloodshot eyes. The Polock was a regular in the Liquor Store, a daily customer. "Can't complain. Long as I pay the bills, the old lady leaves me alone."

Tom cracked a smile and handed the clerk two twenty-dollar bills. "Tell me about it," he said, agreeing. His wife's face flashed though his mind.

Norm entered the price of the four fifths into the cash register, added the state sales tax, and then fiddled inside the change drawer. He handed Tom back three one dollar bills and some change.

"More than usual," Norm said.

Tom shot a questioning look at the cashier while stuffing the bills and change into his pants pocket. "What?"

"Just noticed, you usually buy only one or two bottles of Beam at a time," Norm replied.

"Oh," Tom said. "Going deer huntin' next week. I may need some extra ammo." He winked at Norm, as if telling him an inside joke only he would understand. A wry smile covered his face.

"Shit yes!" Norm agreed. "Them deer are a lot easier to shoot when you got a little booze in ya to help aim your gun." He put each glass decanter filled with the golden amber liquid in its own brown paper bag and then placed all four in a big grocery sack.

Tom snatched up the heavy sack and placed it carefully in the crick of his left arm between his forearm and elbow. "See you later, Norm."

"Yeah, Tommy. Bag a big one."

Tom went back out into the chilly November evening. He put the grocery sack with the four bottles of bourbon in the bucket seat next to him and fired up the engine of the GrandAm. The eight cylinders roared to life; the dual chrome exhaust pipes purred with a deep, satisfying rumble.

His wife, Ginger, would be at home, but not necessarily waiting for him. She'd already eaten over an hour ago. By now, she had gotten used to him showing up late from work every night with the stench of alcohol on his breath. Tom would just have to eat his supper cold, like he usually did…along with at least half a fifth of one of the bottles of Beam he'd just bought.

He put the Pontiac in gear and took off, squealing the tires slightly on the asphalt parking lot. But once he got on the road, Tom kept the speed of the car at five miles below the posted limit all the way until he got home. He couldn't afford another D.U.I. violation. It had only been a month since the local cops last picked him up for driving after he'd had a bit too much to drink. Already driving on a suspended driver's license, Tom Karrski didn't need any more grief. The next time he got caught, he'd end up spending some time in the pokey.

* * *

A fat T-bone steak, smothered with onions and mushrooms and yellow sweet peppers, sizzled in the frying pan. Brenda brandished a stainless steel spatula and flipped the sixteen ounce slab of meat over, trying to keep it the way Jimmy liked to eat it; *rare*.

"Bloody and pink. Just like my women." He liked to joke.

Brenda didn't like it when Jimmy acted so crass. She'd give him a good piece of her mind if it happened too often…near relatives or children, in church, or around friends…especially her's. Jimmy had better behave if he knew what was good for him. She worked hard civilizing her man; the chore seemed perpetual.

They had a good marriage though. No kids. Something must have happened to Jimmy once as a kid. Doctors said he had low sperm count. Jimmy liked to brag that he was, "Shootin' blanks." They had one another, and that was always enough. Jimmy never strayed and neither did she. Brenda handled the finances around the house, which consisted mostly of balancing the checkbook every two weeks right after payday. Nothing in savings, they spent most of paycheck on various "toys and stuff" they bought for each other or for themselves. Jimmy stored most of his "stuff" in the garage and along the outside of the house; the boat, the camper, and the snowmobiles...his and hers. Brenda kept her "stuff" in the house; the new furniture in the living room and bedroom, the big screen digital television set for watching daytime soaps, and all the crafts and country knick-knacks she collected and had displayed all over the place. They both figured Jimmy would one day get a good retirement paycheck from G.M., so they could afford those extra "little" luxuries. So far, their simple financial plan had worked, although every now and then Brenda wondered if they should be saving a little more money for retirement.

She turned the gas burner down on the steak and ran a wooden spoon through the cast iron pot of green beans, simmering next to the frying pan. The steam rising from all the burners kept fogging up the glasses that she wore for close work such as cooking or sewing or reading her latest favorite romance novel. She removed the glasses and placed them upside down on the orange Formica countertop they had installed when they first bought the house some fifteen years ago.

Jimmy should be home any minute, she thought, glancing at the kitchen clock. As if on cue, she heard the clatter of the electric garage door opening and Jimmy's pickup pulling inside. Jimmy was right on time. She smiled to herself. But she'd have to remind Jimmy for the umpteenth time to work on quieting that noisy garage door.

It had been rattling like that for over a month now, ever since Jimmy had accidentally banged into it with his pickup one day while changing the oil.

She grabbed a dry dishtowel and wiped her moist hands gingerly, then went over to a mirror, which was hanging in the little mudroom that led into the garage. She adjusted the neckline on her fuzzy sweater, Jimmy's favorite, and unbuttoned the top button so that showed a little more cleavage than usual. After all, Jimmy planned to be away deer hunting for a whole week, and…well, that usually meant they'd cuddle at some point later that evening. Jimmy had cruder expressions for making love. She'd give him a good slap in the face if she ever heard him use them around her. Finally, she loosened the rubber band holding her brown ponytail in place, letting her hair cascade down to just below her shoulders.

She patted down the sweater around her tummy, took in a deep breath, which had the effect of lifting up her breasts, and got ready to greet Jimmy with a big kiss.

The door opened and Jimmy came through.

"Hi, honey," he said, not really noticing her. He placed an annoying little peck on her cheek, hung his jacket and baseball cap onto a wooden peg on the wall, and then handed her his empty lunch pail before sitting down in his usual chair at the kitchen table.

Brenda unpuckered her lips and just shook her head with one of those, "why do I even try," sort of gestures.

She dropped the pail near the sink and went over to the stove to finish cooking. Jimmy reached for the newspaper lying on the table and buried his nose in the sports section.

"So how's your day?" she asked him, mashing some potatoes with an increased vigor.

"Oh, fine," he answered.

Brenda created a vindictive ruckus around the kitchen while empting all the pots and pans, mixing this and that, and filling all the bowls and plates. At times, the noise approached the volume of the injector assembly line. Jimmy returned to planet Earth and eventually came up for air from his ardent newspaper reading.

"Shit," he said to himself. He recognized Brenda's fuzzy sweater, leaped out of his chair, and grabbed the frying pan from her. "Let me get that," he said, suddenly realizing the hot handle was scorching his fingers.

"Eeeooowww!" he cried, releasing the handle so the pan landed back on the burner with a crash. Hot grease splashed onto the stovetop. He shook his hand like it was on fire and popped several throbbing fingers in his mouth.

Jimmy winced; Brenda smiled.

"You idiot," she remarked, half joking.

He laughed. "You got that right." He yanked her close to him and kissed her hard.

"Sorry." That's all Jimmy had to say. Brenda had already forgiven him. "Nice sweater, by the way," he added. He snaked a playful finger down the front of the fuzzy sweater between her breasts.

"Later," she teased, pushing him away. "Let's eat."

Brenda was a good cook, and Jimmy's burgeoning stomach attested to the fact. Like so many married couples, they ate their evening supper with few words spoken between them. Events changed little from day to day; life tended to unfold like a long, warm spring season. When something important happened, such as a relative dying or the furnace blowing up, as it did last fall, then they talked. Important events, however, occurred only now and then, requiring a minimum of communication effort on their part.

Jimmy relished chewing on a good steak and Brenda relished Jimmy chewing on a good steak. They were comfortable with each other, in their marriage, and in life.

The telephone rang about the time Jimmy had finished enjoying the last tender morsels of his T-bone, and he had begun to take notice of Brenda's cleavage, peeking out from under her fuzzy sweater.

Brenda answered on the third ring. "Hi, Sam. How're Martha and the kids? Good. Yeah, he's right here, stuffing his face as usual. Sure, I'll put him on. See you tomorrow. Bye-bye."

She cupped the receiver and handed it to Jimmy. "It's your brother."

He took the phone from her, leaned back in his chair, and allowed his bare gut to extend outward from under his tee shirt. "Hey buddy. What's up?" The line buzzed; Jimmy frowned a little. "Hell, can't Martha take 'em over? Yeah, yeah. Well, get your ass over here as soon as you can. I was planning to get on the road by eight or nine in the morning. Just hurry up over, damnit. Okay." He handed the receiver back to Brenda.

"Problem?" she asked.

"Aaahhh...Sam's got to take his kids over to some kind of church camp first thing tomorrow, 'cause Martha has to work on a special project at her office. Said he'd be an hour or so late. Means we won't get outa here 'til after ten most likely."

"That's not so bad." Brenda said, trying to be sympathetic. She knew how much Jimmy looked forward to deer hunting season. "Do you need to call Tony Gianinni and Tom Karrski?"

He thought a second or two. "Yeah. I'll tell 'em not to come over until nine, nine-thirty."

Disappointment showed on his face. Brenda went over to him and gently rubbed his belly. "Tell you what. Why don't you go finish up packing the camper for your trip and I'll clean up the kitchen?"

He nodded.

* * *

Jimmy and a welder friend built an armor-plated cabinet of his into the wall of the garage and anchored it to the cement foundation. The vault contained Jimmy's most valued possessions - not cash, securities or gold - but his guns. Along with Jimmy's cigarette smoking, the guns represented another commodity Brenda barred from inside the house.

"Right two turns, thirty-six...left a full turn, fourteen...right to twenty-one." Jimmy spun the large combination lock on the hasp.

He pulled on the lock, unlatching it. The door swung open with a nails-on-the-chalkboard screech. Jammed into the crowded cabinet were three rifles, two shotguns, a couple of pistols, along with a deer hunting bow, a six-inch bowie knife, and a samurai sword his Granddad claimed he had taken off the dead body of some Japanese officer on the island of Guadalcanal in the Pacific. An assortment of ammunition in brown cardboard boxes was stacked on some shelves, while several loose bullets and red shotgun shells rolled around on the floor. The odor of gunpowder and the light oil used to clean the weapons permeated the air inside the cabinet.

Jimmy pulled out a twenty-gage shotgun and a 30-30 Winchester rifle, "Old Faithful," and stacked them on the floor next to him. Then he retrieved the two pistols he used to "finish off the job" on any animal crippled or maimed but not yet dead. One shot through the ear hole usually did the trick. He holstered one of the pistols in his pants, letting the belt hold it in place cowboy style.

Trying to read and determine the appropriate caliber on each cardboard ammunition box, Jimmy squinted at the fine print in the dim light of the garage. He grabbed about a half dozen containers and stacked them up on one of the work counters. A dog-eared newspaper clipping came tumbling out from behind the boxes. Jimmy picked it up.

"The Flint Journal. Sports Section." The banner headlines read.

Jimmy unfolded the newspaper that had already gone somewhat brittle and stained with age. The page contained a picture of Jimmy and his Dad with both men grinning from ear to ear while holding up the head of a large buck by its antlers. The deer was lashed across the hood of Dad's old Chevy station wagon. Hanging limp off the side of the animal's mouth was its fat, bloated tongue.

The caption underneath the picture read, *"James Roland Sr. from Flint Township and his son display a whitetail buck taken in Crawford County first week of open rifle season."* The article underneath the picture went on to discuss deer hunting season in general without ever mentioning them again. A photographer from the Journal had snapped the picture at a rest area along the interstate, where they had stopped after their weeklong annual hunting excursion some twelve years ago.

Two years later, Dad was dead. The picture brought back both happy and bitter memories. It was the last deer Dad had gotten.

Jimmy folded the newspaper along the crease lines and carefully placed it back behind the cardboard boxes. Then he closed the door to the cabinet and replaced the combination lock. He gathered up all the things he had taken out of the vault and went out a door along the side of the garage. His hands were full as he fumbled with the keys to the WindStar.

He opened the door to the camper, went inside, and turned on the light.

The bright phosphorescent light fixture on the ceiling of the camper made Jimmy's eyes wince until they better adjusted. The cramped quarters smelled of perch and walleye and beer and rabbit and northern pike and cooking oil and stale cigarette smoke; the residue of untold fishing and hunting trips taken by Jimmy and his cohorts over the years. During those trips, the small ten-by-fourteen foot camper acted as hotel, kitchen, bathroom, limousine, flophouse and casino. A person walking barefoot on the cheap, permanently stained shag carpeting could feel countless fish scales underfoot. The place had witnessed more carnage in its ten years of existence than most battlefields during the civil war, albeit a non-human carnage.

The place was a dump, but Jimmy viewed it as his castle on wheels.

A batch of memories filled the place. A dent in the wall made last summer is where Tom Karrski, half drunk, conked his head and fell off his chair while playing the best damn poker hand Jimmy had ever seen dealt in a game of five card poker. Some deer blood got dribbled over in the corner by accident a couple of years ago, when the boys were taking the animal's severed head with them to get mounted. It had slipped out of a big garbage bag when Jimmy took a turn off the expressway a bit too fast. No amount of scrubbing could remove that stain. The cracked window above the kitchen sink ended up that way when a feisty walleye, pulled out of the cold waters of Lake Erie, objected to his rude beheading. The uncooperative fish tasted pretty good anyways, Jimmy remembered.

Jimmy puttered around inside, doing this thing and that thing, comfortable as a bear in its winter den. He double-checked on the refrigerator and both coolers, making sure the beer was still cold, the most important task of the day. Then he stored all the guns and ammunition in wooden compartments, located just below the two beds at either end of the camper, and replenished the flushing fluids used in the toilet, so the stuff would not freeze in the pipes if they encountered colder than expected temperatures.

Finally, Jimmy sat down at a small square table bolted down in the center of the room and surveyed his realm. Satisfied all was well, he opened a cold bottle of beer for himself and quaffed several refreshing gulps.

"Aahhh," he smacked his lips together as the amber liquid coursed down his food pipe.

Life was good.

A light tap sounded on the camper door, and Brenda stuck her head inside.

"Hey, babe." Jimmy greeted her. "C'mon in."

She ducked her head through the low doorway. Once inside, her nose wrinkled, sniffing the air.

Jimmy noticed. "That bad, huh?"

"Yep." She produced a can of lavender scented bathroom aerosol and sprayed the room, as if she were being attacked by horde of wasps.

"Crime-o-nittely." Jimmy pinched his nose. "That stuff's worse."

Brenda kept spraying until a thick fog developed.

"Put that damn thing down and come over here."

Taking her own sweet time, she strolled over to Jimmy, plopped down in his lap, and threw her arms around his neck.

"So are you ready to go?" She asked, fiddling with the hairs on the back of his thick neck.

"Uh-huh."

"And you called Tony and Tom to tell them Sam's going to be a little late?"

"Uh-huh." Jimmy raised the bottle up to his lips and took another swig of beer.

"Well then…I just don't know what you're going to do until tomorrow morning," she said. She nuzzled closer to Jimmy, the fuzzy fabric on her sweater tickling his nose. The bright florescent light reflected off the mounds of her chest.

He put his meaty hands around her waist and kissed her long and hard. He started to pull her sweater up when she stopped him cold.

"Oh no you don't, buster. Not in here. Not in this smelly place." She grabbed both his hands and pulled him up from his seat. "Let's go inside."

He paid no attention to her, reached up, and turned off the light.

Chapter Four

"There's no thrill in easy sailing when the skies are clear and blue, there's not joy in merely doing things any one can do. But there is some satisfaction that is mighty sweet to take, when you reach a destination that you thought you'd never make."
Spirella

The city of Flint didn't so much slumber as lay in a coma.

Tony Gianinni stared up into the cold morning sky, a uniform sheet of gray slate, and dug his knuckles into his still half-closed eyes. He stretched and yawned and took a sip of jet-black coffee, strong, the way he liked it. He replaced the little red, rubber lid back on top the thermos, saving the rest of it for the long trip to the Upper Peninsula, and climbed into his pickup truck, a mirror image of Jimmy's. The engine rattled in protest, not liking the rude awakening. Tony gunned the motor and flipped the defroster fan to high. During the night, Jack Frost had nipped the windshield with thick layer of ice. Tony's icy breath coated the insides of the windows with another layer of visual impenetrability while he waited, shivering, for everything to warm up. Somewhere in the cab there must have been a scraper, but that would have required him to get out of the truck and clear the windows by hand. It was far too chilly and too damn early to require such effort. Besides, it was Saturday, the start of his vacation. He snuggled down in the fake leather truck seat, zombie-like, until tiny clear ovals began to appear just above the defroster vents. He put the truck into gear and pulled away from the curb. He tried to navigate down the street while struggling to see through two narrow ovals expanding slowly on the windshield.

The middle-aged man, born of Italian immigrants, lived alone in a plain vanilla mobile home on the north side of town. He had to check on his mother before leaving her alone for a full week. She owned a small, two-bedroom red brick home near the old A.C. Spark Plug plant over on the east side, the same house where Tony and his six other brothers and sisters had been raised. An alcoholic, his dad had died of a liver ailment when Tony was still in grade school.

A depressing stretch of road took him past a battery of dilapidated buildings and abandoned factories that lined both sides of Dort Highway. In prior years, the street would have been clogged with a busy conglomeration of truck and heavy machinery traffic, going to and from all the industrial sites. Tony, however, found the streets nearly deserted that morning. The facades of crumbling brick walls, with blackened windows and tortured smokestacks, were eerie. He could almost sense the spirits of the thousands of men and women who had once worked there. He sometimes wondered his own fate.

Some seven miles later, the pickup swung into his mother's driveway where he parked and turned off the engine. He could see the chubby silhouette of his mom already waiting for him behind the aluminum storm door.

Tony waved at her as he retrieved a grocery bag from the back seat.

She held the door open for him.

"Hi, Mama." He kissed her weathered cheek, went right into the kitchen, and placed the bag down on the kitchen table. A big, five-gallon pot boiled on the stove. The pungent and friendly smell of olive oil and garlic filled the room. It had to be at least eighty degrees inside; his mom seemed always cold, ever since she left southern Italy for good over sixty years ago.

"Whatcha you bring me?' she asked in an Italian accent thicker than one of her homemade tomato sauces.

"Some bread from Auntie Gina. She called me last night and told me to come over and bring you some fresh bread she baked yesterday afternoon before I left on vacation today."

She smiled and peeked into the grocery bag. Several round loaves of focaccia rested in the bottom. "Smells good," she said, savoring the aroma of basil and ripe tomatoes.

"Auntie Gina said to tell you 'hello,' and that you can call her if you need anything next week." He sniffed the air with his nose. "What you got cooking, Ma?"

She shuffled over to the stove and removed the lid on the big pot. A cloud of steam arose like an Indian smoke signal. She stirred the contents then replaced the lid. "Some rigatoni for your brother. He's comin' over later today with the family."

"Good, Ma."

"Why don't you stay? Eat something." She stood next to her tall lanky son who towered over her squat, four and a half foot frame. She pinched his cheek and squeezed it hard. "You need more food. Look at you, nothin' but skin and bones. You got no wife. I pray every day to Saint Anthony that you won't die because you don't eat enough."

Tony sighed, exasperated. "For crying out loud, Ma. I'm over forty years old. I'm not gonna die soon, I hope, and I'm never gonna get fat. I'm not like uncle Joey who looks like a walking plate of spaghetti about to have a heart attack."

She rapped him hard on the head with a wooden spoon.

"Owww! What'd you do that for?"

"You treat your uncle Joey with respect."

"All right, Ma," he said, rubbing the tender spot on his head. "Anyways, I wanted to tell you I probably won't be back 'til next Sunday. You need a ride to church tomorrow or should I ask Auntie Gina to come and pick you up?"

"No, I gotta ride. Mrs. Pagani and her son next door will come and get me."

"Good." he said, anxious to get on the move. He leaned over and kissed the tippy-top of her gray head.

"Don't you go getting killed by one of your friends," she implored. "And make sure you wear your Saint Christopher medal."

"Yeah, Ma."

"Lemme see," she insisted, not believing him.

Tony rooted around down the front of his shirt and pulled out a religious medal attached to a twelve-inch silver chain. "See."

"You're a good boy." She patted his skinny butt. "You bring me back some good venison, you hear?"

"I hope so, Ma."

"Take some bread with you."

He hurried out the door before she had him eating a full course Italian meal at eight-thirty in the morning. "No thanks, Ma. I gotta go. The boys are waiting for me over at Jimmy's."

* * *

Tony pulled up at Jimmy's house ten minutes later. The camper was parked in the driveway, pointing toward the street, ready to go. Jimmy and Tom Karrski were in the process of loading it up with all their gear and provisions and more beer. When Jimmy saw Tony, he waved him on to the space along side the garage where the WindStar had been parked, since Tony would be leaving his pickup truck behind.

Once settled, he got out of the cab and retrieved a heavy duffel bag and several canvas carrying bags with his guns inside. As he brushed along the chain link fence, the neighbor's dog let out a menacing bark and charged the fence.

"Jesus Christ!" Tony yelled, surprised.

Jimmy immediately leaped to his aid. He grabbed a shovel that was leaning against the side of the garage and whacked the fence near where the dog stood snarling.

"Get the fuck away from here." He swung the shovel another time. The chain link fence rattled in response. "Sorry 'bout that Tony."

Tony just shrugged his shoulders and went about putting his things inside the camper.

In the meantime, the next-door neighbor stuck his baldhead out the rear screen door of their house in response to all the racket. "What the hell's going on?" he yelled.

The hairs on Jimmy's neck bristled. "Your goddamned mangy dog, that's what."

The bald guy scowled. "If you'd leave her alone she wouldn't bother you."

The incident was a repeat of several similar ones they had had in the past.

The neighbor summoned the pooch to come indoors. "Here Precious. Come to daddy. C'mon girl."

The dog's ears bent backwards while its attention sawed back and forth between its master and Jimmy, wielding the shovel.

"C'mon girl. Get in the house."

The beast relented and scurried inside. The neighbor slammed the door.

Jimmy mumbled a last obscenity and replaced the shovel.

"Where you want me to put my things?" Tony asked, his provisions piled in the middle of the camper's floor.

"Next to Karrski's stuff…along the back wall there." Jimmy answered.

Tom Karrski ducked his head though the narrow entrance right then.

"Hey you crazy Polock." Tony said, standing up. The top of his head brushed against the metal roof of the camper.

"Hey you ugly Wop."

The two exchanged handshakes and several back slaps as if they hadn't seen each other for ages.

Tom Karrski wore an autumn-colored, one-piece camouflage suit, including an Australian style cap with a wide brim, which covered a head full of curly blonde hair. He had a ruddy complexion and rosy cheeks, caused by the combination of the chilly morning air and his life-long love affair with bourbon. Tom loved a bite from the hair of the dog, unfortunately, on an all too frequent basis.

"I forgot to ask you at the Smokehouse last night, what's this I hear about you landing a twenty-three pound bass last August?" Tony asked.

Tom answered with a broad smile. "Caught the big bastard on Torch Lake up near Traverse City. Scared the hell out of me, actually. We was mostly fishing for perch when all of a sudden…wham…something big hits. Hell, I was only using twenty-pound test line. Fought that guy for near ten minutes before landing him. They tell me it's the second biggest bass anybody's caught out of that lake. Jimmy helped net him so we could get him in the boat before he broke away."

"Surprised we did, drunk as we was," Jimmy added.

"Speaking of which…how about a little liquid refreshment this morning?" Tom asked.

Jimmy flashed a broad Cheshire cat smile and flung open the refrigerator cabinet. Every conceivable space inside was packed with beer. He took three cans out, tossed one to Tony and another to Tom, and popped the tab on his own.

"You guys didn't already start without me didja?"

They all looked up at the same time. Sam Roland, Jimmy's younger brother, barged through the front door into the camper. To get past the narrow entranceway, he had to turn sideways to accommodate his protruding stomach and a waistline at least ten inches larger than his older brother's. He wore a pair of glasses with thick plastic frames and had a fat cigar sticking straight out of his mouth, like a chubby Groucho Marks, along with a full mustache that curled across his upper lip like a fat, black caterpillar.

"Sammy!" A chorus of greetings

Tony came over to him and shook his hand. "Well if it ain't Jimmy's little brother. Long time no see, little fella." He delivered a couple of fake punches to Sam's soft belly.

Although Tony's remark was good-natured in its intent, it hit a real sore spot with Sam. All his life he had always been known as, "Jimmy's little brother", and for most of the kids growing up in their neighborhood as "Jimmy's *fat* little brother." He never liked having to follow in his older brother's footsteps or to live up to the expectations other kids had of him. Sam had always been fat, "big-boned" like Dad used to say. He wasn't as popular as Jimmy and never became "one of the boys" in whatever circle of friends they shared over the years. The years had removed much of the resentment for Sam, but the feelings still lurked in the back of his mind at times.

Sam managed a smile. "Yeah...how's it going, Tony."

"'Bout time you got here," Jimmy added.

Sam hunched his shoulders. Actually, he had burned rubber most of the way from Port Huron, where he worked and lived, covering the fifty some miles commute to Flint in about thirty-five minutes on mostly two lane roads. Despite their differences in growing up, Sam shared Jimmy's enthusiasm for deer hunting and similar outdoor activities.

"Had to drop the kids off at 'Y-Camp' for some church thing this weekend," he said, flinging his suitcase and gun cases on the bunk that extended over the driver's cab. "Clear sailing after that. Got here as fast as I could. How about a beer? The old lady says to say, 'Hello', by the way."

"Hi, back," Jimmy said, handing him a can of beer. Martha, Sam's "old lady", was best of friends with Jimmy's wife, Brenda. At times, they seemed to get along better than the two brothers.

Sam removed a warm hunting vest he was wearing with a dozen or more pockets stitched across the front and threw the thing on the floor. Beads of sweat were gathered across his forehead just from the simple task of transporting his gear from his car into the WindStar. He wasn't as used to manual labor as the others. "Heard a weather report on my way in. We may be in for a little snow. They said maybe an inch or two 'round Traverse City. The U.P. might see more." He swallowed half the contents of the beer can in one huge gulp, wiped the foam from his mustache, and then let out a loud belch.

"Hey! No belchin' and no fartin' in the camper," Jimmy shouted, straight-faced.

The three other fellows gave him a curious look.

Then Jimmy lifted his left leg and let go a real stinker that rattled off the inside walls of the camper.

Tony buried his head in the bed he was sitting on; Tom laughed aloud; and Sam somehow mustered a reply, tooting like an angry hornet from his rear end.

The four of them, gasping for fresh air, ran out of the camper.

"Holy shit!" Tom exclaimed. "At least a condemned criminal gets one last meal before being sent to the gas chamber."

* * *

If the sovereign nation of Canada ever considered invading the United States, they had better not conduct their territorial expansion during deer hunting season in Michigan. They would find the entire state armed tooth and nail from border to border. Every truck, van, camper, and R.V. was a rolling arsenal on wheels. The Canadian army would be thoroughly decimated by roving hordes of avid hunters, wielding a variety of lethal weaponry such as shotguns, rifles, pistols, slingshots, and, of course, bows and arrows.

The American hunter militias would number several hundred thousand soldiers, anxious to be battle tested. Fueled by massive consumption of beer and alcohol, and an occasional marijuana joint thrown in, these men would enter battle in a crazed frenzy to win at whatever the cost. The inebriated force would also be extremely mobile, supplemented by a variety of two, three, and four wheeled vehicles of all sorts and descriptions. There would be terrible carnage.

Our poor, unprepared neighbors north of the border wouldn't know what hit them.

If the entire Canadian military could be so easily dispatched by such an armed armada of crazed civilian deer hunters, what chance did the unarmed deer have?

Jimmy and his lieutenants headed up through the center of the state on I-75. The interstate was crammed with carloads, busloads, and truckloads of other deer hunters, along with the requisite paraphernalia required to keep most of them alive for at least the next week or so.

The chasses of their vehicles hung low to the pavement due to the heavy loads they carried - much of it beer and alcohol.

Brenda offered the boys some breakfast, eggs and pancakes, before they started on their gruesome journey. Much to Jimmy's chagrin, his companions were just plain hungry and couldn't resist Brenda's invitation to eat at least one more time that day. Sam, of course, ate twice as much as anyone else and took twice as long to finish. That added another thirty-minute delay to their trip. Once on the road, Jimmy drove and Sam rode shotgun, keeping him company in the cabin for the first part of the trip. They got on the highway right around ten o'clock, an hour late, according to Jimmy's reckoning. Tom and Tony settled in comfortably in the backend, either catnapping, drinking beer, or playing cards for the first couple of hours.

A thick blue haze soon settled inside the cab of the WindStar, the result of Sam lighting his fat cigar and Jimmy's cigarette chain smoking. The men were quiet for the first part of the trip. They were well past the city of Midland, about an hour north of Flint, before Jimmy and Sam spoke their first words.

The radio station reported the latest weather forecast, confirming the possibility of light snowfall that Sam had mentioned earlier.

"Doesn't sound too bad," Jimmy remarked.

"Naw." Sam agreed.

Jimmy put his turn signal on to pass a huge recreational vehicle, the size of a Detroit city bus, lumbering in the right hand lane.

"Take a look at the size of that monster. Bet that baby runs better than a couple hundred grand," Jimmy said.

The bus had a large picture window cut into its side with five guys lounging on lazy-boys and watching what looked to be an NFL football game on a wide screen television set.

"Lucky bastards." Sam remarked, twirling one of the ends of his mustache as he surveyed the huge rolling lap of luxury out his window.

"How much snow did they say?" Jimmy asked, changing the subject back to the weather.

"A couple of inches, maybe a little more in the U.P. May not even start until we get there by the sounds of it."

Jimmy didn't like traveling in the snow, especially in the WindStar. Even with snow tires, the cumbersome beast didn't get the best traction.

An oversized Ford S.U.V. came flying past them, then put on its brakes and scooted right in front of Jimmy to get off at the next exit. In turn, Jimmy had to step on his breaks pretty hard. A couple of things rattled loose in the backend of the WindStar.

"Goddamn traffic." Jimmy muttered.

A steady stream of heavy traffic headed was north. It resembled rush hour in Detroit clear out in the Michigan boonies.

"So how's work?" Sam asked, relighting the tip of his fat cigar that had gone out.

"Okay. You know, same ol' shit, every day."

"Any more talk of them closing down more lines?"

Jimmy smirked. "Hell, who knows? They're always talking about closing down something. Shit, half of the town's gone over the last thirty years. There won't be anything left pretty soon. Long as I get enough time to get my pension, I don't give a rat's ass. The company can go 'F' itself far as I'm concerned. Them bastards can kiss my ass."

"Dad and Granddad would crap in their graves if they saw what was happening today." Sam said.

"I'll say," Jimmy nodded. "Back then the union had some power. A fella couldn't lose his job unless the union said so. Being union meant something. Nowadays, the company just up's and move's everything whenever it feels like to some where's like Mexico or Puerto Rico, so they can pay them wetbacks with cheap pesos. No benefits or insurance down there. Those monkeys will work for peanuts. Meanwhile, we're up here busting our butts and loosing jobs like crazy. You're lucky you quit fifteen years ago, Sam, and went to work for the government. Least you'll always have a job."

Sam worked as a border crossing guard between Port Huron in Michigan and Hamilton, Ontario in Canada. The work mostly involved being on the look out for any terrorists trying to make it into the country and protecting U.S. agriculture from the importation of some non-descript insect or virus, inadvertently being transported by some little old lady who bought a fruit or vegetable basket while visiting a relative somewhere in Canada. An occasional drug bust might happen once every two or three years, but most of the time, Sam was bored to death in his job. He was forced to ask the same boring questions, day in and day out, to the hundreds of travelers passing back and forth between the two countries every day:

"Are you a United States Citizen?
What state do you live in?
How long were you in the country?
Where did you visit?
Do you have anything to declare?"

The job didn't pay as well as many of the jobs in the automobile manufacturing sector, but it was far more reliable and dependable. Sam never regretted his decision to quit G.M. and move to Port Huron. It also gave him the opportunity to get away from under the shadow of his older brother and let the scars of his youth time to heal. As a result, Sam and Jimmy actually drew closer together as they grew older.

"Betcha that bus with the big picture window we passed back there is full of a bunch of company honchos from somewhere. Don't know their ass from a hole in the ground. Couldn't shot a fuckin' deer if it stepped right out in front of them." Jimmy said, his lifelong disdain for their kind fermenting inside of him.

Sam chawed on the end of his stogie.

"So how'd you find out about this place we're headed?" Sam asked.

"Went to one of those 'Outdoor' shows down in Ann Arbor last summer. A bunch of motels and hunting lodges had booths set up. Looked like some good deer hunting up in the Upper Peninsula, so I made the arrangements. We ain't never hunted for deer up there. Sounded like a good idea to me."

Sam mulled over the words. "Well, I just hope it's worth the extra four or five hours we gotta drive to get there."

Jimmy nodded. "Me too. Otherwise, it's a mighty far commute and a poor excuse to drink a lot of beer."

* * *

A couple of hours later, Tom and Tony were still in the back end of the Windstar drinking beer like thirsty fish, when Jimmy pulled off at the Gaylord exit, about an hour's drive south of the Mackinaw Bridge. A light snow sifted down from a crowded deck of dirty gray, marshmallow clouds. The temperature was still warm enough that the flakes melted the minute they landed. About a half mile down the road, Jimmy veered a hard right and drove into the parking lot of a local restaurant. It looked as though the building had been hewn from the rough trunks of white pine trees that grew all around the area.

A white, neon sign standing out front along the street announced their bill of fare. "Eggs, Sausage, and Toast - $2.99 - Served all Day. He-Man Lunch Special - $4.99."

A flotilla of trucks and busses and vans and R.V.'s crowded the little parking lot. The place looked like a Disneyland for deer hunters. Men strutted about in a cacophony of camouflage get-ups, wearing bright-colored caps and hiking boots with thick alligator soles. They heaved their overweight bodies out of their vehicles, stiff from long ride, stretching and yawning, scratching their private parts in the open parking lot.

Jimmy flung the door to the WindStar open. "Time to get up off your drunken asses and get something to eat."

Tony and Tom awoke pasty-faced, rubbing the sleep from their closed eyelids, with great rolling yawns. The relaxing buoyancy of the WindStar as it traveled down the expressway, much like an ocean liner on the water, acted as a sedative and had placed both of them into sleepy doldrums. One by one, they filed into the restaurant, after first visiting the toilet for some necessary personal maintenance. A homely local teenage girl seated them at heavy oak table covered with a faded gingham tablecloth that was honeycombed with several large holes in the plastic from burning cigarettes.

Through tired, bloodshot eyes, Jimmy surveyed the greasy menu, a hunk piece of clear laminated plastic built to last for the next two hundred years. The place specialized in the usual fare of fried everything.

A saw-off waitress about four and a half feet tall, wearing a frilly gingham dress that matched the plastic tablecloth, sauntered over to take their order. She also had on a pair of faded clodhopper sneakers about three sizes larger than her feet. Her plastic nametag identified her as, "Trixie."

"What can I get for you fellas?" she asked, poised with pen and little green note pad in hand, obviously in a hurry to service the other twenty or so customers in her assigned area.

Nothing looked that appetizing.

"What do you recommend?" Sam finally asked.

"The 'He-Man' lunch special is $4.99, including your drink," she answered.

"What's zat?" Tony asked.

"A quarter pound steak burger, with fried peppers and onions. Comes with steak fries. Cheese is an extra fifty cents."

"I'll have that."

"Yeah, I'll have the same," they each chirped in refrain.

"With cheese," someone finally added. The rest nodded in suit.

"Cokes okay?"

"Sure."

"Make mine Seven-up," Tom added.

Then Trixie gave the usual response. "No Seven-up. Sprite okay?"

"Yeah."

"Four 'He-Man' platters with cheese, three Cokes, and one Sprite," she repeated for their benefit, as if they needed assistance remembering what they had just ordered. "Anything else?"

"Naw,"

Trixie disappeared through a swinging door into the bowels of the noisy kitchen.

"How much longer?" Sam asked, placing his unlit cigar in an ashtray sandwiched between a couple of old-style plastic ketchup and mustard containers.

Jimmy yanked up his blue, flannel shirtsleeve and glanced at his watch. "Three…maybe four hours at most. We should get there around mid-afternoon."

They were sitting next to a window overlooking the restaurant parking lot, when the expensive bus with the big picture window they had passed earlier lumbered into the lot. The leviathan on wheels had to park across several spaces normally reserved for three or four automobiles. As it turned out, the bus stopped right in front of Jimmy's WindStar.

"Take a look at the size of that son of a bitch," Tony commented.

Several minutes later, seven guys tumbled out of the bus. They all wore perfectly manicured hunting outfits, with plush woolen hats and goose-down vests and fine leather boots, the expensive outfits most likely purchased in one of those exclusive executive sporting goods stores down in Detroit. They headed for the restaurant.

"See what I told you, Sam?" Jimmy said with a bit of distain along with a contemptible nod in their direction. "Bigwigs."

According to Jimmy's jaded perception, the "bigwigs" swaggered into the restaurant as if they owned the place, and sat down at a one of the large center tables without waiting for the restaurant hostess to seat them. Jimmy could smell their cologne, their arrogance. It made him angry. They reminded him of that company weasel, Pete Davis, his foreman on the fuel injector line at the plant, and all the other foremen and bosses Jimmy had ever worked for at one time or another. He didn't like them.

Jimmy snickered. "Bet they're staying at a Ritz Carlton hunting lodge somewhere, with waterbeds and hot tubs."

"Hell, that damn bus of theirs looks like a rolling Grand Hotel," Sam remarked, referring to the famous landmark on Mackinaw Island just about sixty miles north of them.

Trixie was in the process of taking the "bigwigs' food order. One of the gentlemen seemed to be talking to her when she motioned over toward Jimmy and the boys. The man got up and came over their table.

"Excuse me," he said, being almost too polite for the predominantly blue-collar surroundings. "Does that white WindStar out front belong to any of you fellas?"

Jimmy leaned back, a surly look about him. He wondered if these big shots needed even more parking space for their goddamn behemoth bus?

"Yeah, it's mine," Jimmy responded like some grade school bully, challenging another kid to cross over a line drawn in the schoolyard dirt.

"Well, I noticed on my way into the restaurant that you've got something leaking out from under your engine. Doesn't quite look right. You better check on it if you're planning to go much further today."

Jimmy's stone face evaporated. "I do?" he said in disbelief. "Crap, I better go check."

He clambered out restaurant with Sam in tow.

"Thanks," Jimmy muttered to the Good Samaritan with a bit of guilty reluctance.

"No problem," replied the gentleman. "If you need help or something, we got plenty of tools in our bus."

Sam nodded in appreciation and then followed Jimmy who was already half way out the door.

* * *

A pungent puddle of frog-green liquid had accumulated on the asphalt pavement beneath the hood of the WindStar and a curlicue of steam rose from the radiator. The same frog-green gunk was splattered all over the slightly rusted engine block and all the paraphernalia connected to it.

Jimmy stuck his index finger into the radiator hole. "Looks bone dry. Must have blown a hose or something and then lost all the antifreeze," Jimmy said, lifting the UAW baseball cap off his head and scratching his scalp with the same hand.

"Good thing we found out about it here in town, where we can get someone to fix it," Sam commented.

"Yeah," Jimmy answered, preoccupied with his own thoughts. He grabbed the top of the hood and slammed it closed hard. "Well, let's go inside, finish off lunch, and see if we can get the blasted thing fixed somewhere close by."

They went back in the restaurant and walked past the bigwigs.

"Anything wrong?" the Good Samaritan asked.

"Blew a water hose or something. Shouldn't be too hard to get fixed," Jimmy answered.

"Well, if you need some help or a lift somewhere?"

"There're a lot of gas stations right around here. Thanks anyway."

"Good luck," the gentleman offered.

Jimmy smirked with his back to him and went back to his table. His "He-Man" platter awaited him.

They ate quickly, silently; their thoughts all concentrating on the prospect of how long it would take to get the WindStar fixed. They were anxious to get on the road and start their deer hunting adventure.

Twenty minutes later, Jimmy steered the R.V. into a grimy little cinder-block gas station across the street. An attendant, in greasy overalls, the spitting image of Goober on the old Andy Griffith television show, crawled out from under the chassis of a Ford pickup where he was changing the oil. He looked like some ugly insect, emerging from its underground nest. Jimmy couldn't tell whether the man was black or white.

"Kin I help ya?" He wiped some oil smeared across his forehead with an oily rag that just left more oil.

Sam, Tom, and Tony were playing a game of "pitch" in the back of the WindStar, leaving the negotiating to Jimmy.

"Think I got a busted water hose. All the fluid in the radiator leaked out while we were eating lunch." Jimmy pointed to the pine log restaurant across the street.

"Awright," Goober remarked. "Lemme see."

He got Jimmy to release the hood latch and then raised the metal canopy open himself. He peered into the engine compartment as if it might harbor some kind of creature that was apt to bite him on the hand.

"Yeah. I'd say so." He agreed with Jimmy's diagnosis. "I kin have 'er fixed in a coupla hours so's ya be on yer ways an outa here fast like, if ya want me to."

"Couple of hours? Just to change a water hose?" Jimmy griped.

"Changin' the dad-gum hose 'tain't the problem. Don't stock them kinda hoses here for R.V.'s, especially old ones like yers. I kin get one in town, but it'll take a little time, an' I gotta finish the Ford in there first."

Jimmy let out an audible sigh. "Okay," he agreed with some reluctance. What choice did he have? "How much?"

"'Bout fifty, seventy-five bucks…plus the hose an' parts." Goober smiled with only a handful of teeth showing.

"Go ahead." Jimmy resigned.

"I'll get on it soon's I finish up here's." Goober crawled back under the Ford pickup and left Jimmy's hood up.

Just then a horn sounded on the street. It was the Good Samaritan who had told Jimmy about the leak in the WindStar. He waved at Jimmy as he pulled the massive bus with the big picture window onto the road, heading for the entrance ramp back onto the expressway.

Automatically, Jimmy waved back. When he realized what he had done, he quickly withdrew his hand. Jimmy knew he owed the man his gratitude for bringing the leak to his attention, otherwise they might have ended up stranded somewhere in the Michigan boondocks with a broken down vehicle and no way to get it fixed. Better to be stranded at some crummy gas station where he could at least play some cards and drink a couple of brewskis until the repairs were complete.

* * *

"Holy shit." Jonathan Briggs, the meteorologist up in Traverse City, glanced around making sure no one had actually heard his profane remark. His wife had warned him not to use "such language" at home, at work, in public, around the kids, not anywhere. Not that anyone was there to hear him anyway. No one was. Usually, only one person was required to come in on Saturday's into the office. Jonathan Briggs worked every third Saturday of the month.

He placed his Daffy Duck mug down and reviewed the latest meteorological data. The cold front that had been approaching the upper Midwest had stalled right above Lake Superior and decided to take up permanent residence in Southern Ontario province. A satellite map of the region showed a series of tightly packed isobars that went right over and through the lake, looking like the concentric whorls of an enormous, greasy fingerprint.

For the lower peninsula of Michigan, the condition meant that only a light amount of snow would be expected. However, for parts of the Upper Peninsula the effects of lake snow due to the cold winds blowing over the slightly warmer water in the lake could be quite heavy. Amounts of two to three feet in some areas could be possible, a far cry from the puny two to four inches previously predicted.

Jonathan checked the clock on the wall. Two-eighteen exactly, at least according to some atomic timepiece located deep in the bowels of the Colorado Rockies by which all the national weather service clocks around the country were synchronized. He still had time to get an updated forecast out to local print, radio, and television news outlets.

He fingers flew over the keyboard with the revised heavy snow warnings for the U.P. and a new forecast for the rest of the state. He pushed the send button, which would transmit the data to about a hundred and fifty locations. Then he flipped on the television set they had there in the office and tuned into the twenty-four hour weather channel to see if they agreed with his assessment.

To his surprise, they did. He toasted them by raising Daffy to the screen.

* * *

Three frustrating hours later, after Jimmy's "He-Man" lunch had begun to churn suspiciously in his stomach, Goober finished installing a replacement water hose on the WindStar.

"Let me borrow your cell phone," Jimmy said to Sam, putting an end to the card-playing marathon. Beer cans littered the floor of the cabin of the mobile home and an acrid cloud of cigar smoke rolled out the door.

"What for?"

"I gotta pay for the repairs with my debit card. So I need to call Brenda and tell her to make sure there's enough money in the bank account."

"Sure," said Sam, searching his jacket for the phone and then handing it to Jimmy.

Jimmy trotted over to the gas station office, where Goober was punching a bunch of numbers into an old-style adding machine, the kind with rows of tiny red and white numbered buttons on the face and a spool of paper attached on top, like a roll of miniature toilet paper.

"A hundred nineteen dollars and forty-five cents," he said, handing the proof of his calculations to Jimmy.

Jimmy shook his head while handing his debit card to the dirty attendant. He punched his home phone number into the keyboard of the cell phone and jabbed at the send button. About five rings later, the telephone message machine at home picked up. Brenda's voice crackled on the well-worn tape.

"This is the Roland residence. We're not at home right now. Please leave a message at the tone and we'll call you back as soon as we can."

"The Roland residence." That sounded so highfalutin' fancy to Jimmy every time he heard the message.

"*Beeeep.*"

"Brenda, this is Jimmy. We had some engine trouble and I had to get the thing fixed. I put the charge on our debit card, about a hundred and fifty bucks. Why don't you hold off mailing one of our payments for a while, otherwise our checks will go bouncing all over tarnation like a bunch of basketballs. Thanks. So far, the trip's going okay. Call you sometime next week…if I can. Bye."

He punched the red "Stop" button and placed the phone down on a dilapidated display cabinet made entirely of glass and held together by duct tape on all four corners. The display contained packages of Wrigley's spearmint gum and an assortment of candy bars whose wrappers were faded and well past their expiration date.

"Sign here." The receipt Goober handed Jimmy to sign had several smudged fingerprints on it. "Where ya headed?" Goober asked.

"Luce County. Up north."

"Deer huntin'?"

"Does a bear shit in the woods?" Jimmy retorted with his usual response.

"Wouldn't know about that," Goober answered as if he had never heard the phrase. "Supposed to be some snow headed that-a-ways."

Jimmy hadn't heard a recent weather forecast. He had been playing poker with the guys in the camper while Goober did his thing to get the WindStar back to driving condition.

"Suppose so." Jimmy just wanted to get the hell out of there and on the road as fast as he could. As it was, they had already lost close to a half a day and now would be faced with driving the last part of the trip in the dark along with the prospect of running into some snow. He handed the signed receipt to Goober.

"Thanks Mister Roland." Goober said, checking the signature as if it was an autograph belonging to a famous person. The "s" in Mister whistled through the spaces between his missing teeth.

"Yeah…thanks."

* * *

They were tooling down in the right hand lane of the interstate at about seventy miles an hour, while anxious traffic in the left hand lane zipped passed at eighty. Jimmy would like to have gunned the R.V. a bit faster, but he knew he'd be asking for problems if he pushed the ten-year old WindStar any harder. Damn thing just might decide to throw a rod. That's all they needed, another delay. The sky overhead unfolded into a gigantic checkerboard tablecloth with an invisible giant on the other side having poked holes through it with massive fingers. Pillars of brilliant snow fell through the holes and obscured the forested land beneath.

Tom Karrski, brown eyes sparkling despite his consumption of prodigious amounts of beer and bourbon, was in the process of telling a joke, the last in a long line of knee-slappers and one-liners contributed by each one of them over the course of the past half hour. His elbows leaned on the bucket seats, where Jimmy and Sam were sitting, while Tony listened and rested comfortably on the back bunk.

"This beautiful woman comes on to the bartender real strong, like she's flirting with him. She asks, 'May I speak to the manager?' He looks around and says, 'Nope. He went home for the evening.' The woman moves in a little closer to the bartender, stroking his beard with her fingers, egging him on. Then he says, 'Is there something I can do for you, honey?'"

A big double-bottom semi rumbled next them on the left, making considerable racket. Tom waited for the truck to pass while prolonging the suspense to the eventual punch line in the process.

He continued. "The gorgeous woman says, 'Yes, there is. I need you to give the manager a message,' she said, popping a couple of her fingers into the bartender's mouth, allowing him to suck them gently. The bartender by now is really turned on, of course. So he says, kissing her fingers, 'What would you like me to tell him, honey?' She pulls him over a little closer to her and then whispers in his ear, 'Tell him that he just ran out of soap and toilet paper in the ladies room.'"

Howls thundered through the cabin. Jimmy just about lost control of the WindStar because he was bent over the steering wheel in almost painful laughter.

He sobered up quickly, however. "All right guys, we gotta cool it for awhile. Toll booth coming up."

A turtle green road sign, stark against the fresh coating of snow, announced the approach to the Mackinaw Bridge, which spanned the cold waters of Lake Michigan and connected the Upper Peninsula to the lower part of the state. A couple of minutes later, Jimmy forked over the one dollar and fifty cent fare to a woman tollbooth attendee. She looked kind of funny, wearing a tan uniform that resembled the exact one the nutty park ranger wore in the old Yogi Bear cartoons. Jimmy chuckled to himself.

The WindStar lurched up the two and a half mile incline toward the soaring Mackinaw Bridge suspension towers, the engine whining like a over-extended sled dog at the effort. Gradually, as they rose up to the eventual five hundred foot level above Lake Michigan's frigid wasters, the cold horizon of the massive body of fresh water came into view. The water churned murky and gray, a mirror image of the angry clouds above. To their left lay miles of open water and the state of Wisconsin, hidden somewhere behind an opaque curtain of lake-effect snow squalls. Mackinac Island, deserted by summer's tourist hordes, floated off on the starboard side, seemingly suspended by a kind of strange magic somewhere between the earth and sky. The delicate red and pink roofs of the houses and souvenir shops dappled the pure white shoreline in bright colors, while a tiny lighthouse on the bay twinkled in the dimming daylight.

Memories of past childhood vacations flooded Jimmy's mind as he glanced over at the mystical island. His parents had taken him and Sam to the island many times when they were kids, mostly in the summers when lilacs bloomed and cherry trees blossomed. That's the way Jimmy remembered his mother; fragrant, like the island, smelling of lilacs and cherry blossoms. Mom, Dad, and little brother Sammy loved the homemade chocolate fudge made on cold marble slabs, right there in Murdicks on the Main Street. Jimmy, however, preferred the Salt Water Taffy he could buy for a nickel apiece in a small candy shop a little further down the narrow brick street that was always packed with constant pedestrian traffic. As a young lad, he enjoyed watching the strange tinker-toy machine, struggling in the front window of the candy store that pulled and stretched the soft, sticky goop between spindly frigile spikes. He never did learn the names of all the various flavors he liked to eat, hundreds of them, and only knew them by colors; pink and yellow and sky blue and lavender and a rainbow of neon shades sometimes mixed together in grand confusion. A "yellow one" might just as well taste of lemon or banana or vanilla or of some other exotic perfumed flavor. Taffy, by the mouthfuls, stuck to his molars and could only be pried loose by an adventurous index finger, much to the chagrin of his mother.

Rarely did the family spend their nights on the island, preferring instead to stay at one of the more affordable motels in Mackinaw City, the northern most town on the Lower Peninsula. Dad's union wages had its limitations, the hotels on the island being quite expensive for anyone having to pay for them with their meager hourly wages. Each day they would board one of the many ferries that worked the coast and transport them out to the always-chilly island for a day of hiking or bicycling along the rocky island coastline. Most times, they would not return back to the mainland shore until near dusk when the sun set fire to the lake. Jimmy remembered the Grand Hotel on the island with its manicured gardens and colossal front porch, where every chair was occupied with lovely women, sitting in pastel dresses, and gentleman, wearing bright silk ties and the finest of suits. Rich people stayed there, not folks like Jimmy, little Sam, or Mom and Dad. The rocky island seemed like heaven to Jimmy, a place impossible to attain for a young boy from Flint whose Dad worked in the factory.

Surrounded by the icy waters of the lake, Mackinac Island lay as frozen as Jimmy's memories, and as distant, and soon vanished behind a curtain of falling snow. The massive suspension towers on the bridge, holding the huge structure in place, gradually faded in the rearview mirror. Jimmy switched on the windshield wipers and lit the end of another Marlboro. Heavy, wet snow began pelting the windshield as they turned off the expressway and headed westward.

* * *

Sheriff Svenson watched the snow swirl on Newberry's main street through the open slats of the dusty Venetian blinds hanging in his office front window. He could already hear the prattle of several snowmobile engines churning in the distance. If the weather predictions were correct, travel by any means other than snowmobile would become all but impossible within the next forty-eight hours or so.

He went back to his desk, littered with unread stacks of documents and reams of papers waiting to be filed, and returned to reading one of the missing person's reports from several years earlier. The report involved a retired lumberjack by the name of James LeClair, who lived in a dilapidated "A" frame cabin he had built himself located just off the shoreline of Lake Superior. A loner, the old man had been somewhat of a colorful fixture in the area since most folks could remember.

An old cousin of his from Marquette on the western side of the U.P. reported him missing, after Mr. LeClair failed to return several of their regular weekly telephone calls. A brief three or four day search for the man turned up nothing and he'd been listed as missing ever since. Most local law enforcement authorities assumed the man either wandered off on a hunting excursion or drowned fishing in some local lake or river, most likely the body ending up in the depths of Lake Superior, the largest fresh water lake in the world. If indeed that was his fate, the hungry sturgeons and other fishy scavengers prowling the depths of the great lake would have made short work of his earthly remains.

What intrigued sheriff Svenson the most, however, was the timing of Mr. LeClair's disappearance, estimated in late October some four years earlier. The time of year matched a similar pattern of other missing persons scattered across the Upper Peninsula of Michigan that had been reported over the past twenty-five years, the entire period of time where records were available. The sheriff had determined that of the over fifty cases of missing persons reported in the last quarter of a century, almost all of them occurred during the months of October and November.

One further statistic worried him even more. In years where missing persons had been investigated, multiple occurrences were common, usually anywhere from four to eight cases had been reported. All the cases remained unsolved.

The bell to the entrance door rang loud enough to shake the mercury fillings in the sheriff's mouth. He glanced up from his work to see Frank Finnerdy, the supervisor in charge of highway and road maintenance for the county, blunder through the doorway. The visitor's meaty hands brushed away a coating of fresh snow off the arms and shoulders of his winter parka.

"Howdy, sheriff," he said, stomping his leather boots on the worn carpeting that led into the office area. Chunks of wet snow slid off his boots and went flying over the floor. "Looks like we're in for a good one for the first of the season, maybe a couple of feet by the time its done."

Ollie removed the half-rimmed reading glasses from the end of his cherry nose and placed them upside down next to the open reports on his desk. "Yah, for sure, Frank. By the looks of things, you fellas down at the county garage will have your hands full, plowing out all the roads and highways."

The supervisor went over to a small table sandwiched between two metal filing cabinets where the sheriff had a pot of hot coffee on the burner. He grabbed a Styrofoam cup and filled it half way to the top with the dark, syrupy liquid that had been simmering on the burner for at least the past four hours. He added two packets of non-sugar sweetener to the brown concoction and stirred it with a dirty plastic spoon.

"Well, that's exactly why I come over to see you, sheriff," Frank said, taking a sip of the hot brew. "The boys over at the weather service down in Traverse City think we may be in for two or three feet of snow. There ain't much sense clearing the highways when Mother Nature's just going to cover them back up ten minutes later."

"Yah, I can see that," the sheriff agreed.

The road supervisor continued. "So I'm telling my crews to hold off until this thing blows through, if that's okay with you." Local regulations required the County road supervisor to coordinate such activities with the sheriff's department.

Ollie considered the ramifications of their decision briefly in his mind. "Yah...sure, Frank. Most of the folks living here got no problem with that. I'm sure we got some tourists passing through the area, most likely some deer hunters from downstate. Hopefully, they got enough brains in their heads to go to a motel or something until the storm lets up. I'll try to get the word out about the road conditions here in the U.P. soon as I can."

"Thanks, sheriff. I've got to make some phone calls as well." Frank turned to leave when he remembered something. "Understand you found a dead woman from down in Kalamazoo this morning up north of here."

"Well...actually, it vas my deputy, Freddy, that found her." The sheriff omitted going into the details of only finding the lady's bones and not much of the body.

The supervisor shook his head. "Too bad," he said. "I understand the husband's still missing as well. He'll be harder to find or track because of this storm."

The sheriff wanted to say that the husband was probably long since dead by now, but he merely agreed with Frank. "You betcha."

"Well...I'd better be heading back over to the county garage," Frank said, taking one last sip of coffee, grimacing slightly at the taste, and throwing what was left in the wastebasket. He replaced the fur-lined hood on his parka over his head. "See you later, Ollie."

"Yah, Frank. See you later."

Cold air blasted through the open door as Frank left, rattling some of the papers on the sheriff's desk. The brisk wind slammed the door closed hard.

The sheriff's eyes stared blankly at the rift of unsolved reports cluttered atop the desk, while his thoughts drifted elsewhere. He thought about tourists and hunters, traveling through his county, perhaps getting stranded in the bitter winter storm, and about the strange tracks he and Freddy had seen earlier that afternoon along with the remains of Valerie Pearson. He also realized it was the middle of November, and how all this sounded familiar, only too familiar.

* * *

Propped up on one elbow and laying on the back bunk of the camper like some sexy, male Mata Hari, Tom Karrski took another hard swallow of smooth Kentucky bourbon from a shiny metal flask. His lips drew aside like an angry wolf to reveal a straight line of teeth clinched tightly together. The flask, containing the cheap five-year old bourbon he'd picked up at the grocery store the night before, reminded him of the battered aluminum canteen he had been given by army supply at boot camp down in Missouri decades earlier when he was a buck private in training. That's where his drinking started, with the military. That career came to an abrupt end twelve years later because his drinking had become a "problem". His former unit commander at the time said, "Tom, you're a good soldier; unfortunately, you're a drunk soldier ninety percent of the time and the other ten percent of the time, you're looking to get drunk." It was a complaint that was to be repeated throughout his working career by a variety of disappointed employers. In Tom's defense, when he was sober, he did good work. Even when he was drunk, he was surprisingly reliable, usually showing up for work on time, even through he might be harboring a hangover and a headache the size of New York. Somehow, Tom managed an alcoholic lifestyle with a working career in the automobile assembly plants in Flint, as did a lot of other guys who were in the union. He wasn't the first guy to do it and he wouldn't be the last.

He replaced the flask in the wide elastic band on his Australian brimmed hat. The constant road bumps in the back of the WindStar seemed magnified from where Tom was lying, trying to relax. He flopped around and repositioned his lanky frame on the lumpy mattress, when he felt a sudden stabbing sensation in his side. He peeled back some of the covers on the bunk in order to determine the origin of his discomfort.

"For crying-out-loud!" he yelled. Tony and Sam turned to see what was the matter. "Will you look at this for Christ sake." Dangling from his hand by its rubbery tale was the bony skeleton of a fish with its mummified head still attached, apparently a left over from one Jimmy's past fishing excursions. No telling how long it had been there.

Jimmy gave a quick glance back as well from his driver's seat. "Well, what the hell's wrong with that?"

Tom crooked his face into the shape of a question mark. "Whatta ya mean, what's wrong? It's a goddamn dead fish."

"Fuck it is." Jimmy replied, smiling. "Looks like a good-sized bluegill from here."

Tony and Sam smirked.

"A bluegill?" Tom repeated in a pale imitation of his sarcastic pal. "A goddamn dead bluegill." He tossed the bony carcass forward so that it landed between the two front bucket seats. The stench of the thing quickly overpowered the cabin.

"Pee-you." Sam pinched the ends of his nostrils. He rolled down the window, grabbed the fish's calcified remains, and threw the skeleton over in the general direction toward Canada. "Catch and release," he commented with a shitty little grin stretched across his broad face. He quickly rolled the window back up as snow streamed in through the opening.

Jimmy rolled his eyes.

Heavy, wet snow stuck to the wiper blades like someone was outside, throwing gobs of sticky bread dough at the windshield. Evening had fallen and a narrow two-lane highway had replaced the broad expressway since Jimmy turned off some thirty minutes earlier. The road ahead glittered with what seemed to be a millions of mayflies caught in the beams of the yellow headlights on the WindStar. They encountered fewer and fewer vehicles traveling in either direction as they headed further into the wilderness of the Upper Peninsula.

Jimmy's eyes were firmly set on the road ahead, his concentration intense as the snow continued to mount outside.

"Two to four inches." Sam remarked sarcastically, peering out the snow-clogged window. "Gotta be half a foot out there already."

Tony, in the back, expressed a bit of growing concern. "Maybe we should stop up ahead somewhere in a motel and call it a night?"

"Ahhh…it ain't that bad," Jimmy insisted. "A couple more hours and we should get to the lodge. Besides, finding a motel up here in the boonies ain't gonna be that easy." He decided it would be better to get everyone's mind off the road. "Anybody else getting hungry?"

The skinniest one of the group seemed the most anxious. "I'm starvin'," Tony said.

"You'll find some sandwiches that Brenda made last night over in the red cooler somewhere in the back. Should be some chips in there too."

Tony rummaged around and found the cooler. He retrieved a handful of sandwiches, each carefully wrapped in its own individual plastic baggie, and handed them out the same way he dealt cards when playing a game of poker.

"What kind are they?" Tom asked, eying his with suspicion, in the dim light of the moving cabin.

"Who the hell cares?"

Tom shrugged his shoulders. "Right." He took a big bite into his. It was ham and Swiss cheese spiced with a swath of hot mustard. "Tastes good," he mumbled with a mouthful that made his remark all but unintelligible.

* * *

A blinding blizzard waged all around them, as they snuggled comfortably inside their cozy mobile hide-away.

"Where the hell are we?'
"I dunno."
"I can't see a goddamn thing."
"Shit."
"Blasted snow."
"Maybe we should head back?"

Jimmy considered the suggestion, but only briefly. "Hell," he said. "We passed the last good-sized town over an hour ago. It'll take us twice that long to backtrack. We should be coming to our turn off toward the frigging lodge any minute now."

The northern gales off Lake Superior had created over a foot of lake-effect snow already; heavy, wet, and slippery. The rear end of the WindStar swayed back and forth on the slick road like an exotic dancer showing off her derrière to a rowdy crowd of enthusiastic union officials in some cheap Detroit bar. Jimmy had to constantly adjust the steering wheel to avoid spinning out of control. Just following the highway was a difficult enough task. They hadn't seen another car or truck for a least half an hour.

Sam, riding shotgun, spotted a murky road marker up ahead. "There," he said, his chubby finger pointing out the frosty windshield just in case Jimmy hadn't seen the sign. Jimmy applied the brakes, but the WindStar just kept going forward, sliding through the unlighted intersection until finally coming to a hair-raising stop about a hundred yards past the spot where they should have stopped in the first place. He threw the transmission into reverse, tires spinning wildly in the slush, barely moving backwards at two or three miles per hour.

"Can you read the sign?" Jimmy asked, squinting. Snow stuck to the sign so that only the top third of the numbers were visible.

Sam rolled down the passenger side window and careened his head outside. Falling snow, mixed with sharp pellets of sleet, slapped into his pudgy face and glistened on his black mustache. It felt like a hundred tiny pinpricks on his cheeks. "I think it says, 'M33', or something like that?"

"That must be it," Jimmy chirped, somewhat relieved they were heading in the right direction. "I think the Lodge should be fifteen or twenty more miles up the road." He didn't sound so sure of himself, not quite certain of which direction he should take. He studied the intersection. You could see the little wheels in Jimmy's head thinking, "Eenie, meenie, meinie, moe." He spun the steering wheel sharply to the right and stomped the accelerator. The bulky cruiser moved slowly forward like one of those giant ore freighters, plying the great lakes and burdened with a full load of Minnesota taconite below decks.

Along with the dense curtains of milk-white snowfall, the dark of the night seemed impenetrable. The puny headlights of the WindStar were but dim candles in a vast outdoor auditorium of sheer blackness. The highway soon gave way to a narrow, seldom-traveled corridor that twisted and turned through a bulky forest of massive evergreens, their boughs hanging low, burdened with the weight of heavy snow and ice. Jimmy felt as if he was driving in one of those computer game mazes with a series of heart-pounding blind turns and an endless monotony of sameness in whatever direction he looked. Each moment blended into the next as if time itself stood still.

They encountered several jarring roller-coaster bumps, which threw the passengers dangerously about the inside as if they were riding in an old-fashioned buckboard wagon being pulled by a team of out-of-control horses. Tony's head crashed into the ceiling with a deafening thump.

"Ouch!" he yelled.

"Sorry," Jimmy replied unable to turn his attention to anything but the terrible conditions ahead of him.

A few agonizing miles further, Jimmy muttered under his breath. "This just doesn't look right."

The road had all but disappeared.

"What the fuck is that?" Sam yelled.

He had hardly enough time to spit out the warning while Jimmy swerved in order to avoid hitting the thing. The WindStar veered hard to the left, sliding sidewise in the hubcap-deep snow, but still managed to strike something that sounded like a gunnysack filled with potatoes smashing into the grill. Next, the thing came flying over the hood of the truck and crashed against the windshield, raining shards of glass, plastic, and metal on the inside.

Jimmy lost all control. Several out of kilter visions flashed through his mind at that moment. He thought about his Dad and Granddad buried in Woodlawn Cemetery, and Brenda preparing breakfast with the sweet smell of bacon frying in the pan, and an endless procession of engine parts passing by on an endless assembly line.

Seventy-five yards later, the vehicle spun and left the road in full flight. The five-ton missile careened off several large pine trees on its way down a steep embankment with everyone inside holding on for dear life. Contents from all the drawers and compartments and niches spilled into the cabin and became lethal missiles, hurtling against anything or anyone that impeded their chaotic trajectory. The right side of the vehicle suddenly rose upward off its wheels, throwing the R.V. on its side, where it continued the wild toboggan ride down the steep slope. They could hear the sound of rocks and trees, scraping violently against the aluminum sides. Finally, the WindStar came to an abrupt and noisy end when the engine compartment collided with the gnarled trunk of a stubborn oak tree that had stood in the same lonely spot for the past eighty-four years.

Chapter Five

Then at the dawning, as day was breaking, the might of Grendel to men was known; then after wassail was wail uplifted, loud moan in the morn.
Beowulf: Anonymous

Crimson snow, deep and red; the rosy slush reminded Jimmy of one of those delicious cherry snow cones he used to buy as a kid on a hot summer day for fifty-nine cents down at the Seven-Eleven store, around the corner and about a block away from his house. Except it wasn't a cherry snow cone. It was blood, his blood, dripping from his bruised head. A vision flashed through his mind, a vagrant memory of the time he and Sammy as young boys had decided to build tree house in the friendly branches of a large sugar maple that grew in the back yard at their old house on Saginaw Street.

Sam had been pounding three-inch nails into the upper levels of the construct when his clumsy foot sent a claw hammer sailing down toward Jimmy, who was working some ten feet below him. The heavy projectile struck Jimmy dead center, right on the top of his fresh crew cut, while jarring his upper and lower jaw together in the process. He remembered the utter surprise when he lifted his wet hand from the wound and saw a palm saturated with his own blood. He screamed bloody murder the entire length of the backyard, running to Mom, who nursed him back to health with a minimum of medication; a dollop of iodine and fifteen minutes of motherly attention.

Some thirty years later, his shaking hand reached up and touched the moistness on his battered scalp and came away bloody, no pain, just a dullness that made him lightheaded. He summoned whatever strength he had and got up on all fours, a blurry world spinning around him like an out-of-whack carousel ride gone mad. Somehow, he had been thrown or fell out of the WindStar. He was kneeling in about a foot of fresh snow some twenty yards from the toppled vehicle that listed ninety degrees on its starboard side. The WindStar resembled dead road kill, its wheels up in the air still spinning slowly, a twisted pile of bent rubble with aluminum panels, seat covers, clothes, beer cans, instrument panels, and all sorts of metal and plastic debris scattered about the accident site, quickly being buried by the heavy snowfall. The whole scene resembled an Oklahoma chicken coup that had been leveled by a class four tornado.

Jimmy's head spun dizzily, thoughts not making much sense to him. He had no memory of how he got where he was. Gradually, his wits returned and he made the correct neural synapses that someone might still be trapped inside the mangled hulk. He staggered over to the WindStar, his boots constantly slipping in the snow. He kept falling down and having to pick himself up again.

The yellow beams of the headlights flared into the emptiness. It was still snowing hard and it was pitch dark. Jimmy reached the cab, shimmied up the side, and peered down through the shattered driver's window. He recognized the brooding, unconscious bulk of his brother still strapped in securely by the shoulder belt. He tried opening the bent door on the driver's side but to no avail.

He heard a groan coming from a darkened cubbyhole right behind the front seat. "Jimmy, is that you?" The familiar, but strained voice of Tony Gianinni asked.

"Tony?" Jimmy's sore eyes strained to see him. He heard shuffling, shoes scraping against metal, and then Tony's tiny owl face popped up at the entrance of the small cave.

"I'm okay. I need a hand. My legs are kinda pinched in here." His arm extended toward Jimmy as if he was swimming and in need of a life preserver.

Jimmy latched on to his arm and pulled him up through the window. It was like being extricated from the hatch of a sinking submarine.

Sam moaned.

"Careful not to step on him, Tony."

Once free the two men turned their attention to Sam.

"Sam."

"Yeah," he winced.

"You all right?"

The front cab, what was left of it, was filled with sound of heavy breathing as Sam tried to access his situation. Billows of murky frost came pouring out his mouth in regular spurts. "My right arm hurts. I think the dang thing got whacked pretty good." He sighed with obvious discomfort and shifted his ample girth, trying to unlatch the seatbelt with his left hand. It snapped with a distinctive pop from the sudden release of tension.

"Here, grab on to us," Jimmy instructed. "Try to stand up."

Sam tried to turn his body as best he could in the tight confines while nursing his right arm all the while. He braced his chubby legs and feet against the frame of the door and pushed up as hard as he could with his sore thigh muscles. After considerable effort, Jimmy and Tony were able to wrestle him around the armpits of his coat and pull him up and out through the narrow window opening.

"Watch the glass," Jimmy warned.

The three of them spilled into the cold snow with a muted thump. It took them a minute or so to catch their breath.

"How's your arm?" Tony asked Sam.

Sam clinched his teeth while holding his right arm outward with his left hand gripped around it tourniquet style. "Hurts like hell. I don't think it's broke though. Won't know 'til I get this coat off." He grimaced at the prospect.

"What about Tom?" Jimmy asked.

Tony rubbed a stiff neck he hadn't noticed before. "Last thing I knew, he was laying on back bunk."

"Let's see if we can find him. You stay here," Jimmy ordered Sam.

Jimmy and Tony clambered around the camper's backside in search of the side entrance. The camper was bent in two, like a discarded beer can run over on the freeway, with the center section completely smashed. If Tom happened to be located in the center when all hell broke loose, he'd be a goner for sure. They went toward what remained of the rear end of the vehicle, now the shape of a twisted aluminum teepee. A four-foot gash of twisted metal marked the entrance to the battered wigwam. Jimmy stuck his bloody head through the gap. The odor of gasoline and motor fluids hit his nose.

"I can't see nothing," he said. "How 'bout seeing if you can get into the glove compartment back upfront, Tony. I need a flashlight."

Tony scurried off while Jimmy buried his head back into the jagged fissure. Half a minute later, Tony handed him a bright yellow plastic flashlight that cast a sharp beam like Darth Vader's light saber in the falling snow. Jimmy aimed the beam inside. Debris lay scattered all over; Jimmy didn't even recognize the place. Over in one of the collapsed corners, under the remnants of a splintered bunk, lay the limp form of Tom Karrski, unconscious.

"There he is," Jimmy said with some relief. "I can't tell if he's alive or dead. We gotta try an' get him outa there."

Quite by instinct, Jimmy tried squeezing his rather ample girth through the jagged edge of the opening. He was just too big.

Tony yanked him aside. "Here, let me try." He snatched the flashlight from Jimmy's shaking hand, took one look to locate Tom's exact location, and plunged his skinny frame through the crevasse as if he was diving for pearls in the ocean's green depths. The junk around Tom clattered at Tony's approach. He bent down close to his injured friend, accidentally cracking his own head on a piece of exposed metal.

"He's got a big knot on the side of his noggin, but a least he's breathing, far as I can tell," came the answer Jimmy wanted to hear. "Looks like his legs are wedged in here pretty good as well."

Upon closer inspection, the beam of the flashlight revealed Tom's right leg, the pant ripped and a patch of bloody bare skin beneath. His leg appeared bent in an unusual angle as if the framework underneath was broken. It reminded Tony of the time when he and one of one of his old union buddies went drinking and tried driving home on one of those unstable three-wheeled ATV's. Both of them were hammered out of their gourds. His drunken pal managed to lose control of the ATV and overturned the motherfucker on a hairpin curve in rural Genesee County. Tony escaped with only a few scratches on his ass, while his inebriated friend fractured his leg in about three places.

"Jesus," Tony remarked. He looked up at Jimmy's face peering down through the open fissure. "Looks like he busted his goddamn leg. Gonna be hell getting him outa here."

Jimmy rested on his elbows, his eyes spacing off into the night sky choked with angry clouds, as if they might provide him an answer. Wet snow pelted his face. He thought a minute.

"Maybe we just leave him in there until we can decide what to do. Snowing like the devil out here; at least he's dry in there." Then Jimmy had an idea. "Stay with him Tony. I'll be right back."

He slid off the camper and trudged through the deepening snow to where Sam was wrapping his arm with some rags he made out of debris material lying about.

"How's the arm?"

"I think I just sprained my wrist. It'll be fine. Didja find Tom?"

"Yeah. He's out cold in the back end of the camper. His leg's broke," Jimmy answered. "I don't know where the hell we are, but we better start finding out real quick. Gimme your cell phone and we can try getting some help."

Sam nodded. He padded his coat pockets where he usually kept the phone. "Hey, didn't I give it to you when you got the water hose replaced in the WindStar?"

A perplexed look crossed Jimmy's bloodied face. "You gave it to me?" Then he remembered placing the phone on the glass display case about ten hours earlier in Goober's gas station, as the greasy country bumpkin touted up the bill for fixing the broken water hose. "Shit!" he cursed himself. Sam looked at him, questioningly. "I left the fucking thing back in Gaylord at that stupid gas station."

Sam's face took on a look of panic. "So we don't have any way of getting some help?"

Jimmy swallowed hard, the guilt not going down quite so easy. The silence was deafening with only the snow swirling around them.

"We better go check on Tom."

Jimmy helped Sam to his feet and they went back to the twisted remains of the camper. Tony was still inside with the beam of the flashlight shining on Tom. His face grimaced with pain.

Jimmy nodded toward Tony, attempting to give him whatever assurance he could. Tony understood the unspoken communication.

"How are ya, Tom?"

"Okay." The Polock's head bobbed up and down quickly as he breathed fast and labored, almost spasmodic.

"I can't move him," Tony said, beads of perspiration and dirt splattered across his forehead. "There's some kind of metal strut or pipe holding him down. I need a crow bar or something. Maybe I can bend the damn thing enough so we can pull him out."

"We'll see what we can find," Jimmy responded.

Debris of all sorts had been strewn around the accident site. Whipped by a stout wind, however, the constant deluge of falling snow quickly covered up everything on the ground. Jimmy surveyed the scene.

"See what you can find, Sam. There was a fair-sized tire iron where the spare tire attached to the back of the camper. Maybe you can find it."

"Will do," Sam said. He finally noticed a light rivulet of crimson trickling down the side of his brother's face. "Sure you're alright, Jimmy?" Sam asked, wiping the blood away from Jimmy's cheekbone with the rags wrapped around his sprained wrist.

"I'm fine. Just go," Jimmy chided, impatient.

Tony tried to remain calm and spoke quietly to Tom within the wreckage of the cabin as if they were in the middle of a church service. "We're gonna try to get you outta here, Tom. How's your legs feel?"

Lying on his back, Tom propped himself up slightly on his elbows. He tried to reach for his limbs, but couldn't because of all the rubble on top of him. "Feels sort of numb," he said. "I think the circulation's cut off."

"Lemme try getting some of that trash off of you," Tony said. He handed the flashlight to Jimmy who looked in at them from above. There wasn't enough space for

Jimmy to jump down into what remained of the cabin and help in the process.

Tony braced himself as best he could in the narrow confines and started clearing all the loose debris. He handed Jimmy pieces of wood and paper and plastic and glass of all shapes and sizes, which Jimmy threw down to a burgeoning pile along side the toppled vehicle. Among the objects discarded were a pair of broken binoculars; an assortment of cracked dishes and plates along with a cornucopia of plastic cups, knives, forks and spoons; several pillows and blankets; a variety of food and condiment containers; and scores of cans and bottles of beer, some undamaged, most smashed or leaking their precious cargo. The parade of garbage seemed endless.

Several minutes later, Sam clambered back up the listing R.V. He handed Jimmy several pieces of twisted metal with his good hand.

"Is this the only stuff you could find?" Jimmy questioned, viewing the items with a degree of suspect.

"Couldn't find that tire iron you said you had. I'll look some more," Sam answered, frustrated. "But everything's scattered all over the goddamn place. We crashed down a pretty big fuckin' ravine. Far as I can tell, things are spread over a quarter of a mile. Plus it's snowing like the fuck and darker than hell. Can't see a damn thing."

A sharp gust of wind ruffled Jimmy's hair, making it stand on end.

"I did find your friggin' hat." Managing to muster a slight smile, Sam handed the familiar blue and gold baseball cap with the "UAW" logo plastered across the front up to Jimmy.

"Thanks." Jimmy stared at the union emblem with a bit of nostalgia then put the hat on his head. The tight band of the cap rubbed sore against his battered skull, but the brim kept the distracting snow from falling into his eyes.

He handed the metal bars Sam had gathered down through the hole to Tom.

"This is the best we can do, Tony," Jimmy remarked. "Looks like parts off the frame."

Tony examined the pieces, trying to determine how best to use them as a lever in order to extricate their trapped companion. "Shine the light over here," he instructed Sam. The beam of the yellow light followed Tony's hand to a location near Tom's pelvis where two aluminum "L" shaped strips had pierced the outer skin of the cabin and cut across Tom's legs near his knees.

Tony wedged one of the bent bars underneath the strips and tried lifting. The bar slipped out of his hands, clanging against the floor of the cabin. He tried a second time, and again the bar slipped

"Shit!" Sweat poured off the end of his nose. He discarded the one bar, exchanging it for the other and tried again. The nervous flashlight beam danced in the dark. Tony strained every muscle in his gangly body, his determination evident on his clinched face and searing bright eyes. The strips holding Tom finally released with a sudden and deafening screech. Tom screamed in pain as Tony grabbed him by the jacket to prevent him from sliding down on his broken leg and injuring himself further.

"We've got to get him out of here," Tony yelled up to Jimmy. "I'll lift him up as best I can. You and Sam will have to get him from there."

Jimmy motioned for Sam to join him near the jagged entrance to the cabin.

Tony struggled while trying to raise Tom up to a level where Jimmy and Sam's outstretched arms awaited and keep his own balance without falling down himself. Tom's face contorted in agony, doing his best of stifle his screams. Pangs of unbearable sharp pain shot through his shattered leg.

"Aaurrghh!" Tom yelled unable to control himself. He fainted, leaving Tony to hoist his limp, one hundred and eighty-five pound frame alone.

Tony mustered all of his strength and lifted Tom's rag doll body upward as far as possible. "Got him?" he pleaded, unable to take the strain another second longer.

Jimmy and Sam grabbed hold of the unconscious man's arms and used their own body mass to leverage him out the cabin. The three of them landed with a dull thud in a snowy heap. Tony crawled out of the cabin a half a minute later like a cockroach emerging from a messy trash pile.

* * *

They huddled together in the darkness like homesick schoolboys on their first camping trip away from home, as a freight train of a wind howled out of the northwest. The cold gale crossed the three hundred or so mile expanse of Lake Superior before dumping the moisture it had accumulated in the form of snow on the unsuspecting lands in the Upper Peninsula of Michigan. Such gales of November were the legends of song and the direct cause of the sinking of a famous ore freighter some decades earlier. What normally should have been a reasonable accumulation of several inches turned into an avalanche, measuring two to three feet in depth. In most areas of the United States, such weather conditions would have been easily classified as a "blizzard," but in the U.P., where the winter-hardened residents were used to such common occurrences, it was euphemistically referred to as "lake effect snow." But it didn't just snow; it fell in huge cotton drifts like some wintry blight bent on destruction. It became a whirlwind, a hideous white tempest.

Jimmy shivered and raised the collar on his coat up closer around his exposed ears, his eyes unfocused on the makeshift splint encased around Tom Karrski's injured leg.

They had lashed two metal strips on either side of his leg with rags and electrical wiring from the crashed camper in an attempt to stabilize the limb from further injury. Despite drinking a half a pint of cheap Kentucky hooch in a futile attempt to desensitize him, Tom had screamed wildly and then blacked out again, as the two brothers held him down with their bulky weight and Tony reset the bone with the makeshift splint. Sickened by the sight of it all, Sam spewed whatever remained of his He-Man platter from the cheesy diner they had visited in Gaylord. The smell of his vomit and spittle hung in the tight lean-to they had slapped together from sections of panels and siding broken off during the crash to protect themselves from the elements.

Although in dire straits and lost in a blinding snowstorm, Jimmy could not escape a sense of childhood nostalgia, as he watched the snow accumulate with each passing hour. Memories of endless snowball fights, back years ago with his friends in the Theodore Roosevelt Grade schoolyard, played over and over in his mind like an old black and white videotape from a 1960's television program. He wondered why he would think such silly thoughts at a time like this of obvious peril, when he suddenly realized that he was half asleep.

"Jimmy, what's that?" someone whispered.

His eyes flicked open like the lens on a camera. He didn't know what to look for or what he was looking at.

Sam touched the sleeve on his arm. "Over there," he whispered in an ominous tone, while pointing with the hand wrapped in rags toward the open side of the lean-to and the snow-covered trees beyond.

Daybreak had just begun. A glimmer of light reflected off the snow, but most everything was still shrouded in darkness and shadows.

"I can't…quite see…" Jimmy stopped. He thought he saw something, something dark and looming, with eyes that reflected the white snowfall like highly polished marbles. Whatever the thing was, it seemed to be watching them from off in a distant grove of pine trees, toward the precipitous ravine the WindStar had plunged down. Jimmy leaned forward and focused his sleep-worn eyes on the dark caves between the crossed limbs of the trees. He could barely make out the darkened hump of something that might not even be there.

"Oooowwww!" Tom cried out in delirium.

"What's the matter?" Tony rose to his elbows, awaked by the noise.

"It's just Tom," Sam replied. "I think he's okay."

Tom fidgeted uncomfortably, resting atop the only intact sleeping bag they had been able to find in the dark. His chest heaved with a long, painful sigh but then he lapsed back to unconsciousness. His breath smelled of stale bourbon, the remnants of the failed anesthetic.

While Tony attended to Tom, Jimmy and Sam redirected their attention back to the point in the grove of pines where they thought they might have seen something. A cascade of white powder fell from one of the branches as if something my have brushed past, but more likely caused by a capricious gust of wind.

"We need to make some plans," Jimmy spoke suddenly of the thoughts he had been mulling over in his mind over the past hours. He motioned with a nod of his still blood-encrusted head for Sam and Tony to join him in a conversation outside the lean-to.

They gathered near the battered front grill of the WindStar, snow still swirling about them. Giant sized snowflakes drifted down from the sky like miniature ballet dancers dressed in frilly tutus. A dark and foreboding sky churned overhead, the feeble sun unable to show its way through the impenetrable layers of clouds as it rose.

"I don't need to tell you guys, we're in some trouble here," Jimmy began while lighting up his first cigarette of the day. Sam and Tony studied the deep snow piled near their feet, listening earnestly to Jimmy, but not looking at him directly either. "I'm not sure where the hell we're at or how we can get out. The camper's completely wrecked, so it looks like whatever we have to do, it's going to be on foot. Although for the life of me, with all this fucking snow, we're gonna have one devil of a time getting out of here."

"I'm not sure Tom is in any condition to travel," Tony stated, with Sam shivering agreement.

"Well, let's face that when we have to. In the meantime, a fire would sure help to get us warmed up and signal our location to anyone living nearby. Things look pretty disserted around here though."

"How far is it to the lodge do you suppose?" Sam asked.

"Dunno. We may have even taken a wrong turn sometime last night. Things got pretty confusing with the snow and everything. We need to get back to the road and try to figure out the best way to go."

"Right."

"Sam, why don't you try to get a fire started? There's enough crap around here from the accident, you shouldn't have much of a problem finding enough stuff to burn. Tom and I will see what we can salvage from inside the cabin and whatever else is left. We lost a lot of our stuff coming down that ravine last night; most of its covered up with snow by now and spread all over the fuckin' place." He took a drag on his cigarette, causing the end of it to flare like a forth of July sparkler.

"What about Tom?" Tony asked.

"I guess we just let him rest for right now. When he sobers up, he'll be pretty sore. Like I said, we need to figure out what the hell we're all gonna do." Jimmy tossed the lighted butt in a drift where it sizzled like a hot piece of bacon frying in a pan. "Let's get going."

While Sam went to check on Tom's condition and gather items for the fire, Jimmy and Tony made their way over to the toppled wreckage of the WindStar. They needed to salvage as much material as possible.

The whole vehicle lay twisted on its side and covered with a least half a foot of fresh snow, with no easy way to get in or out of the doors. With his extra weight, Jimmy would have a hard time navigating inside the wreckage. "Why don't I give you a boost, Tony, so you can check up in the truck cab first and see what you may be able to reach?"

"Sure thing boss. But this don't appear to be exactly union work to me," Tony tried joking.

"That's right…it ain't," Jimmy chuckled. "It's work for stupid motherfuckin' Dagos. Now get your spaghetti ass up there and take a look around." He held his arms out, with fingers lashed together like a stirrup on a saddle to give Tony a boost into the overturned cab. Tony bounced off one of the bucket seats and landed inside with a slight crash.

* * *

By mid-morning, Jimmy and Tony had rescued a variety of useful items needed for their expected journey to find permanent shelter. They stacked the stuff on a large army surplus blanket spread out next to the lean-to. Besides warm clothing, they gathered a sufficient supply of food and beer still intact, to make sure they wouldn't starve for the next twenty-four or forty-eight hours. They also found enough guns and ammunition to arm a small army, but decided to take only one rifle and two pistols with them because of weight limitations and what each of them could reasonably expect to carry on their backs. After all, the weapons would not be needed for hunting in lieu of their accident. What they lacked most were items required for emergencies, such as medical supplies and shelter materials. One good flashlight survived, but it had only one set of batteries. Most of the other stuff was either lost or destroyed in the crash or just not needed. The problem would be getting anything out of their present location and up a steep ravine a quarter mile long, which they had plunged down the night before. They would only be able to bring the items they carried themselves, including the injured Polock, who was incapable of rendering any assistance himself. The deep snow made matters only worse.

"We can't stay here," Jimmy told Sam, assessing the current situation while warming the palms of his hands against the flames of the campfire Sam had started. "We could be stuck here for…shit…who the hell knows how long, and no one would be able to find us. We've got to get back up to the road and see if we can find more permanent shelter."

The snow, at least three feet in depth and with drifts sometimes over their heads, would be their main obstacle. Just walking through the stuff loaded down with supplies would be a difficult task. Tom's medical condition was the other problem. They couldn't just leave him; somehow they had to figure a way to transport him along.

Jimmy couldn't help but regret his own stupidity for leaving Sam's cell phone back at the gas station. Without it, they had no way of communicating their situation to anyone.

Tony's head popped up out of the backend of the mangled cabin with another load in hand. "Here's some more stuff we might need," he said. He handed down the treasure trove to Jimmy; a compass broken off the dashboard of the truck, some knives used mostly to fillet fish, one small axe, a hundred yard coil of bright orange rope, two more pistols, several boxes of ammunition, and Jimmy's favorite deer hunting rifle, the 30-30 Winchester rifle he called "Old Faithful". "There's more guns in here, but I'm not sure we're gonna need 'em for anything," he added.

Jimmy surveyed the cache. "You're right, Tony. We got enough to carry without getting weighted down with stuff we can't use. We're not gonna be doing much hunting, I'm afraid. Fuckin' deer get to live another day."

He had been the first to say that aloud, although the unspoken subject had been on all their minds. What had begun as a much anticipated, weeklong deer-hunting vacation had turned into a snowy nightmare with the need to find warm shelter for all of them and help for Tom.

They ate some of the food, left over sandwiches and pretzels, and discussed their strategy around the warm fire. Some Sam even managed to find a donut from the morning before, but it was frozen solid and difficult to eat. Afterwards, Jimmy said, "We need to figure out how we're going to take Tom with us. We've got to build a sled or something."

He didn't have to say anything more. "I'll do it," Tony replied, already planning the project in his head. He was the natural one to slap something together with his acknowledged expertise as a handyman and Jack-of-all-trades. Ever since Tony was five years old, when he cobbled a birdhouse out of a cardboard macaroni box for his mother, he had been building things. Although lanky in appearance and sometimes downright gawky, Tony knew his way around a hammer and a saw. Most men marveled at his gift; housewives swooned. He had constructed more patio decks, refinished more outdated kitchens, and built more family rooms for his friends and family than most small construction companies in Genesee County. He approached every project with a vision of what it should look like when it was done, and it did. His modest mobile home was a testament to his unique woodworking and carpentry skills. The place was filled with handmade cabinets and furniture that he had crafted and better than anything available on the commercial market.

Within an hour, he had fashioned a crude sled from the remnants of the WindStar. He ripped off a large piece of aluminum siding that was still somewhat intact and pounded it into the shape of a small boat. To this shell, he attached one of the bucket seats from the truck, so Tom had a place to sit while being transported, and a couple of ten-foot lengths of the orange rope up front. The contraption would require two of them to pull Tom over the deep snow dogsled style. While Tony worked on the sled, Jimmy and Sam made several makeshift backpacks out of canvas and seat cover materials salvaged from the wreckage for them to carry provisions.

The whole time, snow continued falling. A brisk north wind would occasionally gust and pelt them mercilessly with snow and ice crystals off the ground. When they were ready to leave, the wreckage of the WindStar was about to be completely overtaken by an immense drift that had been gradually building around the metal corpse like some giant white amoeba bent on devouring its prey.

With all their might, Jimmy and Tony leaned into the rope harness on the sled. Tom, in tow, looked the part of a Grand Poobah of some wintry kingdom being regally transported by a couple of minions dressed in hunting gear. Sam, with his ample girth, plowed ahead of them, bulldozing a path that would make the task of pulling the sled a bit easier. It didn't.

They had more than a quarter mile worth of hard work ahead of them to reach the crest where the WindStar had left the road the night before. They labored under a gray sky that spat at them with huge hunks of flakes that tickled their noses and wet their brows. They rested every fifty yards or so, panting hound dogs tired of the chase. Soon they were encased in snow, abominable snowmen, with chunks of ice hanging from their clothes like a squadron of fat albino ticks gorged on a winter's feast. Jimmy's uncovered ears turned a fiery red although feeling quite numb to him.

"On Donder, on Blitzen." Tom commanded, trying to insert a little sense of levity in their otherwise serious situation. "Sorry fellas," he sympathized, his leg aching despite the apparent comfort of the free ride.

"Let's stop a minute and rest," Jimmy said, removing the rope tethered across his chest.

"Good idea," Tony agreed.

"Hey, Sam. Hold up a minute." Jimmy yelled up to his brother who had managed to distance himself from the main pack by several hundred yards.

Sam stopped, looked back at the human dogsled below him, gave a friendly wave and plopped down into a six-foot snowdrift to rest. The foolish thought of making of snow angels the way his twin daughters did every first snowfall of the winter season occurred to him. He spread his arms and legs askew and sculpted an angel in the fresh snow. It made Sam think of home and his family back in Port Huron.

Jimmy glanced at his wristwatch; the face read a quarter past ten. Brenda would be at Sunday services right about then, with Preacher Thompson probably sermonizing about some important subject that usually had the same effect as a tranquilizer on Jimmy. An uneasy quiet settled in all around them, the surrounding groves of snow-laden pine trees absorbed sound like thick earmuffs. Their hot breaths formed welling clouds of mist that tumbled out their mouths.

"Ever get the feeling you're being watched?"

Jimmy and Tony faced Tom.

"I get this funny feeling every now and then that something's lookin' at us...following us." Tom continued. "I dunno. Sounds stupid I guess."

"Maybe you're just seeing some of them bastard pink elephants?" Tony retorted, laughing. "You better take another snort of that bourbon you been drinking all morning an' maybe they'll go back to the jungle where they belong."

Tom gave him a half smile. He was serious.

Jimmy recalled Sam's similar observation during the night. "Probably just some kind of animal," he offered as an alternative. He glanced about the surrounding forest, suspiciously. He thought it curious how they hadn't seen or heard any sign of life since they had arrived. Jimmy had spent plenty of time in the woods, hunting, camping, fishing, and hiking, and he couldn't ever remember being in a place more peaceful, other than the occasional roar of the biting wind. On the other hand, he felt like they were being watched by something off in the woods as well.

He looked up and saw Sam coming back down the steep incline toward them, retracing his path. His pudgy brother looked like an icebreaker plying through the water and trailing a long silver wake. His black mustache had silver icicles hanging close to his nostrils.

"Another eighth of a mile or so," he offered on his arrival. "I was almost at the top when we stopped. Let me push the sled from the back, it might make it easier for you two up front."

"Good idea," Tony said.

They took up their assigned posts with Sam in the back, Jimmy and Tony lashed to the ropes up front, and Tom secured in place. The four of them headed for the ridge where the WindStar had begun its plummet downward.

* * *

The splintered trunk of a pine tree toppled off to the side of the narrow road marked the exact location where the R.V. had left the road and then cascaded down the quarter mile ravine. No other signs of their passage remained on the snow filled road.

"Holy Mackerel!" Sam remarked as the four of them peered down the snowy incline they had just ascended. It looked as if a giant caterpillar had crawled up from its earthy lair and left huge tracks of its passing. Some two thousand yards below lay the sprawled wreckage of the WindStar, a mere speck, barely visible from their lofty perch.

"Damn," remarked Jimmy, trying to catch his breath after sharing the load with Tony, as the two struggled pulling Tom up the steep incline. Two decades of Brenda's good home cooking and the extra weight around his ample girth hadn't prepared him for such a formidable physical task.

"What the hell happened?" Sam asked finally.

They had not talked about the incident since they had been so enmeshed in sheer survival all this time.

Jimmy shook his head trying to remember exactly what had happened. "I hit something. Don't know what the hell it was though. Snowing too blasted hard. It was just there, nothing I could do. I hit it and we went spinning, then we hit that tree over there and went down the ravine after that. Lucky we didn't flip over a couple of times. Could've killed us all. As it is, Tom's fucked up, Sam's got a bum arm, and I bashed my head against something. Good thing I got a thick enough skull and nothin' vital got hurt. Looks like only the Dago ended up without a scratch."

"The lord loves a good Italian," Tony smiled.

"Fuck!"

It was hard to tell whether they were standing on a road or not. The deep snow had a way of masking everything and making things look the same in all directions. Jimmy dug at the ground with the heel of his boot. It took several strikes before he reached a patch of black pavement.

"I'm not sure which direction we even came from," he said. His head swayed from side to side as if waiting for traffic to clear at a busy intersection before proceeding. The image of the jackass who gave him the finger just two short days ago flashed through his head. "My guess is we came from that way." His gloved hand pointed to the narrow path, which curved off into the woods to their right.

Tom jiggled the compass taken from the camper and held it up for everyone to see. "That would take us south, if that's the way we came." The steady rain of snow obscured anything further than a half a mile in all directions.

"So do we go back or head the other way?" Tony posed the question.

Jimmy's eyebrows snuggled closer together. "I don't recall seeing much on the way here. I say we head north. If we're lucky, we might run into the lodge. Who knows, maybe we can find a house or something up ahead. We have to try find a telephone for some help and get us outa here."

"Sounds okay to me," Tony said with Tom in the sled nodding his agreement. Tom's face flushed red due to the combination of cold and bourbon he'd been drinking since daybreak.

"Hey, fellas! Look at this." Sam, wading in waist deep snow off to the side of the road, was bent over at the waist, inspecting something hidden underneath a growing drift.

Jimmy and Tony pulled the sled with Tom in it over to where Sam stood. An ominous dark cloud hovered in the sky directly overhead.

"I think I found whatever you hit last night, Jimmy," Sam said at their approach. "At least what's left of it." He rooted around down in the fresh powder just like he did in the backyard sandbox when he was a fat little kid, Jimmy remembered.

The butchered remains of an animal, all bloody and scraped, rested in the small depression Sam had dug. Apparently, the bloody carcass had been dragged under the chassis of the WindStar and then torn apart. Some of the legs and its head were completely missing. A bloody mass of ragged entrails was spilled and hanging out a partially exposed cavity of the creature's hindquarters, or what was left of them. An accumulation of reddish liquid along with globules of yellowed pus and the contents of the ruptured organs mingled to form a puddle of dark brown goop. The smell of freshly killed game tantalized their nostrils.

"What is it?" Tom asked, careening his neck from side to side, trying to see around Jimmy, Sam, and Tony, who were standing in the way.

Tony joined Sam to conduct his own inspection. He poked at the disassembled parts of the creature with the tip of a long knife he had retrieved from his canvas backpack. "Beats the crap outa me," he muttered. "Doesn't look like anything familiar to me, but that's a pretty big fuckin' animal by the looks of things. Without seeing the front end, I'd say this sucker would come in at a hundred and fifty...maybe two hundred pounds or better, whatever the hell it is"

"Whatta you mean, you don't know what the hell it is?" Jimmy asked quite emphatically. "It's gotta be something...a deer or an elk. Hell, maybe it's a goddamn cow."

Tony continued his coroner's post-mortem inspection. The rough hide and coarse fur covering the thing resembled nothing he had ever seen before. "I dunno, Jimmy. There's just not enough of it here for me to make out what it is." He paused, rubbing his bare hand over the rump of the carcass, a gentle glide over the hairy surface. "Maybe if we could find the front end of the thing, we could tell what it is. Be your luck you bagged the biggest damn something or other in the U.P. by running it over with your goddamned WindStar."

Jimmy snorted, a failed laugh bordering on disbelief. "It doesn't much look like a deer to me either. The other half of whatever it is could be a hundred yards anywhere around here, buried in the snow somewhere. Might take us half the day just finding it."

"What the hell's that?" Sam piped in.

"What?" Tony answered.

"There...on the thing's leg, over on the side."

Tony reached over and lifted the leg, already stiffened by the combination of the cold temperature and the ensuing rigor mortis. "I'll be goddamned."

"Look at that, would you." Sam exclaimed.

The eyes of the whole group focused on the spot.

"It's...a claw...or talon, something like that," Tony remarked, wide-eyed.

"You're crazy." Jimmy stated, jumping into the depression for a better look himself. Twenty or so years of prior deer hunting experience hadn't prepared him for what he saw. His finger ran along the smooth, six-inch curve of a deadly spike made out of the same hardened material as on the animal's hooves. It looked as though it might belong to a large bird of prey or some prehistoric reptile. The curved weapon, ebony colored, with a serrated edge that ended in a sharp point, had the potential to inflict a nasty if not lethal wound if delivered by a powerful thigh muscle, such as the one to which it was already attached.

"Damn." Jimmy spoke for all of them.

"Never seen anything like that all these years I've been hunting," Tom added, careening his neck for a better view into the depression, the bourbon making his words slur slightly.

"About the size of a claw on a good sized black bear." The hairs on Sam's neck were raised. "Well, if that's what you ran into last night, Jimmy, I can see why we ended up in a goddamn ravine."

"What should we do?" Tom finally asked, as the group stood there, transfixed in amazement. He looked up to Jimmy for leadership and an answer, as his leg began throbbing again.

"Shit. Nothing we can do here," Jimmy concluded. "No telling how far we have to go. I sure don't like the looks of that thing we ran into either. Maybe there's more of them around. We better get moving again."

No one disputed the captain's orders, so they each prepared to resume the hard march. All except Tony, who grabbed hold of creature's talon and began sawing it off with the knife where it was attached to the leg. The hardened talon came loose only after he had hacked at it several times and finally yanked the thing loose from its fleshy perch.

A mournful howl, like a dying wolf off in the distance, split the eerie silence.

"What the fuck is that?" Someone yelled.

Jimmy fumbled for one of the pistols he had placed between his belt and stomach. He drew the weapon and brandished it in the air as if he were about to signal the start of a foot race. His eyes darted in search of the sound. Everyone stopped dead in their tracks.

"Damn. What is it?"

Jimmy scanned the horizon and surrounding forest intensely, but saw nothing. "Dunno. Let's just get the hell outa here." He finally said, yet not holstering the gun. "C'mon Sam...Tony. Get away from that...thing, and let's go."

Tony released the stiffened leg and examined the bloody prize he had severed. The light of the day played across the polished surface of the talon. He replaced the knife, handed the talon to Jimmy who tucked it into one of his pockets, and grabbed the rope on Tom's sled opposite Jimmy.

Jimmy sucked in his gut to make room for the pistol. The steel on the revolver's barrel felt cold against his belly. "Sam, lead the way," he ordered, pointing northward. "Don't get too far up ahead this time," he added, feeling uneasy about the whole situation.

"Sure thing," Sam said. He had every intention of following his older brother's exact orders.

* * *

"Five hunnard and twenty-five dollars!" Bart Bakersfield yelled with a definite hillbilly twang in his gruff voice at the television contestants who were competing on a Sunday afternoon rerun of "The Price is Right" game show. He was folded comfortably in his favorite lazy-boy recliner with his bare feet up in the air, about six feet away from a fifty-two inch, high-definition T.V. screen, wearing only the bottoms of some faded flannel pajamas with the elastic waistband stretched out.

"Six hundred dollars, Bob." Marge Gibson, a middle-aged housewife contestant from Des Moines, Iowa, offered the amount as her price estimate for the Maytag refrigerator-freezer combination up for bid. She had a bright red gingham dress on with matching socks and sneakers.

"Too high, you idiot," Bart barked aloud.

The next contestant, some faggy looking sot from New York City, offered six hundred and one dollars, thinking Marge was pretty close in price; so he offered one dollar over her bid in hopes of blocking her out of the contest. The contestant closest in price to the item, but without exceeding it, won the prize.

"Bastard," Bart blustered.

"The actual retail price," Bob Barker, the game show host, paused for a brief moment of fanfare and suspense. Bart leaned forward in anticipation. "Six hundred and seventy-five dollars."

"*Ding, ding, ding, ding, ding, ding, ding!*" An annoying bell rang in the background.

"Linda Lopez, congratulations. You're our winner. Come on up here," Barker yelled, his steel gray hair plastered firmly in place on is head.

The saucy Latino lady from somewhere in southern California jumped up and down, clapping her hands wildly; happy that her six hundred and fifty dollar bid was best. Bart suspected she was an illegal alien by route of the Rio

Grande, by the looks of her. The country was just full of 'em Mexican wetbacks as far as he was concerned.

"Dang." Bart remarked, speaking aloud. "That thang ain't worth that much. Got the same ones down at the Sears store for a hunnard bucks less than that." He shook his head.

Doris, Bart's wife, sat next to him on the sofa in their trailer home, about a half mile south of the tiny town of Newberry in the U.P of Michigan. She glanced up at the television screen from the quilt she had been laboring on since Mother's Day. "She's probably from California," she commented, trying to help her dumb husband figure it out. "Folks out there's pays almost double what's we pay fer things. That's probably why's."

"Hell, then why don't they do their shoppin' round here?" he wondered. He scratched an itch on his hairy chest with ragged fingernails loaded with an accumulation of black gunk underneath. "Stuff's lot cheaper here's about. Save the show some money. Barker's an asshole."

Doris's eyes rolled back in their sockets. "Ain't Christian referring to folks that ways, Bart. Shut yer trap if you keep on with it."

He stroked the day old stubble on his chin, paying her no attention.

The telephone rang.

"Hello," Doris answered on the second ring, her voice sweet, professional. The caller might have thought he dialed a business office or a hotel, certainly not the Bakersfield residence. "Bart? Yes, just a minute please." She cupped her hand over the receiver while handing it over to Bart at the same time. "Sounds like Frank Finnerdy down at the county garage."

Bart had been expecting the call. He was one of eight drivers in the County hired to plow roads in the winter. He pushed the mute button on the T.V. remote and took hold of the phone in his meaty hand. "Hello. Yep. Snowed like crazy and still snowing. Heard the wind's supposed to kick up a notch or two later on today too. It'll drift like crazy." There was a long pause while his listened to Finnerdy's buzz on the line. "Makes a lotta sense to me, waiting to clear off them roads until it stops. They'd just drift over again anyways. Plus, the trucks get stuck. What good's a snow plow that's stuck in the snow? Ain't worth a tinker's damn. I don't wanna get stuck out in the boonies somewheres. I'll just sit tight until I hear from you, Frank. Yeah, bye." He handed the phone back to Doris and put the sound back on the television.

"You ain't having to go to work yet?" she asked.

His eyes were focused on the screen. "Nope. I guess him and sheriff Ollie agreed thar's too much snow."

She stopped mid-quilt. "Too much snow?"

"Yeah. Finnerdy's afraid all the drivers'll get stuck. He's thinking we should wait until it stops blowing around. Good idea if you ask me. Most of the county's roads is shut down anyways; lottsa phone and power lines down too. Probably won't have to go out until late tonight, maybe not until t'morrow morning. He'll give me a hollar when he thinks it's okay."

Doris rolled her eyes again at the prospect of having to be cooped up with her lame-brained husband for another twenty-four hours in their small, one-bedroom trailer. Liked to drive her nuts, he would.

"Twelve hunnard dollars even," Bart yelled at the television screen. A new round of overly eager contestants were bidding on a solid oak bedroom suite that would have taken up most of the space available in Bart and Doris's entire one-bedroom trailer.

* * *

The wind picked up. By the time the tiny winter caravan of deer hunters trudged a mere fifty yards along the flat plane of what they though was the road, the shifting snow had obliterated their prior tracks as efficiently as a grade school teacher, erasing the class chalkboard at the end of the day. It was as if they had never been there. Even though they followed in Sam's bulldozing wake, Jimmy and Tony labored hard, toting Tom in the makeshift sled behind them. In the meantime, Tom just kept guzzling down huge gulps of the bourbon anesthesia to thwart off his increasing pain. He got more and more drunk with the passage of time.

An hour or so later, Jimmy torched another cigarette and adjusted the reins around his other shoulder. "We haven't seen a goddamn thing," he commented, exhaling a blue fog. The tips of his ears had turned a pearl white and his fingers and toes had gone numb. It was the same for all of them.

"Bet we only made a mile or so since we started. We can only go fifty yards or so at a crack until we gotta stop and rest. I'd rather be climbing one of them big sand dunes up in Leelanau County on a hot summer day," Tony said. He gathered a hocker toward the back of his throat and spit it out in one sticky glob that whirled through the air like the fast moving blades on a helicopter.

"No houses, no barns, not even a friggin' road sign." The words emerged out of Jimmy's mouth through teeth clinched together tightly.

Tony sucked in a deep breath of cold air. "Told you before, Jimmy, not a lot of folks live in the U.P. I've been up here fishing sometimes and you end up not seeing a living soul for days."

"Yeah, I know." Jimmy began feeling the ponderous weight of his own personal guilt for causing their predicament. He was the one that had suggested going up to northern Michigan for deer season this year, and he had been the one driving the WindStar when he lost control and crashed. He felt like a fucking idiot for accidentally leaving Sam's cell phone back in Gaylord. He wished he could kick himself in the ass for that mistake.

The whole situation reminded him of the time when he and Sam went on one of those infrequent weekend fishing trips with their Dad, when they were teenagers. It took close to thirty minutes for the three of them to boat out to a secret little cove, known only to their Dad, on Torch Lake where hungry schools of bluegills and perch loved to congregate in late July, favoring the cooler, deep waters. When they finally got there, Jimmy realized he had left Dad's tackle box with all their stuff inside back on the boat dock now some fifteen miles away. By the time they retrieved his mistake and returned to the cove, well over ninety minutes later, a line of thunderstorms storms hit. The bad weather lasted the rest of the weekend, ending their family fishing foray before it had even started. They returned home without catching a single fish, all Jimmy's fault. Dad let him know about it too. He didn't talk to his careless son for nearly two weeks afterwards. Jimmy felt terrible about what he had done, and now he felt the same way about their current predicament, only much worse.

They continued their strenuous trek the rest of that afternoon, stopping occasionally to rest, grab a smoke, or eat a quick snack. They encountered not the slightest indication of civilization on their route other that a couple of highway road signs, warning of a tight turn or a reduced speed limit. Snow kept falling from the churning sky above their heads but not at the same heavy rate as the night before. The wind, however, kept up its relentless assault, at times creating a whiteout of blizzard proportions. Eventually, the road took them through heavy forests with trees so thick and uniform, they couldn't see anything beyond twenty-five yards on either side.

"Still don't see a blooming thing," Jimmy said, nearing the point of exhaustion. His arms and limbs ached from the task of pulling Tom in the makeshift sled. He thought it quite strange for them not to have encountered even a squirrel or a bird or some other creature for as far as they had traveled. The woods seemed lifeless, other than an occasional encounter with whatever kind of animal it was that chose to howl at them in the night. Every now and then however, they catch a fleeting glance of something following behind them. For whatever reason, the thing never revealed itself, preferring to stay hidden from their sight.

"Woods are too thick to see anything up ahead," Sam remarked, biting off a piece of beef jerky he bought at Goober's gas station. The thing tasted stale and had the consistency of old shoe leather. He ended up throwing most of it away. Pointy icicles hung off his thick mustache.

They had stopped for another rest, their cold feet aching with a dull numbness from constantly being underneath the deep snow. Their stoppages became more frequent as their strength and stamina began to weaken with each passing hour. Their diet of mostly snacks and crackers and jerky, washed down with whatever beer they had brought with them, had grown tiresome. They had also underestimated their physical needs for such an arduous journey and had consumed most of the provisions by mid-afternoon. They had thought, erroneously, that they would have found shelter by now. They began to appreciate the vast wilderness of the Upper Peninsula and the true challenge facing them. It was close to four o'clock and darkness would soon fall. They'd been out walking exposed to the harsh elements since daybreak, although their progress, when measured in terms of the distance they had traveled, was miniscule.

Tony surveyed the formidable landscape. "See that hill up ahead…over there?" He pointed to an area off on the right hand side of the road that rose several hundred feet with sparse vegetation on the bony summit. "Maybe if we climbed up to that small clearing, we might be able to see something."

"I dunno," Jimmy remarked, giving the Dago's suggestion some thought. "Haulin' Tom that far cross-country doesn't make much sense, especially since we'll be off road. No telling what we might get into or how deep the snow cover." He glanced at Tom, who sat slumped over in the bucket seat a little blurry-eyed.

"No, you fellas go on." Tom spoke slowly from his cozy nest in the sled, his senses dulled by alcohol. His voice slurred like a friendly drunk who you'd find in most any neighborhood bar. "Get me out of the wind and I'll be fine."

The plan sounded good, Jimmy thought. "Sam, why don't you go on further up the road a bit and check it out, while Tony and me will see if we can see anything from the top of that hill. We gotta run into something sooner or later."

Sam nodded without saying a word. Jimmy noticed how tired and aged his younger brother looked, carrying an extra fifty pounds of "baby fat", as Jimmy liked to call it. Icy clods of moisture had replaced his bushy mustache. Jimmy remembered when Mom used to dress him Sam for school on cold winter days in black rubber galoshes up to his fat knees, a pair of warm woolen mittens, and a bright red stocking cap with a fuzzy ball dangling off the top. Jimmy wanted to yell up to him, "Sammy, wait for me," and then let him have it with a snowball on the side of the head when he least expected it.

"Let's get going," Tony said, handing one of the ropes on the sled to Jimmy.

Jimmy took hold of the reins and they pulled Tom over toward the side of the road and placed him beneath the boughs of a massive white pine. The thick overhang of evergreen branches laden with heavy sheets of powder resembled a warm, cozy cave. The pleasant aroma of Christmas Trees filled the dark cavity. They made the Polock as comfortable as possible before heading toward the summit.

"Stay here, Tom." Jimmy ordered. "We'll be back soon as we can."

Tom nodded. He was in obvious pain. A smattering of blood showed on the rags that held the makeshift splint together on his leg.

* * *

The view from the top of the rise, for all their efforts, proved worthless. A tangle of impenetrable forest spread before them in all directions. Blowing snow obscured objects in the distance, while a darkening horizon in the east heralded the eventual coming of nightfall. The two men tried catching their breath from the difficult uphill journey before heading back. It had taken them fifteen minutes to climb a hill that in the summer would have probably required three or four minutes of effort at most.

"So much for that brilliant idea," Tony remarked, clouds of white haze billowing from his open mouth.

Jimmy shook his head with disappointment. "Damn. You'd think we'd be able to see something." His chest heaved up and down like the bellows of an accordion.

Both their eyes strained, trying to find shelter or anything familiar. The snow blurred the entire panorama, creating dark, brooding mounds of far off objects.

"Hell, I can't even see where Sam went from up here," Tony commented.

"I was hoping we'd at least see some smoke rising from a cabin or farmhouse or something. Not even a fuckin' telephone pole," Jimmy commented. He rubbed the sore bruise from the accident under his baseball cap and tried warming his reddened ears numbed by the wind with his bare hands. "Nothin' but trees and snow and more goddamn trees."

"Waste of time coming up here, I guess. Worth a try though," Tony said.

"Too much work." Jimmy's face turned sullen and stony. "I gotta take a piss before I bust." He turned his back to Tony and took several paces off to the side. He loosened the zipper on his pants and felt the cold air on his genitals. A crystal yellow stream of urine disappeared through a small pinhole in a deep drift. When Jimmy was a youngster he would have drawn designs of various shapes or attempted to write his name in the snow. Jimmy recollected a sweatshirt he had seen once in a souvenir store on Mackinac Island. The shirt had picture of Snoopy, the playful cartoon beagle, on the front, frolicking in the snow and giving his little birdsie friend, Woodstock, a bit of sage winter advice.

"Don't eat yellow snow." The caption read underneath.

Jimmy wondered how he could think about such foolish things in a time of crisis. He shook loose the last glimmering drops of liquid and tucked his privates back in the warm folds of his pants.

The quiet solitude was suddenly interrupted by a distant howl, similar to the sound of wolf baying at a full yellow moon.

"You hear that, Tony?" Jimmy asked. His head rose in the air like a hound, sniffing the scent of prey on the run.

"Yeah," his companion answered doing the same.

A second howl started, floating ominously in the air in concert with the first. They had heard the same bloodcurdling sound when Tony sliced off the talon on the creature run over by the WindStar.

"There it goes again," Jimmy said. "It's coming from over that way," he indicated with a nod. "In the direction from where we came."

Their eyes locked on each other's. They spoke but one word to each other.

"Tom!"

The two men started down the incline as fast as their legs would carry them in almost perfect lock step. The deep snow dragged at their sore limbs and slowed their progress considerably, as if they were running in waist deep ocean surf. Tony, being thinner and in fair physical shape, made better headway than his chubbier companion and was soon more than half a football field ahead of Jimmy. About three quarters of the way down, the sharp peal of gunshots stopped them in their tracks.

Tony glanced back toward Jimmy. "What the hell?" he yelled.

Jimmy hollered back. "Beats the shit outa me. Go on Tony. Get going. I'll catch up with you soon as I can."

Tony rambled on ahead with an extra burst of speed and was soon out of Jimmy's sight. Jimmy followed his snowy wake in a slow, arduous trot. Unconsciously, he had drawn the pistol. He waved the weapon over his head with each labored stride across the snowfield, his index finger poised on the trigger with the safety knob released. Several minutes later, he saw Tony and Sam off in the distance engaged in a heated conversation. They were bent over, examining something on the ground near the evergreen tree where they had left Tom. All he could hear were their elevated voices and an occasional swear word.

"Damn…Fuck…Jesus…Holy fuck!"

He knew something was terribly wrong.

The two men caught sight of him.

"Jimmy. Come quick." Sam yelled, brandishing the 30 – 30 Winchester rifle they had left behind with the injured Polock. "It's Tom. He's…he's dead."

Chapter Six

*The hellish hurricane, which never rests,
drives on the spirits with its violence:
wheeling and pounding, it harasses them.*
Dante Alighieri

    A map of the lower peninsula of the Michigan is said by some to resemble a giant mitten, a left-handed mitten at that. The "mit" consists of most of the central and western part of the State, while the "thumb" part of the mitten is a swath of fertile farmland that extends some forty or fifty miles into the shallow, blue waters of Lake Huron. Jimmy recalled the first time he had field dressed a whitetail deer one early December years ago. He shot the two-year-old buck on a cold, snowy day up in the "thumb" area of Michigan, near the sleepy city of Alpina. Since Jimmy was the one who had killed the creature, his proud father thought it only appropriate that his teenage son learn how to complete the gory task of "dressing" the dead animal in honor of the special occasion.
    He and Dad hoisted the prize trophy up by its antlers on a convenient tree limb and lashed the limp but heavy carcass in place with some sturdy rope. His father took out a twelve-inch long bowie knife, with a razor edge sharp

enough to cut strips of thin paper into tiny little shreds with only a feather touch, and handed it carefully to his young son. After showing his son how to remove the buck's genitals and then tie off the anus with some nylon twine, Dad instructed his young son to make a large incision all the way from the deer's pelvis clear up to the base of the skull. He finished off his lesson to a wide-eyed and nervous Jimmy with a wry grin plastered across his weathered face.

"Boy, he's all yours," he said. "Go at it."

The brutal process required Jimmy to slice through the deer's tough ribcage and sever its esophagus and windpipe in the process. After a fair amount of hacking and sawing, Jimmy placed his bare hands on either side of the long incision and pulled the two sides away from one another with every ounce of his strength. A cascade of vital organs and entrails tumbled out from the eviscerated carcass onto his boots and covered the fresh snow underneath their feet in a river of blood and guts. The young lad gagged at the sight; the breakfast of pancakes and eggs he had eaten earlier that morning roiled in his stomach. He promptly puked his guts out. Dad just smiled.

The torn and dismantled body of Tom Karrski reminded Jimmy of that gory teenage incident with his father. Tom's dismembered corpse lay askew beneath the big pine tree, where they had left him only a short time ago. The bloody scene resembled one of wartime carnage.

"What the hell happened?" Jimmy pleaded for some explanation as he tramped through the drifts on his way to where Sam and Tony stood with sorrowful expressions on their faces. His face grimaced in repulsion at the horrible sight that greeted his eyes.

"Shit!" Sam replied, massaging his temples between his thumb and forefinger as if trying to rid himself of the numbness he felt inside. "We don't know what fuck's going on, but something's killed the Polock."

"Jesus." Jimmy couldn't believe his eyes. His mind did not want to accept what his senses perceived.

"I heard Tom yelling...screaming...so I started back as fast as I could. Didn't know what the hell was wrong, but it sounded like he was in some kind of trouble. He just kept screaming and screaming. Damn snow. I tried to get here sooner." Sam searched for his breath, trying to hold back from breaking down completely. "I got here too late and found him a torn apart. What on God's green earth would do something like that?" The distressed expression on his face pleaded for an answer.

The entire center portion of Tom's body, from his neck down to his waist, was gone, with only remnants scattered all over the ground. One of his severed hands was lying right next to Jimmy's boot with the palm up and fingers extended, as if beckoning one of them to come closer. Another arm was hanging from a tree limb right above the bloody corpse, its hand locked tightly around a narrow branch, as if its owner had been trying to climb the tree in a failed attempt to escape whatever was attacking him. Tom's head, battered and bruised, rested five yards north of the body in the crook of some pine branches beside the tree. One of his eyeballs dangled from an open socket on to his cheek. The other eye was open, staring soldier straight at nothing.

"Gunshots. I heard gunshots." Jimmy said.

Sam continued. "I didn't see a thing until I got here. The Winchester was lying on the ground right next to him. I don't know why he didn't or couldn't use it. Maybe he never saw what hit him. I tried yelling for you guys, but with the wind and all, you couldn't hear me. So I just picked up the gun and fired a couple of rounds, hoping you'd hear and come back."

"Jesus 'F' fucking Christ!" The realization that Tom was dead seemed an impossible notion for Jimmy, or any of them for that matter, to accept.

Jimmy bent down on his knees and touched the stiffened fabric on Tom's bloody pant leg. He stroked it the same way he petted Brenda's cat at home when it purred comfortably asleep under the rays of a late afternoon sun while laying on the warm living room sofa.

"Maybe it was a…bear…or a wolf, some kind of wild animal?" Sam posed the question.

Tony had been down on his haunches, inspecting the ground for clues. His fingers probed the hard-packed snow. "I don't think it was a bear or a wolf," he finally said.

Jimmy turned to Tony. "Why not?" He asked.

"Things just don't add up, Jimmy. All the wolves were hunted down years ago. The only place you'll find them now in Michigan is on Isle Royal, smack dab in the middle of Lake Superior about two hundred miles from here. There could be some black bears around, but I don't see any sign of them. Bears just don't normally attack a man like that. Besides, Tom had a gun and he knew how to use it, whether he was drunk or not." He paused a few seconds for thought. "Look at some of these tracks around the Polock's body. I haven't seen anything quite like 'em before." He pointed out a variety of indentations left in the snow by whatever had attacked Tom.

Jimmy and Sam studied the evidence. The ground was thoroughly trampled as if a company of infantry solders had bivouacked in the area. It was hard to identify any individual imprints or recognizable markings of any kind except for the partial impressions left in the snow that could have been caused by almost any kind of animal.

"Take a closer look, fellas." Tony said. "These markings look like they were made by the kind of animal you hit with the WindStar. See those indentations next to each print…holes about the size of your middle finger? Looks exactly like it was made by a talon or claw, just like the one I took off the hindquarters of that animal, Jimmy."

Jimmy smirked at the notion. "You crazy Wop. Are you saying that damn thing followed us here?"

"Not that one, of course, but there's probably others," Tony said. "By the looks of these tracks, there must have been at least three or four of 'em."

The two brothers listened intently to the Dago's sober analysis. Something was trailing them and staying out of their sight on purpose, but they had no idea what it was.

Jimmy turned his attention back to the bloody hulk of his former friend. He shook his head in disbelief as tears gathered in his eyes. Sam ventured over to his brother and placed a reassuring hand on his shoulder.

Then Jimmy stood up and went over to the Winchester and picked it up. He reloaded the rifle with ammunition and chambered a fresh round. "Well...if they're comin' after us," he said, "let's be ready for them."

* * *

For their own safety, Jimmy knew they shouldn't waste more time than necessary out in the open vulnerable to any more attacks. The men needed to find shelter. After discussing alternatives, they decided the best course was to leave Tom Karrski's remains in the grove of white pines where he had died. They gathered and carefully wrapped the remaining parts of their former hunting companion and placed them in a brown plastic poncho that had been salvaged from the wreckage of the R.V.

Worried that other animals or scavengers might be attracted to the carcass, they wrapped the remains as tightly as they could with the rope from the makeshift sled Tony had built. They planned to return eventually and retrieve the body once they found safety for themselves. As an added precaution, they hoisted the body into some of the higher branches in one of the trees and carefully secured it in place.

From a distance, the plastic bundle with Tom's remains inside, hanging from the tree limb, resembled a huge cocoon spun by a giant caterpillar. They further marked the location by tying strips of cloth to the outer branches on several surrounding trees. As a final measure, Tony suggested that they all urinate around the site, thinking the strong scent of humans might detour any woodland scavengers from disturbing the body. What might otherwise have been a humorous suggestion, they took in all seriousness, considering the gravity of their circumstances.

By the time their gory task was completed, dusk came upon them. They were cold, tired, and hungry. Despite everything that had occurred and their carefully made plans, they were still no closer to finding shelter than when their adventure had started. Bitter cold and darkness without ample provisions now faced them.

"We've got to keep going in the direction we were headed," Jimmy suggested. He noticed the surprised look on his brother's face, since Sam had already gone several hundred yards down the same route and had seen nothing. "I know, Sam," he said. "But we don't have any other choice. We can't go back. It would take us more than a half a day just to get back where we started."

"And we can't go cross country," Tony added. "Snow's heavy and the woods are too thick to make any headway. Naw, Jimmy's right. We need to stick close to the road and take our chances that we'll eventually run into something."

Jimmy handed Tony the 30 – 30 Winchester rifle and one of the pistols they had brought with them to Sam. They were all armed. "Whatever killed Tom is still out there. Don't be afraid to use them."

The three survivors exchanged worried glances.

"Don't worry," Tony replied, his index finger resting with confidence on the trigger housing.

"I'll lead the way for a while, but we'll need to take turns." Jimmy adjusted the collar on his coat over his ears. He looked back one last time at the brown poncho suspended from the boughs of the pine tree. The image of Woodlawn Cemetery behind the mile long wrought iron fence back in Flint flashed through his mind. "Let's go," he said.

* * *

Gradually, as they moved forward, the evergreen forest changed character to one that contained a variety of hardwoods; oak, hickory, walnut, birch, maple, and sycamore. The gnarled branches and twisted trunks provided a stark contrast in color against the mounds of albino snow despite the darkness. The woods seemed more menacing...more alive.

For several long arduous hours, Tony and Sam followed Jimmy's lead, single file, forming their own little caravan of snow covered Eskimos through the artic wilderness. They alternated the lead every ten minutes or so, giving each of them an opportunity to rest somewhat after the brutal task of forging the way for the other two. The frigid wind scraped at their exposed faces as the sky above them gradually darkened into night, and the forest closed around them in a chilly embrace. The combination of Tom's gruesome death and their own growing perilous situation turned their thoughts inward. Conversation was at a premium, each man left to stew in his own thoughts, as they waded through the immense snowfield.

The narrow road hugged the hilly topography of the area and rarely provided a straight shot of more than a hundred feet at any one time. The winding route added an enormous amount of distance to the path they followed. For every mile they traveled, a crow flying in a straight line would have gone half the distance. Their lonely walk continued for over three hours without them encountering shelter of any sort, whether natural or manmade. Their frustration grew with each ponderous stride.

"We better keep our guns ready," Tony recommended. He clicked open the chamber on the Winchester, insuring that a round was securely in place. "Just in case."

Jimmy and Sam were not about to spurn what seemed as eminent advice from their experienced friend. Both of them carried the two forty-five-caliber pistols salvaged from the wreck. Colt Model 1911's, the pistols packed quite a wallop, especially at close range. The older of the two guns had belonged to their Dad, the one he liberated from the army while serving in Korea. He'd given it to Jimmy just before he died, with frail hands that showed the devastation of his loosing battle with cancer. It was a fine gun many a hunter would envy. Jimmy had purchased the other one at a local department store in Flint before the most of the stores stopped selling handguns all together.

As useful as their weapons might be, Jimmy wished they had brought more of the high-powered rifles and shotguns they had left behind in the cold wreckage of the WindStar. The pistols might not have much of an effect against an attack by intruders the likes of which they faced.

They began to detect sounds, ever so slightly at first, in the remote distance, the crackling of wood and the splintering of sticks under heavy footfall. It sounded as if someone or something was stalking them, yet staying out of their sight on purpose.

Jimmy's cold fingers held fast to the smooth surface of the Colt's aluminum frame that rested in his coat pocket, while Tony gathered up the rear like an infantry foot soldier ready to protect his small squad.

Sam held up his arm Indian style, signaling for them to stop, but without saying a word. The noise of twigs and brush crackling in the invisible distance kept on for several uncomfortable seconds and then stopped. Only the sound of wind whistling through the naked branches overhead remained constant.

"Yeah, I hear it," Jimmy whispered to Sam. He was tempted to light a cigarette but thought otherwise.

"Been following us for most of an hour now," Tony said. "On both sides."

A chill spun along Jimmy's spine, like someone had dropped an ice cube down the back of his shirt.

The long wail of an animal echoed eerily in the distance. The disturbing commotion droned on for some twenty or thirty seconds, increasing in intensity and then fading slowly away like the lonely whistle of a freight train from afar. They shifted around, trying to determine the source. Then a second bellow started off to their left, and a third in the direction from which they had come. The exact source of any of the sounds remained elusive, almost as if whatever the cause was on the move.

"Let's keep moving," Jimmy urged. "We're sittin' ducks out in the open like this."

"Think what's following us might be what got Tom earlier and attacked us?" Sam asked.

"Probably. Anyway, don't be afraid to shoot if you see something."

All three of them kept their weapons off safety.

* * *

"There's something right behind us," Tony said after a time, almost whispering. The hairs on Jimmy's neck stood up on end.

They had stopped in a grove of slender birch trees long enough for Jimmy to grab a quick smoke and for all to them to rest briefly.

Tony retrieved the Winchester he had placed down at his feet, while Jimmy carefully snuffed out the burning coal in the snow. The Dago raised an extended index finger to his lips as if to say, "Shhhh," while his eyes carefully surveyed the dark terrain to their rear. The whiteness of the snowfield provided an eerie sense of dull illumination creating a shadow world of fantastic, hazy shapes. Finally, his gaze came to rest on a darkened mound of what may have been fallen timber or a tangle of thorny bushes on a steep rise off to their left side. "Over there," he whispered, nodding in the direction.

Both Sam and Jimmy tried to follow his line of sight, but nothing moved.

"Fire a round up in that direction. Let's see what happens," Jimmy said in a soft voice.

Tony clicked off the safety with his thumb, brought the stock of the weapon against the pit of his shoulder, and fired up toward the mound.

"*Zing!*" The rifle snapped like the crack of a bullwhip.

At that exact moment, something flashed out from a bushy thicket right behind them. The thing let out a blood-curdling yowl and charged toward them.

"Look out!" Someone yelled.

It hurtled out of the darkness toward them. The massive chest of the intruder brushed by Jimmy, knocking him into Tony in the process, and then careened into Sam. He went flying some ten feet, eventually landing in a heap on the ground. Whatever hit them blazed back into the darkened forest with surprising speed. It left a musty, animal scent in its terrifying wake.

Jimmy ran to his brother's aid.

"Sam! Sam! Are you all right?" Jimmy yelled, almost frantic for his brother's safety.

Sam gasped for air like a drowning man, struggling to regain his breath, the air knocked from his lungs. He sounded like an artic seal, horking up a mouthful of mackerel. It took half a minute for Sam to recover. Eventually, he rose on all fours and, with his brother's assistance, got back up on his own two feet. Jimmy brushed the snow from his clothing and noticed a laceration clear across Sam's chest that left parts of his coat hanging in threads. Had it not been for the thick fabric and the layers underneath, Sam would have been cut quite severely.

"I'm okay," Sam huffed. "Did you see what hit me?"

"Not really," Jimmy said. "The thing came up from behind us, I really didn't get a good look at it. I only know it was bigger than hell." He turned toward Tony. "Did you see anything, Dago?"

Tony recovered the Winchester that had been pried from his grip during the brief attack and had fallen in deep snow. He wiped the weapon clean of moisture and immediately prepared it for use if required.

"No...no, I didn't see it very well either," Tony replied. "Happened so fast and it's still dark as hell." He kept a sharp lookout in case the thing decided to double back.

Sam shook the cobwebs from his head. "Hit me like a ton of bricks."

Jimmy glanced off to the rise on their left where they had seen the dark mound. It was no longer there.

"Look at these tracks," Sam said, examining the prints left by whatever had just attacked them. "Looks just like the ones we found all around Tom's body."

Jimmy got the flashlight out of his backpack and shined the beam on one of the prints. "I'll be damn," he said.

Tony kept scanning the blackened nightmare forest, staying on guard. He didn't tell Sam or Jimmy what he thought he had really seen. He didn't tell them about the horrible face of the monster or the long sharp teeth with incisors the size of daggers that came ever so close to slashing Sam's throat, as it passed by and narrowly missed him by just a couple of inches. He didn't tell them because he couldn't believe it himself, but he knew they were in trouble, and he now understood exactly how Tom Karrski had died.

"Sam…Jimmy, we need to go, now. They're comin'!"

* * *

"Too late," Jimmy yelled.

A dark shadow flashed through a stand of bone-white birches some thirty yards from them. Jimmy drew the Colt from his pocket and fired several shots. The bullets missed their target and collided with several trunks, splintering them in the process.

Another shadow appeared off to their left. Tony pumped several rounds in the direction of the intruder. The first and second missed, but the third hit pay dirt. The creature, whatever it was, let out a loud painful squeal and then quickly disappeared back into the darkened forest.

"Damn!" Tony remarked.

Suddenly, they detected swift movements in several locations around them. Quite naturally, the three men merged together, pinning their backs tightly against one another, each of them firing when one of the creatures revealed themselves. The pitch-blackness of the night made it impossible to see anything clearly. The men aimed and shot at anything that moved. Both Jimmy and Sam had to reload their pistols a couple of times.

The forays of their attackers appeared staggered, both in location and time. They didn't attack all at once, preferring instead to show themselves briefly and then, just as quickly, dart back in the dense shrubbery, maintaining a safe distance from the humans at all times.

"What the hell are they doing?" Sam asked, the pistol smoking in his grasp. "What don't they come closer?"

Jimmy fired three more shots to his front. The muzzle on the pistol flashed like thunder bolts in the night, lighting up the frightened expressions on the men's faces. The rounds again missed their marks to his frustration.

"The goddamned things are keeping their distance on purpose…as if they're checking our defenses."

"They're quicker than hell too," Tony remarked. "Seems like they become visible for about a long as it takes us to see 'em, by the time we react, the bastards scurry off back into the woods."

Several more darkened shapes ran between two drifts of snow on the edge of the forest. Tony raised the rifle as fast as he could and pulled the trigger twice. One bullet missed, the other ricocheted off an object buried under the snow and went whistling into the blackened, cloud-infested sky.

"The snow doesn't seem to slow them up neither," Sam said.

Just as suddenly as the attack had begun, the creatures stopped showing themselves. Jimmy, Sam, and Tony stood back to back against one another for several more minutes, but the surprise assault had apparently ended.

"Now what?" Sam asked finally.

"We need to get out of here," Jimmy said, still staying on full alert.

"I think I got that first bugger that came after us," Tony said.

Jimmy hesitated while thinking what they should do next. "Let's check it out, but we need to need to keep our eyes peeled. Maybe we ran into a nest of them or something."

Tony nodded. "No argument here." He started through the deep snow toward where he thought the animal had been hit. Jimmy and Sam followed, all three with their guns drawn.

When Tony arrived at the spot, he bent down and examined a dark splotch against the snow. "You got that flashlight Jimmy?" he asked.

Jimmy reached into his backpack and retrieved the flashlight. He handed it to the Dago, who in turn shined the yellow beam on the splotch. A dark crimson stain soaked through several inches of fresh powder. "At least the god damned things bleed," he stated triumphantly. He directed the light around the area until he saw some more familiar tracks in the snow along with a trail of blood, leading back into the deep forest.

"Looks like it got away," Sam said. "If we follow those tracks, maybe they'll take us to what you hit, Tony."

Jimmy didn't like the notion. He glanced over toward the dark forest. "We better not fellas. If we get off the main road, there's no telling where we'll end up. That thing may be injured and all the more dangerous. Besides, if the rest of his friends decide to attack us again, we're better off in the open where we can see them."

Just as Jimmy finished talking, they heard more branches cracking in the woods.

"Sounds like they're headed this way again," Tony said.

"Let's just get the fuck outa here," Sam added.

All the while, Jimmy had been reloading his handgun. He snapped the magazine closed with the palm of his cold, numb hand. "We better hustle our asses as fast as we can and find some kind of shelter," he said. "I sure as hell don't want to end up like Karrski."

The snow and wind continued to swirl around them as the three men took up their journey with a terrifying sense of fear driving them forward.

* * *

Tired and sore from their recent attack, the three weary survivors had barely gone a half a mile through deep drifts of snow, when the cold and their own fatigue made them stop for a brief rest. They stood in the middle of what they thought was the highway, with thick brush and heavy timber on both sides. For the past five or ten minutes, they hadn't heard any more sounds coming from the woods.

Despite the welcome respite, they remained on heightened alert, their fingers poised on the triggers of their weapons at all times.

They stopped long enough for Jimmy to light one of his few remaining cigarettes. An impenetrable blanket of jet-black clouds appeared to be snagged on the very tops of the tallest evergreen trees. It seemed to Jimmy as if he was inside a long, dark tunnel with no end to it. He took one impatient drag off the cigarette and tossed the butt aside. The tobacco tasted flat and unsatisfying.

"We need to keep moving," Jimmy said, anxiously looking around in the dark corners all around them. Smoke crept out of his mouth and nostrils as he spoke. "Those...things could be back any time."

Sam stomped his feet against the crushed snow in the little area where they were all standing. "I can't hardly feel my toes," he said. "It's hard enough walking through all this white crap and having your feet numb at the same time."

"That's another reason we need to keep moving. We gotta find some place inside where we can warm up and get some rest," Jimmy said. He glanced over towards the Dago who seemed to be preoccupied in his own thoughts. Despite the darkness, Jimmy could see the whites of his friend's eyes rolling in their sockets as he methodically surveyed every nook and cranny nearby. "Hey, Tony! Whatsa matter?"

"I don't like it." Tony sighed.

"Whatta you mean?"

"It's just too quiet," Tony said, squinting up into the night sky and seeing nothing.

"Well...maybe those things just quit following us. Now that you shoot one of them and we know they can bleed, maybe they'll leave us alone."

"Yeah...maybe," Tony hesitated, not believing Jimmy's speculations for a minute. He had a hunch. He reached into Jimmy's knapsack, pulled out the flashlight, pushed the switch, and directed the beam toward the shadows nearby. A tangled knot of vines and small bushes laden with snow came into view, beyond that an endless forest of tree trunks. Between the gnarled trunks of trees, sinister eyes glowed eerily, reflecting the yellow light back at them.

"Holy Christ!"

Quickly, Tony shined the light in the opposite direction. Another dozen or so pairs of illuminated retinas lay hidden in between the timbers, staring toward the humans.

They were surrounded.

Jimmy shot first. The pistol in his hand exploded. Tony grabbed the Winchester with both hands and fired off several rounds from his hip in the opposite direction without even aiming. The bullets from both guns disappeared into the dark. They could hear wood splintering and an occasional squeal of an injured animal.

"Whatta we do now, Jimmy?" Sam yelled.

"Down the road. Fast!" Jimmy instructed. "I'll cover." He shot twice more and reloaded the colt as Tony and Sam continued to fire while hurrying down the roadway. He could hear a commotion off to both sides and the sounds of branches and twigs snapping close by. Several dark shadows appeared against the white background of snow. Jimmy took aim and shot, but the shadows immediately disappeared back into the forest.

Suddenly, he tripped. The deep snow engulfed him like an angry ocean wave devours a surfer. He floundered briefly, but was unable to regain his balance on the slick surface. He looked down at his icy boots at what may have tripped him. In the dim twilight were two knapsacks abandoned by Sam and Tony in their haste to retreat. But neither did Jimmy have the time to gather them up along with their precious cargos inside. He needed to get out of there just as quickly; unless he was willing to share the same gory fate as Tom Karrski did some hours earlier.

Suddenly, Jimmy felt the strong hands of his two companions clamp down on his shoulders. They had come back for him.

"Get up, Jimmy!" They were both yelling. "Get up."

Shots being fired on either side rang in his ears as Jimmy tried to regain his equilibrium. He was covered in snow and ice. Soon he felt himself being dragged along the ground along by the nap of his coat. Jimmy held on tightly to everything he had brought with him, afraid the stuff might be accidentally lost.

For at least fifty feet, Sam and Tony hauled Jimmy behind them as they fired indiscriminately into the surrounding thicket. Finally, they rounded a sharp bend in the road and encountered a narrow one-lane bridge with a raging stream churning beneath. They yanked Jimmy to his feet.

Jimmy quickly surveyed the bridge. His initial thoughts were that the swift waters of the current might provide a natural obstacle from the things that were chasing them. If they could hold the narrow roadway in the middle of the bridge from their attackers, they might have a chance at getting away. Each of them had the exact same idea.

The men lurched towards the safety of the bridge. They could hear the things chasing them, closing in on both sides, and congregating behind them. The heavy snow dragged at their legs and made their progress agonizingly slow. Soon Jimmy and Sam ran out of ammunition and were unable to reload on the run. Only Tony, with the Winchester, was able to lay down a steady rain of deadly fire. He fired time and time again, forced to run backwards. He felt as if he was back in the army, but this time engaged in mortal combat.

Sam and Jimmy arrived at the bridge first and reloaded, fumbling in their haste. Rushing water, filled to the banks, roared beneath the open wooden slats of the ancient bridge. When Tony finally arrived, they formed a tight knot in the center of the roadway with waist-high steel girders on both sides. The small platoon of armed soldiers stood like eighteenth century British regulators, firing at shadows and elusive targets in the distance. Only now and then would their efforts be rewarded with the scream or cry of an injured animal. On occasion they heard the sound of creatures splashing in the frigid water off to their sides, but nothing ever came of such sideways attacks. Apparently, whatever creatures attempted the watery route either gave up or drowned in the process.

After several minutes, the forays stopped and silence returned along with the frigid current churning beneath them. In the distance, they could see several dark mounds, lying in the snow motionless.

The men were out of breath, completely exhausted and scared out of their wits. A chorus of howls, like the mourning of lonely coyotes, began mounting in the invisible distance again. Suddenly, they heard the sound of splashing off to one side.

"What the hell," Sam muttered. "Don't those bastards ever give up?"

The men could hear the creatures out in the brush diving into the water and then they saw a flotilla of dark shadows swimming downstream toward the bridge. A dozen furry mounds approached the base of the bridge where they massed next to several of the struts supporting the bridge. Several began to climb upwards, their claws raking against the steel supports.

"Holy mackerel!" Tony aimed the Winchester down as if he were shooting from the walls of a fortress under siege. He fired on the center mass of the creatures nearest. They howled in agony and released their precarious grip. Several fell toward others below them also engaged in climbing upwards toward the humans. The collisions sent several of the beasts tumbling into the frigid waters below. Tony kept shooting until smoke obscured his sight and he couldn't see any more of the creatures. The rest of the beasts had either been shot or drowned.

"Now what?" Tony looked to Jimmy for an answer.

Jimmy looked back at the route they came. "We need the supplies in those backpacks you fellas abandoned, but we can't take the risk of going back." He had taken his own backpack off and was looking inside. "I've got some stuff…mostly ammunition, but we lost a lot of the tools and food we brought with us."

Sam and Tony listened to Jimmy's dire assessment of their situation with the faces of guilty felons who had been caught in the act of committing a crime of some sort. More howls floated across the frozen landscape.

"I think they're massing for another attack," Tony said. The men could already hear more sounds of the creatures gathering off in the deep forest.

Jimmy surveyed the area around the bridge. "We can stay here and hold them off again," he said. "The water on both sides of us gives us an advantage. But that means we'll have to stay put and fight."

Tony could tell that Jimmy didn't like the purely defensive strategy by the hesitant tone in his voice. The Dago tried coming up with another alternative when he spotted a heavy accumulation of thick grasses and bushes along the shore on the far side of the bridge. It gave him an idea "Why don't we cut down some brush and set it on fire in the center of bridge. Those things don't seem able to get at us through the water. Maybe we can put something between them and us…"

"A fire!" Jimmy remarked.

"Yeah, a fire."

Jimmy thought hard. "To get to us, they gotta come over the bridge. But with the fire going, they won't be able to cross without getting burned."

"At least the fire may delay them long enough for us to get away," Sam added.

Jimmy nodded, buying into the idea. "Sure worth a try. Tony, if you provide me and Sammy some cover, we'll gather stuff for the fire." He was already heading over to the far end of the bridge. "Sam, come help."

* * *

In ten minutes time, the boys had managed to gather a five-foot pile of grasses, rotting branches, and other debris from under the bridge, enough to make a sizable fire. They stacked the stuff in the middle of the roadway, making sure to the narrow central span of the bridge would be completely blocked. Jimmy added a little precious fluid from his cigarette lighter to the pile, which got the fire going in no time. In the distance, they could hear the howls of their attackers coming ever closer. Flames, well over their heads, leaped skyward and spread quickly to the steel girders marking the sides of the bridge.

"Let's get going while we've got a chance," Jimmy ordered, his pale white skin suddenly ablaze in bright orange from the fire.

They threw a couple of more large branches on top the growing conflagration in the hopes of insuring themselves more time to get away. Already, they could see dark mounds massing along the shoreline on the other side of the swiftly moving stream.

The three of them gathered what little belongings they had left and headed away from the scene as fast as their frozen legs would take them and the deep snow would allow.

With little other choice, the three tired and exhausted men kept on their lonely march for several more hours well into the frigid, endless night. Their tired eyes throbbed in their sockets, sore from having to be on the alert for unseen and unknown dangers lurking in the forest, and the constant bleach-white sameness that accosted them in every direction. They walked along in almost hypnotic trances, unaware of their surroundings and the slow passage of time. The threat of hypothermia loomed along with frostbite to their extremities. It was well past two o'clock in the night and they were about to give up to their exhaustion and the elements.

Then, Jimmy thought he saw something floating off in the distance like a ghostly desert mirage. Thinking unclearly and near the end of his endurance, he paid no attention to the aberration at first. Something in the back of his brain, however, eventually clicked and awakened him from his fatigue-induced mental stupor.

Jimmy surfaced from his deep mental fog. "What's that over there?"

The distinct shape of a rectangular object loomed about a half mile off in the forest, up a fairly steep and long incline.

"Looks like a house...or a trailer, or something," Tony said, knotting his eyelids tightly together to see the thing better.

They studied the object for a while, not quite believing their eyes.

"I don't give a damn what it is," Jimmy said finally. "Looks like some kind of shelter and we need to get inside. If we're lucky, there may be a telephone."

They veered off the road upon which they had been traveling and headed cross-country toward the object, immediately sinking waist deep in fresh powder. Walking up the slope with mounds of fresh snow hindering their way was almost impossible. On several occasions, the men could only proceed when locked together, arm-in-arm, pulling each other along and working as a team. They paid a heavy toll for their physical effort and were near the limits of complete exhaustion. The rectangular structure, that had been their target, stood out against night sky with a ponderous mantle of snow accumulated on its flat roof.

"I'll be goddamned," Jimmy remarked, as they drew closer and finally recognized the object of their efforts. "It's a goddamn railroad caboose."

The revelation brought a slight smile to each one of their tired faces and a stream of pleasant memories to their minds. As children, growing up in an industrial city like Flint, trains were an integral part of the lives and represented a sense of adventure and a door to far off places.

"I'm not sure what the hell the damn thing's doing here," Sam said. "I'm just glad to see it."

"Ditto." Tony agreed.

"Let's check it out."

They covered the last hundred yards with renewed vigor; their stamina bolstered somewhat by the surprising discovery. The caboose looked old and dilapidated the closer they got, with its crimson wooden exterior weathered and bleached from spending years, if not decades, exposed to the harsh elements of northern Michigan. The place also appeared to be abandoned without any signs of recent activity. Unfortunately, there were no power or telephone lines that they could determine leading to the small railroad car, nor any indication of how the thing might have arrived in its curious location in the first place. There did not seem to be a railroad track or even a right of way where trains may have operated within eyesight. Snow buried the once mobile car up to the tops of its rusted iron wheels. The faint odor of oil and petroleum wafted in the air.

"How the hell did it get here?" Jimmy wondered aloud.

His friends shrugged in similar wonderment.

They surveyed the exterior of the caboose first. What little paint remained on the old wooden planks came off in thin strips and crumbled into a fine, gritty powder at the mere touch of their curious fingers. On one side were two small windows with their murky glass panes still intact and thick metal bars bolted to rusty iron frames for added protection. It reminded Jimmy of an old western jail, where the town sheriff might have housed all the local desperados. No other defining marks or identification were visible, not even the name of the railroad line that had once either used or built the car.

Off toward one of the sides, the Sam and Jimmy discovered a large fifty-five gallon steel drum filled to the brim with a black, oily sludge

"Man that stuff stinks," Jimmy remarked, replacing the metal cover back on top. "Some kind of recycled oil. Not much good for anything."

"Hey Jimmy...Sam...over here."

The brothers went over to the rear of the caboose where Tony had been investigating on his own.

"What is it?" Jimmy asked.

"Take a look," Tony said, pointing to a spot on the ground with the muzzle of the Winchester.

They moved in closer.

"I found it under the snow, just like that," Tony said.

The object of their attention was a man's boot by the size of it. A leather shoestring was still lashed in a tight knot and tied around the upper part. A brown sock rested inside, with a jagged end of a bone sticking out the top.

"Jesus," Sam said, his eyes open wide at the grizzly artifact.

"No tellin' how long it's been there," Tony added.

Jimmy bent down to examine the article close up, fumbling with the stubborn switch on the flashlight with his cold fingers. He turned the beam on the mysterious leather boot and was careful not to touch the fragment of bone. "Hmmm...doesn't look that old...a little worn...but otherwise its in pretty good shape," he stated. "They still carry the same brand down at Wal-Mart's. Almost bought me a pair a couple of years ago." He glanced up at his two companions. "It hasn't been here that long probably."

They heard the definite crack of a branch or twig snapping in the surrounding woods. They drew their guns and held them at the ready.

"Yo!" Jimmy yelled out as a fair warning. "Who's there?" His voice carried far in the thin night air, returning an echo back several seconds later.

They waited for a reply; none came.

" We've been in an accident…we need help…come out…we don't want no trouble." He shouted again, aiming the flashlight in the general direction of the noise. Darkness gobbled up the insignificant beam.

"Might just be some critter off in the woods," Sam suggested, hoping the monsters that had followed them had been stopped at the burning bridge.

Jimmy frowned. "Might also be what got Tom and what's been after us half the goddamn night."

They felt an uneasy silence.

Jimmy turned off the light. "Let's see if we can figure out a way to get inside this place. I'm tired of freezing my ass off," Jimmy said.

"Sure thing" Tony replied. He picked up the boot and placed it under his arm.

Sam and Jimmy bulldozed their way over to the side of the caboose and climbed up a rusted metal ladder with three rungs onto a small wooden platform attached to the rear end of the caboose. At one time, the platform must have had a protective overhang or roof. It was missing. All that remained were broken wooden struts, studded with nails and screws, that rose from the floor and suddenly ended up nowhere, looking like an identical pair of old fashioned coat racks, the kind you still might find in a small town barber shop.

The entrance to the caboose was small and narrow, about half the size of a normal door. Jimmy tried turning the straight metal handle several times to get the thing to open. It didn't budge an inch. He sighed and looked around for something to pry the door loose. Seeing nothing useful within eyesight, he drew his pistol.

Sam expression took on a look of alarm. "Maybe someone's still in there?"

Jimmy's face contorted. "For crying out loud, Sammy, we're not the goddamned Avon lady delivering some lipstick and perfume." He shook his head in disbelief. "If someone was in there, they would've heard us by now."

Tony chuckled a couple of feet away.

Jimmy raised the pistol and aimed the barrel at the door just below the metal handle. Sam and Tony plugged their ears.

The gun fired, sounding like one of those a tremendously loud cherry bombs going off the boys used to play with on Fourth of July holidays. The explosion splintered the wood and formed a jagged hole large enough for Jimmy to snake his arm through. He fished around on the inside, searching for a way to unlatch the handle. In a couple of seconds, he pulled on something and the door creaked open. Pitch-black on the inside, the place reeked of oil and kerosene.

"Shine the light inside, Jimmy. No tellin' what the hell's in there." Sam still looked worried. He had always been the cautious, less adventurous one growing up.

Jimmy aimed the narrow beam through the door. The place consisted of only one large room, constructed of the same worn wooden planks as on the outside. They could make out a couple of wooden chairs, a table missing one leg, a small bed or cot at one end of the room, and some shelves attached to the walls stacked with all types of useless paraphernalia. There was definitely no one at home and no indication when anyone might have last been there.

Tony came up behind Sam and Jimmy to gather a look himself. They balked at the entrance, as if afraid they might see a ghost, while the flashlight beam darted about inside, landing on one object and then quickly moving on to the next.

"Well...ladies, I suggest we go inside," Jimmy said. He moved slightly to the side to let Sam and Tony through the door first. "After you," he said, with a sarcastic note of politeness and an arm extended like the maitre d' at some fancy restaurant.

They took turns, going inside, one by one. They had to bend over awkwardly in order to avoid hitting their heads on the top of the doorframe, less then five feet in height. Bundled in heavy clothing, the men squeezed through the tight opening.

As Sam traversed the room, his forehead encountered something hanging from the ceiling and set it clanging. "Damn," he said, wincing at the slight pain while his hand nursed the spot of collision.

Jimmy pointed the flashlight at the object. An old kerosene lantern swayed to and fro, the kind used by railroad men well over half a century ago. The lantern hung from an iron hook imbedded in the ceiling and a piece of rope tied to the handle. He fetched a lighter from his pocket, fiddled with the glass canopy on the lantern, and then lighted the wick with the flame from his lighter. Upon lowering the glass, a warm orange glow enveloped the interior.

Jimmy looked around the place while noting the entrance door was still open. "Whatta ya born in a barn?" he scolded the others, even though he was last to come inside. "Close the goddamn door."

Tony obeyed his commander and went back to shut the door. He secured the latch as best he could, considering the damage caused by the gunshot. "Shot the piss of that," he commented.

They lumbered around the room for several minutes in curious fascination, exploring their new surroundings in the dim light of the kerosene lamp. There were cabinets and shelves and cubbyholes galore to investigate but with very little of anything useful to be found in any of them. Some old clothes, a dusty pile of magazines dating back to the early nineteen-sixties, and a variety of broken tools of various types and sizes were all they found. Of greatest interest and necessity to them, however, was a small, wrought iron stove toward the back of caboose with a neat pile of cut wood lying close by, almost as if they had been expected.

Jimmy packed the stove with some scraps of paper and some of the smaller pieces of wood, made sure the vent on the flue pipe was open, and set the fire to his handiwork. He torched the end of his last Marlboro afterwards and threw the empty box on the growing fire. At first the blackened stove belched a cloud of gray smoke back into the room, but once sufficient heat had built up inside, the stove drew just fine. The men quickly removed their bulky clothing and gathered around the stove, as if they were attending a Boy Scout jamboree around a friendly campfire.

Exhaustion and silence took hold of them as they gradually warmed themselves. The numbness on their ears and fingers and noses soon began to tingle until turning into a dull aching sensation, the result of frostbite each man had suffered in varying degrees. They kept silent while their thoughts turned to their current predicament and to the memory of their dead companion, Tom. The once joyous prospect of a simple deer-hunting trip with lifelong friends had become a nightmare. In the stillness of the caboose, they also imagined hearing mysterious sounds and frightful noises outside in the surrounding forest. They feared whatever it might be, and the darkness only made matters worse.

* * *

Jimmy stretched out across the ram-shackled bed, leaned up on one elbow, and took a few satisfying puffs off the end of his last cigarette that he had extinguished earlier to save for just such an opportunity. He blew a couple of lazy smoke rings into the air that swirled around like fat donuts before finally falling apart. Sam and Tony were seated across from one another at the rickety three-legged table, finishing off the last precious morsels that remained inside a potato chip bag. Several empty plastic wrappers of beef jerky littered the tabletop. Such was the remains of dinner, the first meal they had eaten that day and probably their last for the foreseeable future since all the food was now gone, abandoned in the knapsack left behind in their hasty retreat. The wind still howled outside, hissing softly through all the tiny cracks and crevices of the outside walls.

"So now what do we do?" Although Sam had posed the question, the issue haunted each of them.

Jimmy sighed. "We stay here for the night, get some sleep, and then we see what things look like in the morning."

No one argued.

He continued. "No telephone, no electricity. This place really doesn't do us much good, considering our predicament. Looks pretty damn deserted too."

"How do you explain this?" Tony asked, referring to the hunting boot, resting on the table beside him, that they had discovered just outside the caboose.

Jimmy raised an eyebrow. "Don't know. Maybe some hunter lost it, chasing a deer or a rabbit or something. Maybe some animal found it and drug it over here from god knows where to nibble on the damn thing. Hell, I don't know."

Tony imagined far worse.

"And what about Tom?" Sam asked. "You know, the whole situation."

The terrible image of his friend's eviscerated body clung to Jimmy's mind. As much as he tried to avoid thinking about death, something always seem to come along and remind him of his own mortality in the most terrible way; first granddad, then Dad, and now Tom. He could picture Tom's wife, Ginger, at home now, probably sleeping comfortably, innocently in her bed, completely unaware of her husband's horrible fate. She'd be expecting her husband to return home with the usual stories. It would be a happy time, and she would stand close to him, listening to his every word, laughing at all the humorous incidents that invariably would have occurred during the trip. They'd laugh and hold hands and life would go on.

Now all that would never happen. Tom was dead, his guts spilled across the snowy ground, while what remained of him hung from the branches of a tree somewhere in the goddamn middle of nowhere. What would they say to Ginger?

"I don't know, Sam. I don't know." Jimmy swallowed hard, unable to clear the lump in his throat. "Right now, I'm more worried about us." He rose up out of the bed and came over to his brother's side. "How's that arm of yours feeling?"

Sam held his injured limb out for inspection. His wrist showed signs of swelling from the knuckles clear up to his elbow. He winced just holding it in place. "It hurts," he said. "At least it's not broke, I think."

Jimmy remembered how he and Sammy would roughhouse as kids, Jimmy torturing him for no apparent reason other than the sheer fun of it. Many times, Jimmy would get Sam in a headlock or some other painful position and try to make him say or do something against his will. Sam seldom gave in to his brother under such circumstances. Somehow, he toughed it out, able to remain obstinate despite the pain being inflicted by his older brother. Jimmy wondered if Sam was hiding the pain of his injured arm the same way now.

"Yeah...well, just take care as best you can." Jimmy gave Sam a tender little rap on the head. Then, changing the subject, he asked; "How's our ammo situation?"

Tony emptied the contents from his coat pockets in the middle of the table. Several boxes and loose cartridges of ammunition tumbled out. "We got some ammo left," he announced, while trying to paint an optimistic scenario as possible. "Not enough to fight a war, but enough to give us a fair amount of self-protection."

"Enough to stop whatever got Tom?" Sam questioned.

Tony shrugged. "The Winchester can handle most any fair-sized game, but I'm not sure about those things that attacked us and got Tom. Damn things are harder than hell to shoot, and seems like you gotta hit it 'em dead on before it does much good. They're pretty fucking tough to hurt, let alone kill the bastards."

Jimmy considered his friend's assessment of their situation. He walked over to the stove and put a couple of more pieces of kindling on the fire. Sparks crackled inside the flue pipe. "We've had a hard day," he concluded. "What's say we get some rest and try to figure out things in the morning?"

"I'll stay up a while," Tony volunteered. "Wouldn't hurt for one of us to try and stay awake, keeping an eye on things for a while...just in case." He didn't specify his concern any further. He didn't have to.

* * *

The telephone rang at six-thirty. It was still pitch black outside, the sun not due to rise for another hour or so. The ringing awakened Doris Bakersfield. She reached with her arm from under the warm, thick quilt and grappled for the receiver on the phone, resting in its usual place, on the nightstand next to her side of the bed. The chilly air gave her the goose bumps on her bare shoulder and arm.

"Hello," she said with a little phlegm stuck in the back of her throat that made her sound like a one of those Saturday morning television cartoon characters with a high-pitched voice.

A man's voice crackled on the other end.

"Just a minute, Mr. Finnerdy. Bart's right here." She flicked on the small table lamp, turning on a dim light, and cupped the receiver with her hand. "Bart...Bart." she whispered loudly.

Bart was lying on his side with his back to Doris, snoring, with a wadded up chunk of the bed quilt tucked under his arm. He wore a raggedy sleeveless tee shirt that exposed his meaty frame and shoulder blades, covered with a coarse mat of hair. He hadn't budged an inch.

"Dagnabit, Bart...get up." She took the end of the receiver and knocked him upside the head. The plastic made a dull thud on impact.

He bolted upright, blubbering like some sleeping walrus rudely awakened by a cold splash of seawater. "Yeah...yeah...ahem...whatsa matter?" His pudgy knuckles tried rubbing away the light from the lamp.

"It's the phone you idiot," she still whispered, carefully pronouncing each syllable so her dimwitted spouse would understand. "It's Frank Finnerdy, probably wanting you to come out and start snowplowing."

Bart peeked through the narrow slits in his eyelids. He grabbed the receiver from Doris. "Yeah. Frank? Christ...what time is it? Already? Yeah. Yeah. Sheriff Svenson says its okay too. Well...I kin be thar in a little while, but I gotta get me some breakfast and java first. Yeah. In about an hour, huh? Sure, I kin make it. See you thar's."

He reached over Doris and returned the receiver to the phone.

"Gotta goes to work," he announced, stifling a yawn in the process.

Doris wanted to jump up and yell, "Alleluia!" and "Thank the Lord!" She had already spent too much time alone in their tiny trailer with her annoying husband. Thank goodness the weather had apparently improved enough to allow the county snow crews to begin their work of plowing out the streets and roadways. She needed him out of the house if she were to maintain her sanity.

"Biscuits and gravy?"

Bart looked at his tiny, sawed-off pipsqueak of a wife with a perplexed look on his dumb face. "Huh?"

"You want me should fix you some biscuits and gravy before you leave fer work?" she repeated in a hillbilly dialect he'd better understand.

"Huh-huh," he replied.

Doris got up first with several pink plastic curlers, dangling askew off the sides of her head. She grabbed a terrycloth robe, hanging on the back of the bedroom door, slipped it on, and headed off toward the kitchen barefooted.

Bart swung his legs over the side of the bed. He yawned and stretched and itched a couple of spots down around his equator. Then he stood up on a set of thin wobbly legs and went over to the bedroom window. He pulled aside the frilly curtain sash and looked out on to a row of a dozen or more mobile homes parked side by side in the trailer court. The snow was piled two or more feet high in every direction, but at least it had stopped falling. He glanced over at the side of the trailer toward his parked snowmobile, covered by a tarp and buried under a heap of snow. He'd have to clear all that white crap off before cranking her up and heading down to the county garage some three miles into town. Finnerdy said he'd be down there around seven-thirty or so to open up the place. Bart wanted to get there early, if he could, so he'd get assigned one of the newer trucks with big double blades on the front and a stereo player in the cabin, so he could listen to country music all day while he worked. They'd be plowing most of the week, no doubt, starting with the big four lane highways first. Some of the smaller roads would probably have to wait until mid-week before they could get to them.

Bart wasn't in a big hurry anyway. The longer the job took, the more overtime he got, and the more money he got paid. He smiled, gums wide. He went over to the nightstand, next to the telephone, and grabbed the water glass with his teeth bobbing around the bottom, uppers and lowers.

"Time to go to work," he muttered under his breath, putting his choppers back in his big mouth.

* * *

The flame inside the kerosene lamp danced slightly, causing ghost-like shadows to quiver on the walls inside the caboose. An old "Look" magazine, dating back to nineteen sixty-eight with the back cover missing, rested on Tony's lap. Just before he dozed off, he had been reading an article on the Winter Olympics to be held that year, featuring an attractive young figure skater on the cover by the name of Peggy Fleming. The room resonated with the sounds of the three men snoring soundly from their day's adventure.

It had finally stopped snowing outside. Bart Bakersfield was just sitting down to a steamy hot breakfast of biscuits and gravy inside his cozy little mobile home near the town of Newberry. The barest indication of dawn had begun to show in the eastern sky.

Kablamm.

An explosion rocked the caboose.

Kablamm. Kablamm.

Several more hit in rapid succession. The kerosene lamp started swinging wildly from the iron hook where it hung on the ceiling.

Kablamm.

Tony lost his balance and fell off the chair on which he had been napping. He landed on the cold, hard planked floor, rudely awakening him. Jimmy leaped from the bed and Sam quickly followed suit, arising from a warm nest of blankets and coats he had built for himself on the floor.

Kablamm. Kablamm.

One of the walls on the caboose rattled violently, as if someone was outside attacking and trying to break in with a battering ram. Several of the wood planks could be seen flexing with each blow.

"What the hell!" Jimmy yelled, still trying to awaken from a sleepy stupor.

Kaboom. Kaboom.

Suddenly, the attack came from the opposite wall, a complete one hundred and eighty degrees in the other direction.

Kaboom. Kaboom. Kablamm.

Jimmy ran toward one of the windows. He couldn't see anything out the dirty, cobweb-infested windowpane. It was dark outside anyway. Still, he strained, trying to see something.

Kablamm...Kaboom...Kablamm...Kaboom.

The sorties alternated, coming from side and then the other, almost as if planned. Some of the wooden planks on the walls began to show stress, as if they might break apart if the ramming continued.

Tony reached for the Winchester, lying on one of the shelves near the door, raised the weapon, and leveled it in the general direction of the attack. He pulled the trigger once...twice...several more times. Wood splintered on impact and left jagged holes an inch or two in diameter where the bullets smashed through. The ramming stopped on the one wall but continued on the opposite side.

Kaboom. Kaboom.

One of the planks broke toward the bottom, creating a hole about the size of a cement block. Tony saw the vague shadow of something dark moving on the other side. He aimed and rattled off three quick shots, all but making it through the opening. Something screamed on the other side.

Then the attack stopped as suddenly as it had begun. The sharp smell of gunpowder and sulfur and smoke choked the musty air inside the railroad car. Jimmy ran toward the door, flung it open after first fiddling with the latch, and raced outside. The forty-five, caliber pistol held in his nervous grip led the way.

Outside, there was no sign of the attackers, not a sound, nothing other than a cold breeze rushing through the needles on the pine trees. Sam and Tony joined him quickly outside their little shanty refuge, weapons in hand.

Tony jumped down off the rear platform attached to the caboose, landing in a soft drift of snow, and went over to the side of the railroad car where the attack had begun. He had sense enough to bring the flashlight with him. The snow around the site had been trampled thoroughly and pieces of splintered wood from the concussions were scattered about ground. He examined the area for clues in the dim glow of early dawn. A gossamer ribbon of orange clouds marked the eastern horizon. He could find no sign that any of the bullets had hit their mark despite his accurate marksmanship. His hand stroked the battered planks and his fingers explored the bullet holes. He hurried around to the other side of the caboose over by the big oil drum closely followed by Sam and Jimmy right on his heels. He shined the light up and down the surface of the outside wall. Something caught his attention just below the large hole the size of a cement block.

"What is it?" Sam asked.

Tony touched his index finger to the bright red ooze dripping down the wall. "Blood," he announced. It's probably from one of those things that's been following us. The tracks are like all the others we've seen before"

"Sounded like a couple of guys with sledge hammers trying to break through the walls," Sam said.

Jimmy stepped between the two of them and poked his finger into the splatter of blood. "I'd say those things managed to cross the stream somehow and followed us here. I don't know what the hell they are, but they're definitely after us again." He wiped the end of his finger against his pant leg.

A lukewarm sun was in the process of lighting the sky.

* * *

Shortly after daybreak, they surveyed the outside of the caboose for signs of damage caused by the early morning attack. After making some temporary repairs, they went back inside, fearing a return of the creatures. The also braced the door from the inside, using several large pieces of two-by-fours, just in case of another attack.

"What do we do next?" Sam asked, warming his backsides as close as he could get to the iron belly of the stove. "Maybe we should leave and try to get help?"

"Get out of here? Where the hell would we go? We walked through a friggin' frozen wilderness for almost two days without finding a damn thing. We'd better just sit tight for awhile," Jimmy replied. He fiddled with the chamber of his pistol, making sure the weapon worked properly. "No telling if and when we'd find another place." He felt like having a cigarette to calm his nerves and automatically reached into his pockets looking for one. Then he remembered he had smoked his last the night before.

"What happens if we get attacked again?"

"We're better off staying inside than being out in the open without any sort of protection."

Tony joined in on their conversation. "At least we can hole up here for as long as necessary. Sooner or later something's gotta come down that road we were following. I just hope they don't decide to wait until next spring."

Sam considered the situation. "I don't know...I just don't like it. I think we need to get prepared in case there's another attack."

"Good idea, Sammy," Jimmy said. "I've been thinking about this. First, none of us should go outside alone...even if it is to take a piss. If we stick together, we'll have less of a chance of getting attacked."

"Yeah," Sam and Tony nodded.

"Second, we don't have any food left. We ate or lost everything we brought with us from the WindStar. Either we figure out something or we're gonna get mighty hungry."

"Water's not a problem," Sam said. "Easy to melt snow from outside on the stove."

"You take care of that, Sam. The other thing we need to figure is how to get out of here…alive. Seems to me we should build some sort of signal fire. We're a long ways from the road and the snow's deeper than hell. The smoke might attract some kind of attention as well."

"So what do we do first?" Tony asked.

Jimmy thought a few seconds. "Well…let's make sure this place is as secure as we can make it. We don't need something bustin' in here and killin' us all in our sleep."

In the distance, they heard a long howl.

"Let's get crackin,'" Jimmy ordered. "But first I do have to take a piss." He glanced at his two companions.

"Pissin' don't sound like a bad idea," Sam said. "We better all go out together."

"I got a bladder full too," Tony announced.

The three of them got their coats on and went outside in a tight knit group, keeping their wary eyes on the forest and their weapons close at hand the whole while. At times, Jimmy couldn't believe that he was not on a regular hunting trip with his friends. The tragedy of the situation still had not sunk into his stubborn brain. He missed all the card playing and beer drinking and hunting, the camaraderie normally associated with the fall deer hunting season. He missed his cigarettes too, but he missed Tom Karrski even more.

* * *

Toward midday, while Jimmy was busy cutting wood for the signal fire at the far end of the caboose a safe distance away from the oil drum, while Tony and Sam made repairs to the outside walls damaged in the attack earlier that morning. Considering the size and quickness of their attackers, they stayed within close proximity to one another for their own safety in light of all that had happened to them. Tony found several loose boards inside the railroad car, and he and Sam were in the process of replacing the damaged planks below the barred windows on the southern end of the caboose.

Sam saw them first.

"Take a goddamn look at that," he said in a low voice to the Dago, working right beside him.

Tony glanced over toward a spot where some pine trees had grown together in a thick knot to form a small natural amphitheater a stone's throw from the railroad car. Twenty or thirty deer milled about the clearing, pawing and scratching the deep snow with their sharp hooves in search of tender grasses to eat underneath. All the animals were healthy and plump, the result of a temperate autumn along with an abundant, local food supply. The congregation of game animals was about the largest Sam and Tony had ever observed in the wild, particularly in the middle of hunting season.

"Holy smoke," Tony whispered, not quite believing such a fortuitous stroke of good luck.

"I never seen so many in one spot before," Sam said, admiring the unique sight.

"Me neither."

The deer kept foraging and seemed oblivious to the humans despite their close proximity.

"I wonder what would make them gather in a pack like that?" Sam questioned aloud.

Without making any sudden moves, Tony carefully leaned over for the Winchester, balanced against the wall of the caboose. "Beats me. Maybe they got shit for brains. Their mistake, our luck," he said, while bringing the butt of the rifle up against his shoulder and taking dead aim at one of the larger females closer in from the others.

"What...what are you doing?" Sam asked, his eyes widening at the sudden revelation of what Tony was about to do.

Tony never diverted his eyes from the sights down the barrel. "We came up here to do a little deer huntin', didn't we? Well, I'm just gettin' us some fresh meat for supper," he replied with a wry smile. He winked his left eye shut as his right eye placed the sights on the end of the long barrel right between the eyes of the unsuspecting doe. His finger squeezed the trigger.

A single shot rang out.

The stunned doe rose merely twitched its long, slender ears and then toppled over sideways. The bullet snapped right through the animal's skull, killing her almost instantly.

"Yeehaaa!" Tony whooped in a fit of joy and accomplishment. "Got the bitch dead on."

At the sudden sound of gunfire, Jimmy jumped and careened his neck toward the violent sound. He dropped everything and sprinted as quickly as he could to where Tony and Sam were working. In the distance, he could see several deer dispersing back into the pine forest in full flight, jumping helter-skelter in all directions. The reverberation of the gunshot echoed through the forest and off the thick trunks of trees.

"What the hell's going on?" he yelled, slightly out of breath and fresh adrenalin pumping through his veins.

"Got us a deer, Jimmy," Tony announced with pride. "Got her with one shot."

Jimmy looked over toward the direction where Tony had fired. The remains of a deer, dappled with patches of tan and white, lay lifeless in the snow some fifty yards from the caboose. "Damn...I'm not sure that was a good idea." Jimmy shook his head.

Tony looked perplexed. "Whatta you mean? Man, we're in bad shape; we gotta eat."

"Yeah, I know." Jimmy seemed unsure. "Maybe we just shouldn't have..." He never finished the thought. "Crap...I don't know."

An uncomfortable silence settled in around them. A slight breeze that had been blowing stopped. The tan hump of the deer lay motionless surrounded by what looked like mounds of snow-white cotton recently picked from southern fields.

Sam finally said something. "Well...maybe we should go see what the Dago got?"

"Yeah," Jimmy finally said, resigned to what had happened, but suddenly feeling on edge. "Let's go check it out. But keep an eye out, just in case."

The nervous trio stepped into the undulating drifts, leading toward the small clearing. Their wake looked as if a farmer had come along with a plow and carved three rows of earth turned alabaster.

"I think I got her with a clean shot right through the head," Tony remarked as Sam and Jimmy examined the fresh carcass. A pool of fresh blood gathered on the ground beneath the exit hole on the underside of the skull. Wet mucous dripped from the doe's black nose where the faintest hint of mist vented out the nostrils for the last time. The brown eyes were still open and bright. In the back of their minds, they each wondered if the pretty doe might still somehow sense her dire situation.

"Whoowee!" Sam yelled, suddenly caught up in the enthusiasm of the moment. "Looks like we'll be eating some venison tonight, Jimmy."

"I guess so," Jimmy replied. "Let's get her back to the caboose and we can figure out what to do next. I don't like being out in the open like this."

Tony, however, was suddenly not listening to them; something else had caught his attention. The herd of the deer, which fled at the sound of gunfire, had returned, and they were running full steam out of the forest directly toward the men. The color quickly faded from his face.

"Jimmy...Sam...Get out of here. Fast!"

The two brothers glanced up and saw the herd headed their way. Tony raised the Winchester ninety degrees straight up into the clouded gray sky and fired three warning shots. Several of the deer veered off at the last second in order to avoid a collision with the men.

"Go on," Tony ordered. "Get back inside. Run!"

Just then, more deer appeared, running wildly out of from the woods with panic clearly evident in their large eyes. Jimmy grabbed the sleeve on Sam's coat and twisted him violently toward the railroad car some fifty yards distance. With their backs to the forest they took off running through the deep snow, following the tracks they made but minutes earlier. Behind them, they heard what sounded like the bloodcurdling scream of a panther, soon followed by other similar screams, coming from slightly different directions than the first. Jimmy knew then, that there was more than deer chasing them. He tried looking back, but with all the flurry of activity and a herd of frantic deer kicking up clouds of snow and ice, Jimmy couldn't see a damn thing.

Tony, meantime, prepared for the attack upon hearing the same terrifying cries of the hunters. He made sure Jimmy and Sam were headed back safely to the railroad car and then began retracing his steps backwards himself, providing cover for their retreat. He fired a couple more warning shots into the air again as more confused deer approached the retreating men too closely. Suddenly, his eyes caught sight of a massive patch of brown and black prowling through the thick timber. Several more creatures soon appeared slightly off to the left of the first.

The creatures continued with their blood-curdling screams as they negotiated out of the forest and headed toward the fleeing deer and the three men. Tony's head bobbed sharply to the left and right, trying to get a good look at them as they weaved through the gauntlet of timber and shrubbery. They were fierce looking beasts with long furry snouts and rows of jagged, sharp teeth bristling in their gaping mouths. Tony watched them with horrid fascination while his knuckles turned white from the pressure of holding on to the gun.

As the ugly animals drew closer, he began to see them a bit more clearly. The creatures had deep-seated eyes as if carved from pure, cold obsidian and massive heads dominated by a huge open cavity in the center, a maw filled with row upon row of razor sharp incisors. Covered in a mat of coarse hair and rippling with muscles, their powerful limbs propelled the beasts forward at incredible speeds. The front of their legs were studded with dagger-like talons the size of iron railroad spikes, just like the one he had sliced from the remains of the creature Jimmy had collided with on that first fateful night in the WindStar.

A half dozen of the monsters charged full bore out from the timber. A small deer loomed in their path, frantically trying to elude their hungry grasp. The lead creature caught up to the unfortunate animal in mere seconds, its huge gaping mouth grabbing the terrified victim firmly around the neck. Another of the monsters sank its teeth into the flanks of the now squealing and helpless prey. Working in tandem, the two ripped the deer apart and immediately began consuming their bloody catch while resuming the chase at full speed. More creatures emerged from the woods and joined in the fray with the others.

"Mother of God!" Tony said, witnessing the brutal attack. The beasts resumed their relentless pursuit of the herd, driving more the terror-stricken deer in front of them directly toward the three men.

Thick plumes of moisture emerged from the their nostrils in billowing ivory clouds that rose into the frozen air. Tony thought they looked like some devilish steam locomotives with hot fires stoked in their bellies. He could almost hear their iron wheels grinding against a metal track.

"Blam...Blam...Blam!"

Shots rang out from the Winchester as he scrambled backwards, firing the weapon at the leader. Bits of flesh and blood exploded off the creature's head where the bullets struck. Stunned, but not mortally wounded, the injured beast veered off from the rest of the pack and ran back into forest while screaming in horrible pain.

Tony quickly turned around to check on Jimmy and Sam. The roly-poly brothers still had at least half a football field to go before reaching the safety of the caboose. He realized they wouldn't make it in time. He stopped dead in his tracks and stood upright like a revolutionary war soldier engaged in battle and aimed the rifle squarely at the herd of oncoming attackers. One of the creatures was headed straight towards him.

From twenty feet away, the monster leaped as Tony blasted point blank into the creature's soft underbelly. It let out a murderous groan as two of the bullets ripped through its heart and lungs, leaving a left a bloody passage in their wake. The collision sent the Dago reeling where he landed hard on his outstretched arm with the two hundred pound creature pinning his limp appendage underneath. Tony heard the bone snap as intense pain shot up through his shoulder. He could feel the stale breath of the creature on his face as he struggled to free his broken arm from under the dying beast.

Jimmy and Sam had only made it about half way to the caboose when they heard the panther-like cries of the attackers and shots being fired. They tried turning around to see what was happening, but they could only make out dark, hazy impressions through the clouds of snow being kicked up by the fleeing herd of deer running all around them. The deep snow made it feel as though they were running in three feet of ocean surf at the beach, grabbing at their pounding legs and slowing their progress.

Suddenly two of the juggernauts were on them, a conglomeration of limbs and legs entwined in a violent concussion. Jimmy went down, face first into the snow, somersaulting end-over-end before landing in a disheveled pile. The pistol was knocked from his grip. He had no idea where it landed. Intuitively, he balled into a defensive position, expecting the beasts to continue their assault on him, but it never came. The thunderous beating of the hooves moved away from him.

He opened his eyes and saw the two beasts gaining on his brother and then ramming into him. The impact sounded like a sack of overripe tomatoes hitting a brick wall. The creatures stepped up their senseless attack, battering the defenseless human with their hard skulls and tossing him around like a useless toy fought over by selfish school children. Sharp talons attached to their muscular front legs slashed at Sam's throat and chest.

"Goddamn bastards!" Jimmy yelled, observing the carnage on his knees and feeling helpless. Frantically, he searched the ground for the Colt pistol. Eventually, he caught a glimpse of the silver barrel poking up out of a snow bank. He grabbed hold of it and started running toward the marauding beasts.

Blam...Blam...Blam.

Several rounds hit their intended target and exploded in a gory spray off one of the beast's battered skulls. It fell dead in a limp mass next to his brother. The remaining creature took off in a flash, galloping full steam toward the departing herd of deer and its brothers in pursuit.

Blam...Blam...Blam.
Click...Click...Click.

Jimmy kept shooting at the departing target even though the chamber on the pistol was out of bullets. The barrel smoked with heat.

Sam managed to pull himself up on all fours and arched his back like a house cat rising from a long afternoon nap. He gasped, trying to regain the breath knocked from his lungs and then collapsed in a lifeless heap. A glob of bloody spittle dangled from his mustache and stretched in a gooey rope to the ground beneath him. The still warm carcass of the dead creature lay beside him with its brains splattered over the trampled snow.

By the time Jimmy arrived, Sam was not moving at all.

* * *

Bart Bakersfield took a chaw off the end of a plug of hardened tobacco that looked like a piece of five-year-old licorice left outside in the sun way too long. He added the bite to several others he had taken earlier and tucked it inside his burgeoning left cheek. He looked like a man who had developed a bad case of the mumps on but one side of his already pudgy face. A streak of tobacco juice trickled down the side of his mouth, a skinny brown rivulet that ended at the tip of his fat chin in a gooey brown drop that refused to fall.

He turned the big steering wheel hand-over-hand to the left, directing the county snowplow onto the highway, and aimed the big rig westward, away from town. At the same time, he cranked up the volume on the C.D. player a notch higher. One of his favorite country music songs blared from the speakers.

"My Tennessee woman is given me the blues

Looking' so good in her short skirt and high heel shoes.

She's my Tennessee Honey even though she don't wanna be

Tired of cookin', she just walked out on me."

A little off key, Bart sung the chorus out of the right side of his mouth, as he brought the broad steering wheel back to dead center. He stepped on the accelerator and the four hundred and forty horsepower engine roared in delight, gulping down fuel at the rate of three miles to the gallon of gasoline. As the truck gathered speed, he adjusted the cylinders on the Bonnell High Country Plow so that the snow covering the highway was thrown clear of the right hand medium of the road. He would come back at some later time and plow the left side as well. Right now, just clearing the way for one lane of traffic along Route 83 would take the better part of the afternoon. No one had made it down the highway in a wheeled vehicle for over forty-eight hours; no one, except for a raft of local residents using their snowmobiles, who tended to ignore the normal street boundaries anyway. Bart could see their caterpillar tracks crisscrossing the highway this way and that way, in every direction, as he proceeded down the highway. The storm didn't seem to have much of an effect upon them.

He had been plowing since almost daybreak, for over the past ten hours. Bart smiled, thinking of the overtime pay he'd be earning from here on out.

He moved along at a steady thirty-five miles-per-hour pace, watching the snow cascade off the slippery blade like thick ice cream being scraped from the bottom of the carton. He hummed most of the time since he didn't know all of the words to the song, other than the chorus. Then he would break out in a nasal twang in a poor imitation of the singer when it came time again.

"My Tennessee woman is given me the blues
Lookin' so good in her short skirt and high heel shoes.
She's leavin' my heart empty like she done before
With her suitcase packed walkin' out the door."

Bart was a happy man. He'd make plenty of overtime pay over the next couple of days. Plus, he was finally able to get out of the house, away from his wife Doris, who had been driving him nuts with all her quilting and house cleaning and fixing things up over the past couple of days and demanding that he pitch in and do his part around the house. Like to give him a heart attack, she would.

Nag…nag…nag.

He wasn't used to such hard work.

He felt a little chill in the cab of the truck; so he reached inside his coat pocket and retrieved a half-filled pint of some mean Tennessee whiskey that he had bought the last time he and Doris went back home, to a little town by the name of Tellico Plains. Bart had already consumed the other half a little before lunch, which consisted of a meatloaf sandwich and some apple pie that Doris had made for him. He rolled down the window, spit out a huge brown tobacco hocker, rolled the window back up, and then held the bottle against the steering wheel while his chubby fingers unscrewed the cap. He tilted the bottle into his mouth. The liquid inside gurgled with three large swallows and came down an inch or two in volume. Bart gripped the steering wheel hard, as the burning pain of the whiskey trickled down his food pipe.

"Yeow-sir!" he remarked aloud through his clinched false teeth. He shook his head like a housecat with ear mites and replaced the bottle back in his coat pocket.

"Yeah," he thought to himself, smiling. "I'll be making some pretty good overtime these next coupla days. It's gonna take me near the rest of the day to clear this here highway alone. We ain't gonna be touching them back roads fer a good stretch of time yet."

He turned up the volume again on the C.D. player. A new song was playing, a sad one that made the singer sound as if he had a belly ache. Bart saw sparks flying off the plow-blade and dollar signs dancing through the windshield of the big truck.

Chapter Seven

To endure is greater than to dare; to tire out hostile fortune; to be daunted by no difficulty; to keep heart when all have lost it – who can say this is not greatness?
William Makepeace Thackeray

The sight of Sam, resting on the bed with a bleeding chest wound, reminded Jimmy of a fallen medieval knight who had lost a jousting match. He and Tony managed to drag his brother back to the caboose before the monsters could mount another attack, although Tony was not in much better shape. The Dago's right arm, just below the elbow, hung limp and broken with one of the bones protruding through a small hole in his forearm. A gash on his left thigh about the length of a ball point pen had stopped bleeding once Jimmy helped him apply a tourniquet from material left over from his pant leg that had been shredded in the attack. Blood smeared his leg, clear down to his saturated sock. The gapping wound oozed in dark crimson.

"Just stay there," Jimmy ordered. He had just helped Tony lie down on a pile of blankets and old rags in the middle of the floor. "Lemme see how Sam's doing."

Tony nodded without saying a word. He held his right arm with his left hand around the elbow, trying to apply some pressure to alleviate the pain. He and Jimmy would have to splint his broken arm soon.

Jimmy rushed over to his brother, who was lying on his back and holding a wad of bloody dressings firmly to his chest.

"How you doing, Buddy?" Jimmy sat down on the edge of the bed and cupped his hand over his brother's forehead. Jimmy was worried. He didn't like the awful gasping sounds his brother made every time he breathed.

"Not sure, Jimmy," Sam answered, wincing at the effort. He recognized their predicament. "Hell of a mess we're in."

Sam's remark cut deep into Jimmy who held himself responsible for everything that had happened to them, including Tom's horrible death. After all it was Jimmy who had planned the hunting trip to the Upper Peninsula in the first place and crashed the WindStar in the snowstorm. Jimmy had also left Sam's cell phone back in the gas station so that they were now unable to make contact with anyone. He wished he were the one laying in the bed right now rather than his little brother.

"Here," Jimmy said. "Let me take a look at that."

Carefully, he moved Sam's hand aside from the dressings. The talons on the beasts had managed to penetrate through several layers of fabric, including Sam's thick winter coat and flannel shirt. Jimmy used his fingers to tear a larger hole in the fabric so he could see the extent of his brother's injuries better.

The wound in Sam's chest was about an inch above and slightly to the right of the nipple on his left side. Blood pooled around the injury and bubbled every time Sam exhaled. Jimmy concluded that Sam's lung must have been punctured as well. The bony spear on the monster's flaying legs must have missed his heart by a mere fraction of an inch. Things looked bad.

"Well…what's the prognosis, doc?" Sam sputtered.

Jimmy forced a smile. "You ain't dead yet are you?" Jimmy decided not to take any kind of further risk that might worsen Sam's condition. "You need a *real* doctor to take a good look. I think there's some tape left over from the wreck. Maybe if we can get you bandaged up that might help things out. In the meantime, you lay there as still as possible. It ain't gonna do you any good walking around, so just stay put."

Sam figured the injury was pretty serious by the look on his older brother's face and the slight tremor in his voice. What Jimmy didn't know is that Sam didn't blame him for what had happened, that Sam really believed it was just a series of bad luck which led up to their current situation. He had no explanation for the strange creatures that had attacked them, however.

"It's not your fault," Sam tried telling Jimmy, giving him some assurance he was not at blame.

"Just be quiet," Jimmy said, not listening. He went over to the three-legged table in the middle of the musty room and retrieved a roll of the all-purpose duct tape they had used in putting together Tom Karrski's makeshift sled. Jimmy tore a piece of clean material off Sam's shirt and placed it around the entrance to the chest wound, fixing it in place with several strips of tape. He hoped the bandage would prevent further bleeding and lessen the leakage of air from Sam's lung.

"I need to give Tony a hand," Jimmy said. "You gonna be all right?"

Sam wet his thirsty lips with his tongue. "Yeah, go help. I ain't going nowhere soon."

Jimmy gave him a comforting smile and went over to check on Tony.

Mere skin and bones, the slender Italian raised himself to a sitting position, balancing on the elbow of his uninjured arm. "Ya gotta help me put a splint on my arm," Tony said.

Jimmy's eyes widened. "Not sure I know how about doing that," Jimmy confessed.

"Don't worry. I was a pretty damn good Boy Scout once upon a time. I'll tell you what you need to do. Okay?"

"Okay...I guess," Jimmy agreed, reluctantly.

Tony shifted his position again, obviously in pain. "You already got the duct tape. Now we need something strong and as straight as you can get to stabilize my arm, a piece of wood or something."

Jimmy eyeballed the interior of the caboose. He noticed something in one of the dark cubbyholes along the walls and went and got it. "How's this?" he said, holding up an old broom with a long wooden handle.

"Perfect." Tony replied. "If you can cut about two feet off the handle, that should work."

Jimmy found one of the big hunting knives with a serrated blade they had brought with them. He hacked through the handle with a couple of good whacks and brought the piece over to Tony.

"How good were you?" Jimmy asked. Tony had a perplexed look on his face, so Jimmy elaborated. "You know, how good of a Boy Scout were you?"

Tony chuckled despite his discomfort. "Got to be an Explorer after about ten years. Earned most every kind of merit badge the Boy Scout's had. I wore one of them long brown sashes around my shoulder with about a hundred of 'em sewed on it. How about you?"

"Never made it past Tenderfoot," Jimmy answered. "I didn't like the fuckin' scoutmaster; he was a shift foreman out at the tank plant south of town. He made us do all kinds of stupid stuff, so I quit after the first year. That pissed Dad off, so he never let me rejoin."

"Too bad," Tony said, remembering his scouting experiences in a much more favorable light. "I'll need some ice too, Jimmy. That shouldn't be too hard to find. A bucket full of snow from outside will do."

Jimmy got an old tin pan from one of the cabinets and filled it with snow piled from just outside the door. He came back in and found Tony fumbling clumsily with one of the hunting knives with his uninjured hand while trying to cut the remnants of his shirtsleeve away from wound. Jimmy placed the pan down on the floor, took the knife from Tony, and finished removing what fabric remained. Like a narrow branch from a willow tree skinned of its bark, a jagged bone protruded out through the underside of Tony's forearm. The area around the puncture was bruised and swathed with blood as if someone had painted his arm with watercolors. The mere sight of it sickened Jimmy and set his stomach reeling.

Tony noticed a dull pallor on his buddy's face. "Jimmy, hand me that pan of snow," he said, trying to get Jimmy to think about something else.

Jimmy shook the cobwebs from his head. "Yeah, sure. What you need that for?" he handed the snow gradually turning to slush to Tony.

Tony placed the tin pan down on the floor and then carefully lowered his broken arm into the icy compress. He winced several times, his face wrinkling around the nose and eyes, as the fresh wound encountered the cold. "Got to try and get my arm as numb as we can get it." His words emerged from teeth clinched together in a sign of obvious discomfort. "No telling when we might get any help. You gotta help reset the bone, Jimmy, before I go into shock."

His eyes ablaze in panic, Jimmy gave Tony a troubled look.

"It'll be okay, Jimmy. Just do as I say and everything will be all right. I wish we had a little of Tom Karrski's fire water left over. A couple shots of his cheap booze would make this go a little easier."

Jimmy kept quiet, listening to Tony's every word. A minute or so went by while Tony let the numbness from the icy slush penetrate deep into his forearm. At first, the icy bath felt like a rod of cold steel was being inserted through his bones. After awhile, his arm turned a milky white in color and most of the feeling disappeared.

"That's about a good as it's gonna get," Tony said. "Like I said Jimmy, we have to reset the break and then get the splint in place."

Jimmy swallowed hard, obviously nervous in the task ahead. "Okay, you stupid Dago, tell me what to do."

Tony crawled over to a nearby corner of the railcar where some two-by-fours were nailed between the adjoining walls and wedged his legs firmly between them. He grabbed Jimmy's hands, placed them around the wrist of his left arm, and then braced himself. "On the count of three, I need you to pull as hard as you can until the bone resets itself. The bone is the ulna, the one on the outside of my forearm. Hopefully, it'll snap back into place if we do this right. Once it's fixed, you'll need to stabilize my arm using the broom handle and duct tape. You got that, Jimmy?"

"Yeah, I guess..."

"I'll be fine, Jimmy. I just need you to do this one thing...and do it fast."

The two men stared directly into each other's eyes without saying another word. Jimmy's hands coiled around Tony's wrist.

Tony took in a deep breath of air and started counting. "One...two...three!"

Jimmy pulled, applying steady pressure on the arm. The Dago immediately flushed red and grimaced at the intense pain. His lips parted to reveal two rows of shiny straight teeth locked firmly together. "Go on," he managed somehow to say. Jimmy pulled even harder. The broken bone gradually slid back through the open puncture wound. Jimmy felt a sharp snap through his fingers as Tony moaned in agony and finally screamed at the pain

"Quick. The splint." Tony could barely talk. His eyes rolled back underneath the lids.

Jimmy grabbed for the broom handle and lashed the wood strip in place with several strips of duct tape. Tony nursed his shoulder with his right hand, gradually falling into unconsciousness while leaning against Jimmy. A trickle of slobber dripped from the corner of Tony's contorted mouth, while Jimmy cradled his friend in his arms and gently stroked the hair covering his forehead.

* * *

After Jimmy had set Tony's arm and made Sam as comfortable as possible, he made sure they were secure in the caboose. He propped several large pieces of wood against the door and pounded a few rusty nails he found laying around directly into the doorframe itself, leaving their heads slightly exposed however, so they could be removed later on. Jimmy also scraped some of the cobwebs aside from one of the windows which looked out onto the snowfield where the latest attach had taken place. There was no sign of the beast he had shot attacking his brother nor of the fallen creature Tony had killed. He did notice, however, two long bloody trails leading from where the animals had been slain back into the nearby forest. In that brief time, the other monsters must have returned and dragged the bloody carcasses away. Jimmy could only imagine the gory feast that must have ensued.

An hour of so later, Tony woke up. His left arm below the elbow was wrapped several times around with long strips of the all-purpose, gray plastic adhesive with the wooden broom handle fixed securely in place.

"Pretty fuckin' good job for a tenderfoot," Tony managed to say, while admiring Jimmy's broomstick handiwork. The sharp pain, which had caused him to faint, had been replaced by a dull throbbing. His hairy arm would pay dearly when the sticky duct tape eventually had to be removed, however. Until then, the splint provided stability to the disabled limb. Jimmy had also made him a makeshift sling out of some of the rags lying about the floor.

Jimmy managed a smile at his friends compliment. Humor proved a rare commodity in such circumstances.

The gash in Tony's leg was another matter. The cut he received was long and deep, and he needed stitches. Jimmy did his best to patch the wound up while Tony was unconscious, securing a tight bandage around his thigh fashioned out of more rags and more duct tape. The bandage allowed Tony to relieve much of the pressure from the tourniquet he had put on to squeeze the flow of blood. The combination of his multiple injuries put Tony out of commission for any sort of travel outside the caboose or any other kind of help for that matter. The same, of course, applied to Sam who's condition appeared even more serious.

"You're gonna be pretty much on your own from here on out, Jimmy," Tony remarked. "Not much Sammy and me can do to help you. Sammy more than me."

Jimmy considered the harsh reality of their situation. He most worried about the potential of another attack. They didn't appear safe whether they were indoors or outdoors. The massive creatures proved to be a threat wherever the three men might be located.

"You know they're coming back," Tony said after a while.

"Yeah...I know," Jimmy replied.

"Whatta you mean?"

"You know...those things, whatever they are...they already came back. They've been here and dragged the two creatures you and I shot back into the woods somewhere...who the hell knows where."

Tony just stared at Jimmy without saying a word. You could see the fear in his eyes.

"It's almost like...like they were some kinda goddamn solders, coming back to claim their dead and wounded."

"Maybe they are, Jimmy...maybe they are."

Jimmy's face twisted in disbelief. "You sould like they're...some kind of intelligent animal or something."

"We need to get ready for them, that's all I mean," Tony said, dead serious. "We're being hunted by them, Jimmy. Just like when we hunt deer."

Jimmy let the words sink in. "We'll have to stay here, inside, until we get some help," Jimmy finally said. "Thing is we haven't seen a single living soul since the god-damned crash. I'm not sure it's such a good idea for me to be out alone, searching for help either." He shook his head, stymied by their predicament. "I think the best plan is for us to sit tight and wait for someone to come along that highway...the sooner the better. In the meantime, we gotta get this place ready."

Quite unconsciously, Jimmy patted his coat pockets searching for a cigarette. Remembering he had smoked his last only made him feel worse.

"Hell of a time to quite smokin'," he remarked aloud.

"Could be a long time 'til they get around to some of the more remote areas," Tony remarked.

"That's what I'm afraid of," Jimmy said. "Sam's not going to be able to make it that long. He's got to see a doctor...and you're not in the best of shape either."

Tony didn't dispute anything Jimmy said.

"First thing you need to do is try and get the Winchester." Tony said. "It's outside somewhere, Jimmy. The blasted thing got knocked loose when we were attacked. We'll probably need it from the looks of things."

Jimmy kept wishing he had a cigarette. He thought they made him think more clearly. Instead, his brain was a muddle of confusing thoughts as a result of his forced withdrawal from nicotine. The unenviable prospect of going back outside and facing those monsters alone only made matters worse.

"What did you exactly see, Tony? Even though I managed to shoot one of those bastards, so much was going on all around me that I didn't really get a good look at the thing."

Tony could still feel the stale breath from the dying creature rasping against his neck and the ponderous weight on his broken arm. Somehow, he had managed to free himself despite his injuries. "I dunno, Jimmy. I didn't see much neither. I just a shot at anything big, dark, and hairy." He didn't want to worry his drinking buddy and best friend any more than necessary.

Unfortunately, the Dago's good intentions had just the opposite effect. Jimmy was scared to death to go back outside and face the faceless monsters. His own imagination painted a mental picture of them more terrible than any description Tony would have provided.

* * *

A bone white moon winked in and out a string of thin clouds racing overhead and threw skeleton shadows on the hills and valleys below. A brisk wind out of the north howled with a menacing voice of its own, like a phantom prowling through the trees in the forest. Feeling the cold, Jimmy braced the collar on his coat closer around his neck, as he quietly latched the door to the caboose with as little noise as possible, making sure it closed securely behind him. He stood on the platform just outside the door with his back touching the wall for several minutes without budging an inch, his legs frozen in place not from the cold but from fear. Jimmy looked up and saw open sky and stars for the first time since the crash. The moon's bright illumination lit up the snowy landscape in a pure white radiance, which made everything within eyesight easy to see. The dark, imposing forest beyond, however, remained hidden in ghostly shadows.

Nervous, Jimmy took in shallow breaths through his open mouth. The cold, twenty-degree air stung the back of his throat and windpipe. His saucer-moon eyes scoured the artic landscape for any sign of the murderous creatures.

An ocean of snowy drifts lay before him like desert dunes frozen in time. The land was stark and empty and without any sign of the killer beasts.

Despite the cold, Jimmy could feel beads of nervous sweat trickling down his spine. He moved away from the comforting wall of the caboose and made his way down the ladder. Once down, Jimmy measured the distance to the approximate location where Tony had been hit and where he may have dropped the Winchester.

"Forty...fifty yards at best," he thought, trying to bolster his own self-confidence. "Hell...not that goddamn far...half the length of a football field." He surmised that Barry Sanders, the fabulous former running back from the Detroit Lions football team and his favorite player of all time, could cover such a short distance in a mere five or six seconds. Unfortunately, he realized he was no Barry Sanders and the famous football player never had to negotiate through three-foot snowdrifts to reach his intended target.

Jimmy's intent was to go around the side of the caboose, over by the big oil drum, and then follow their tracks and the bloody path back to the spot where Tony had been attacked. Much to his dismay, however, the wind had drifted the snow so that few signs of their rushed retreat remained. He took his first tentative steps away from the caboose, staying vigilant the whole time. His fingers on both hands were poised atop the hair trigger on the pistol and pointed the way forward.

He tramped through the heavy drifts by taking large strides, over and over again, as if gingerly negotiating his way across a swift mountain stream, stepping from rock to rock. Jimmy made good progress and in relatively short order was surprised to find himself at the exact spot where he and Sam had been attacked, about half way to his intended location. He could discern light pinkish areas underneath the fresh powder, remnants of the bloody carnage which had taken place earlier, but blowing snow had all but obliterated the trail where the fallen beasts had been dragged back into the forest by their ravenous brethrens. Now and then he saw evidence of the herd of deer that had been chased as well, bits of fur or markings of their hurried passage. They, like their human counterparts, had become the hunted.

Luck was with Jimmy as he drew closer the foreboding line of woods. Sticking about a foot and a half out of the snow, the metal barrel of the Winchester reflected in the moonlight. Jimmy reached down and resurrected the thing from its snowy grave. He brushed some accumulated clods of ice from the butt and trigger housing, but otherwise, the weapon appeared in perfect working order.

The whole enterprise had been easy so far, too easy…he thought.

Before heading back, Jimmy glanced over toward a slight mound in the snow that marked the place where Tony had shot the deer. Reluctantly, he shined the beam of the flashlight he had brought with him but had been turned off in order to avoid being seen out in the open. The light revealed the partial remains of a doe, half eaten and completely disemboweled. Jimmy could only assume the beasts had returned to claim yet another prize from the bloody rampage. He quickly realized, they might still return. He switched the flashlight off and started back home.

Just as he drew nearer to the relative safety caboose and started to relax, he heard a sharp panther-like cry from deep in the forest. Along with the cry were the death screams of an animal in agony. What kind of an animal, Jimmy could not be sure. But from the terrible sound of suffering carried by the cruel night wind, he was certain of the poor creature's unfortunate fate. Shivers ran down his neck, while he cocked the Winchester as a precaution and quickened his pace. He would not stop shivering until he was safe inside.

"You got it," Tony announced upon seeing him enter the caboose with the Winchester in hand.

"Yeah…I got it," Jimmy said, still surprised at his harrowing adventure, even though nothing had happened to him. "Not that I didn't almost shit in my pants gettin' the damn thing."

Tony sympathized with him and fully recognized the danger Jimmy had faced in retrieving the gun. "We'll need it," he said. "I'm certain of that."

Jimmy understood perfectly. "Well…looks like we're gonna be here a while, and those things out there are probably gonna come lookin' for us." He looked into the Italian's dark eyes. "Let's try to get some sleep. We gotta long night ahead of us."

* * *

The hours passed slowly inside the caboose. Hungry and unable to sleep, the men kept constantly on guard for the terror that lurked outside. They felt abandoned by the world they once knew and at the mercy of events they had no way of controlling. They were afraid.

"You know I hate to say it, Jimmy, but I miss being on the line," Tony said, adding some fresh kindling to the stove and then hobbling back to his warm nest on the floor.

"Dumb Dago, you don't miss working on the line, you'd just rather be any place other than here," Jimmy corrected him. "Me too," he added.

The two men would have many such brief conversations between them during the course of the evening, amounting to little other than an acknowledgement that they were still friends and shared many of the same fears and feelings.

"I'd give anything for a cheap ninety-nine cent burger right about now," Tony remarked after several minutes of uncomfortable silence.

"Amen to that," Jimmy said.

"With plenty of pickles and a super-size order of French fries." The remark came from Sam, over in the corner still stretched across the bed. His voice sounded weak, but nonetheless music to Jimmy's ears.

Jimmy went over and sat on the edge of the bed. He placed the palm of his hand across his brother's forehead. Then he helped Sam with a drink of water from a dented canteen, a survivor from their crash, hanging from a nail on the wall. "How you doing, pal? You've sort of been going in and out of it for the past couple of hours."

Sam managed a smile. "I been better," he said.

"Forget the goddamn burger. When we do get out of here, I'm buying you the biggest fuckin' steak you'll ever eat." Jimmy said, trying to be as positive as possible.

"That's a deal," Sam said.

"I'm buying the beers," Tony chimed in from his bed of rags spread across the floor in the middle of the room.

Jimmy was about to get up and return to his usual place at the three-legged table, when Sam grabbed his arm. "We gotta get outa here, Jimmy." He had a wild look in his eyes. Jimmy didn't know if it was the fever or if his brother was just afraid.

"Yeah, I know," Jimmy said, shaking his head almost apologetically. "We gotta stay here tonight, though. Neither you or Tony are in any condition to travel, especially at night." Then he added, reluctantly, what was on all their minds, "And we got those…those things out there, whatever they are. At least in the daytime, we might be able to see them. At night, we got no chance."

"I don't want to die in here," Sam said.

Jimmy tried to fortify his own resolution. "Neither do I, Sam…neither do I," he said.

He gave his brother a pat on the shoulder, got up, and went over to the window. He tried looking out, but could see nothing clearly through the thick frost that had once again accumulated on the windowpane. He imagined somewhere out there, the beasts lurked, waiting for the men to come outside. After that, he retrieved the Winchester and placed it squarely on top of the table so it would be right next to him at all times.

* * *

Despite the noisy scraping of the tempered steel blade against the hard asphalt pavement going on outside, the two-way radio in Bart Bakersfield's snowplow squealed like an irritable housewife mad at her husband. The transplanted hillbilly turned down the volume control knob and listened to Frank Finnerdy back at the county garage in Newberry, talking to some of the other snowplow drivers who were scattered throughout different parts of the county, doing the same thing he was. Many of the main highways had been cleared of snow, but now Frank was calling the drivers back into town because of worsening weather conditions due to high winds and further drifting. Besides, most of the men had been working close to twelve hours and they needed a rest. Bart's turn to speak with his boss came about third in line.

"Where are you at, Bakersfield? What's you're location?" Finnerdy asked twice, making sure Bart understood the question.

Bart imagined Frank back in Newberry, not working very hard and sitting with his fat legs propped up on an old wooden desk. He'd have the microphone glued to his chubby fingers like some dumb television news reporter doing an interview with an important politician. His warm and comfortable office would be cluttered with all kinds of official looking papers and documents and old calendars tacked up across all the walls and on all the filing cabinets. That's the way Bart always imagined Frank, "sittin' on his dead ass with his feet up in the air." Give the man a cigar and he'd look exactly like some country bumpkin politician right out of the nineteen-thirties, about ready to take in a bribe.

Bart keyed the button on his mike. "Hell, I'm about three or four miles from the Schoolcraft County line on Highway 83, making my third pass and I still only got one goddamn lane open. Never plowed the shoulders more than a foot or so, but at least traffic can make it down one lane pretty good, providing some crazy driver don't go to horsing around and end up spinning into a ditch or something. Not sure they even started plowing over there in Schoolcraft County next to us though. Went 'bout half a mile into Schoolcraft before turning back around. Them County plows over in Schoolcraft still ain't made it down 83. Maybe the boys over there decided to sit out the storm in Macy's Tavern down in Manistique instead. They're probably drinking boilermakers right now."

"Lazy bastards," Finnerdy agreed. "Well, you've probably been listening to the radio conversation enough to know we're pulling everyone off the roads for the rest of the night. Sheriff Svenson and I been listening to local reports about high winds causing real problems out there. We can't afford having one of our drivers stuck, so why don't you call it a night. Come on in from where you're at and then get your ass in here first thing in the morning so we can start the whole ka-bang all over again most likely."

"Shit, Frank! Sounds like a good idea to me. I ain't had hardly nothing to eat other than a cold meatloaf sandwich the missus made when I left early this morning. Damnation to hell, about time you called. I'm hungrier than a damn polecat caught up a thorny tree by a pair of mean hound dogs. Besides, seems like I just get done plowing one section of road and by the time I turn 'round and come back, the snow done drifted her over again."

Frank had heard Bart bellyache before. It wasn't the first time and it sure as hell wouldn't be the last. "What about all that goddamn overtime pay you're making?" he reminded his not-too-intelligent hillbilly driver.

"Overtime?" Bart yelled back into the mike. "Yeah…I like that overtime, but a feller's gotta eat every now and then too."

Frank shook his head, but gave in. Bakersfield was always coming up with some lame excuse not to do work and go have something to eat. "Alright. Go home, get some food and a good nights sleep and be here at the county garage at seven o'clock sharp tomorrow morning?"

Bart wondered what kind of goodies his wife Doris might have cooking on the stove back at the trailer or packed away inside the refrigerator. Whatever it was, his Tennessee honey was one hell of a good cook and he knew the food would taste good. He might even get to watch a little T.V. for an hour or so while he ate. "Sounds like a go to me," he replied.

"Okay. The sheriff will be here in the morning to give us an update on conditions as well. We gotta get them roads cleared soon as we can, otherwise the county supervisor and every other Tom, Dick, and Harry around here will be on my ass."

"Sure thing boss. Over and out."

Bart acted as if he was behind the controls of a jumbo 747-jet airplane, conversing with the control tower. He hung the microphone back on the dashboard, hunkered down behind the big steering wheel, and checked his wristwatch. If he pushed it, he could be back at the trailer park and Doris's home cooking in less than twenty minutes. He made a full one hundred and eighty degree u-turn right in the middle of the road and headed toward Newberry. Then he lowered the blade on the snowplow, stomped on the gas pedal, and throttled the speed up past forty. Bart took out three mailboxes and a couple of road signs along the highway in his eagerness to return home for something to eat and maybe watch a couple of game shows on the television before calling it a night. And if he was real lucky, Doris might want to do a little lovin' with her hillbilly husband before bedtime too.

* * *

In the middle of the night and fighting to stay awake, Jimmy ticked off the list of unfortunate things that had gone wrong since they crashed the WindStar. Tom Karrski was dead. Not only were they lost but also they hadn't eaten for days, in addition to being cold and exhausted. Two of them suffered from serious injuries. And finally, they were trapped inside of an abandoned railroad car, being hunted by animals intent upon kill them. Jimmy could not imagine things could get much worse.

In the dim light of the kerosene lantern, he glanced over at his two injured companions, both sleeping fitfully in the solitude of the caboose. The wind howled outdoors and whistled through a myriad of tiny holes and cracks in the wooden plank walls. Despite fatigue and his own stinging pain from frostbite on his ears and fingertips, Jimmy fought to stay awake. The dim glow on the face of his wristwatch told him that there were at least four more lonely and nervous hours until daybreak.

Like an ancient staircase in a haunted castle, the caboose creaked in a huge gust of wind. Jimmy listened, his ears attuned to every little sound and noise no matter how small or insignificant. Time passed ever so slowly. His eyelids became heavier and heavier, until he finally nodded off to sleep.

"Jimmy."

His eyelids fluttered as the image of the Dago's face slowly resolved in front of him. Jimmy's head lurched up from the top of the three-legged table where he had dozed off. "What..."

Tony held three fingers to Jimmy's lips. "Shhhh," he said, hushing him. "Listen," he whispered.

Jimmy cocked his head like some hunting dog on the prowl. Between the sound of the wind blowing outside and Sam's soft snoring on the bed, he heard nothing.

"Can you hear it?"

Jimmy listened again. This time he heard something, a slight scraping noise of some kind, a sort of rasping. It reminded Jimmy of the time a squirrel had somehow gotten stuck in between the living room and bedroom walls of their home back in Flint. The unfortunate creature was trapped for most of a day. The squirrel kept scraping its sharp claws against the inside of the plaster walls, trying to get out. Like most wives, Brenda went nuts over the noise until they called an exterminator over who was able to rescue the poor animal through a hole in the attic.

"Yeah," Jimmy nodded, finally. "But what is it and where's it coming from?" He kept the tone of his voice low and soft.

Tony shrugged his shoulders, his splinted arm cradled in the sling across his chest.

Jimmy got up from the chair and went over to the center of the room and stood directly under the kerosene lamp. He tried focusing on where the noises were coming from. The elusive sounds would occur only every now and then, confounding them both as to its source and exact location.

Suddenly, the stillness of the night was cut with the loud growls and snarls of wild animals. Immediately, the two men knew exactly from where the sounds were coming.

"Jimmy, the bastards are right underneath us!" Tony yelled.

A chorus of shrill squeals and furious scrapings coming from beneath the floorboards started.

Sam awakened from his slumber. "What's going on?' he managed to ask, barely able to raise himself up on his elbows.

"Stay where you are," Jimmy ordered.

The wooden planks of the floor reverberated as the creatures scratched and clawed, trying to break through the floorboards and get to the men. The beasts snarled and hissed as they tried to figure out a way inside. Somehow the bolts attached to the planks and the metal undercarriage of the railroad car held in place.

Occasionally, Jimmy would catch glimpses of claws and talons wriggling their way between some of the cracks and spaces between the floorboards. It sounded as if a whole nest of the vile creatures had taken up residence underneath the rusted wheels of the caboose.

"God damn it to hell!" Jimmy screamed at their tormentors. Not having any other alternative, he grabbed the Winchester and started pumping round after round into the floor. Every now and then, his ears were rewarded with a shrill scream, which he interpreted as a direct hit on one of the monsters, although he had no real way of telling. Tony soon joined in the fray, hobbling around on one leg, indiscriminately firing shots from one of the pistols with his uninjured hand into the space below the caboose.

Choking clouds of sulfur and ash quickly built up in the tiny room, making things even more difficult to see in the dim light. Gradually, the sounds of squealing and scratching subsided. There was no way of knowing if the creatures had all been killed or had managed to escape the human's lethal bullets.

Sam began coughing violently in the smoke-filled room. Jimmy rushed to his aid.

"We need to get some fresh air in here." Jimmy realized that by opening the door they could be exposed to further attack. For Sam's sake, they had to take the risk.

He walked over to the entrance, quickly removed the nails and braces, and then flung open the door with the pistol drawn and aimed at any would-be intruders. A cold rush of fresh air tumbled into the caboose while outside a sudden flurry of activity took place as several of the beasts emerged from underneath the carriage.

Jimmy raised the pistol and brought the sights on the barrel to rest on the flanks of one of the creatures. "You fucking bastards!" Jimmy yelled through clinched teeth.

He pulled the trigger three times, pointed the weapon at another one of the startled creatures, shot another three times, and reloaded with a fresh clip. The three or four beasts he had confronted fled in a stampede toward the West as fast as their pounding hooves would carry them despite whatever injuries Jimmy may have inflicted.

All Jimmy could think about at that very moment was the savage killing of Tom Karrski and the serious wounds to his brother and Tony caused by the marauding killers. It made his blood boil.

He fired more shots. "Cock-sucking, mother fuckers!" He kept firing even though their speed quickly took the beasts out of range. Soon Jimmy ran out of bullets, but he merely reached into his pocket and retrieved a fresh clip. He took aim again and continued shooting.

"Cock-sucking, mother-fucking bastards…" He kept saying over and over again. Tears welled in his eyes and ran down his cheeks in long rivers as acrid clouds of sulfur swirled around him. Suddenly, he felt the reassuring hand of his friend Tony on his shoulder.

"Jimmy! Stop. Stop. They're out of range. Come back inside. You're wasting ammunition. We may need everything we got for sometime later." It took all the strength Tony could muster to restrain his emotional friend.

Finally, Jimmy came to his senses. His arms fell to his sides as the pistol smoldered in his hand. Utterly exhausted, he looked out into the vast and now still forest.

"Come back inside, Jimmy."

Jimmy turned and confronted his best friend. Lines of worry appeared prominent on Jimmy's face. He buried his head on his friend's shoulder and cried, as Tony helped him back inside the caboose.

* * *

The attack by the creatures, although short lived and unsuccessful, put all three men on edge. They did their best to repair the damage caused mostly by the bullets from their weapons being fired a point blank range into the floor. Several wooden planks bore gapping holes where the shots had been fired. Jimmy stuffed rags and other materials he found scattered on some of the shelves in an attempt to plug them up. In a couple of the larger holes, they placed sharpened sticks to provide obstacles and some protection in the event of another attack from underneath. There really wasn't anything else they could do, except wait and wonder if and when the next attack might take place.

They were exhausted and badly in need of sleep, especially Sam, whose injuries were the most serious. Jimmy, too, gradually recovered from his brief emotional crises and was soon able to regain his position of leadership. He and Tony agreed to take turns, staying awake as a sort of sentry on the lookout for whatever else might happen for the remainder of the night. Jimmy made himself as comfortable as possible on the floor, but a good solid snooze eluded him no matter how hard he tried. When he did finally fall asleep, he dreamt terrible nightmares.

Close to daybreak, Jimmy roused wide-awake for no apparent reason. It took him a little while to regain his bearings after a brief but fitful nap. Then he realized the reality of his situation. It was still pitch black inside the caboose. They had extinguished the kerosene lamp that hung from the ceiling, trying to reserve as much of the precious liquid as possible for later use if needed. He'd been dreaming about being back at work with all his coworkers and fellow union buddies, a crazy nightmare where nothing made much sense.

In the dream, Jimmy found himself standing next to the line back at the G.M. Powertrain Assembly Plant in Flint. When he looked down, however, instead of the usual steady stream of fuel injector components, the metal conveyor system contained the bloody, dismembered parts of dead animals. There were legs and paws and snouts and hunks of raw, bloody meat. Jimmy recognized the head of a cat, its green eyes opened and murky in death. He also saw something that looked like a hand severed from a chimpanzee, and the ear lopped off a goat or small donkey.

Working beside Jimmy were not his usual friends or union buddies. The people looked human enough, but their faces contained lifeless expressions and vacant eyes. They reminded Jimmy of those zombies he'd seen on late night television in old Hollywood movies. Blood glistened on their hands from their gory enterprise. The zombies were busy attaching mechanical parts and wires and different electrical components to each animal segment that went past their station. At the end of the process further on down the line, a strong electric current was administered to the redesigned configuration...now half-animal, half-mechanical...by a set of paddles similar to those used to revive heart attack patients in a hospital. The leg or hindquarter, or whatever part it once was, would suddenly come back to life, twitching in uncoordinated spasms on the surface of the metal conveyor belt in response to electrical stimulation.

The zombie workers acted as if they had been heavily drugged, brainless shadows of once intelligent human beings. Someone or something seemed to be controlling them, regulating their every movement with machine-like precision over which they had no ability to resist.

Jimmy approached one of the zombies. He put his hand on the zombie's shoulder. It turned and faced him. Jimmy recognized the face immediately. It was Tom, Tom Karrski, who had died horribly, and whose body now hung suspended in the branches of a god-awful tree in some unidentified location in the Upper Peninsula of Michigan, where Jimmy and the boys had left his body to rot.

Tom's vacant eyes failed to acknowledge Jimmy; his poor friend merely stared off into distant space, as if hypnotized, unable to respond by voice or in any other way to Jimmy's pointless entreats. A clear plastic tube appeared implanted through a small puncture wound near his carotid artery into his neck. The other end was attached to a vile looking creature of some sort, which had anchored itself by small metal hooks directly to Tom's breastplate. A gray, viscous material coursed through the middle of the tubing, as the alien parasite sucked the human's precious fluids as a source of regular nourishment. Some of the stuff oozed from the end of the flexible tubing onto the floor and splattered on the Polock's work shoes. The terrible image of his friend Tom being slowly digested by the hideous creature disgusted Jimmy and made him sick to his stomach. Jimmy glanced around and noticed that every one of the zombies had an alien parasite implanted on their chest.

    Further down the line, the reengineered animal parts entered a dark tunnel fashioned out of a bright, highly polished material that gleamed in a brilliant copper color. A deep, monotonous sound, like the constant beating of a bass drum, came from within the bowels of the tunnel. Occasional shafts of bright light flashed out the narrow hole, creating a series of brief, but frightening shadows along the walls of the plant were Jimmy stood.

    Jimmy rushed over to the other side of the assembly line, where the end products were being disgorged from the gory industrial process. Apparently, the animal parts were being fused together in some miraculous way inside the metal tunnel, resulting in a twisted amalgamation made out of flesh and metal and plastic. Some of the things that emerged ended up having extra limbs or several heads attached. Other failed experiments lacked essential parts or organs. Most of the creatures had no hides or skin, with muscles and veins and arteries and nerves that were fully exposed, without the slightest protection to their delicate organs. Many of the unfortunate ones writhed in agony on the bloody conveyor belt, as if suffering their final death throws even though their reanimation had taken place only minutes earlier.

Those reanimated creations able to walk or crawl were led off the final stages of the assembly process and taken to a large warehouse attached to the plant by their zombie makers. The rest were pulled or dragged along the cold cement floor, leaving a long, greasy path which Jimmy followed. He entered a cavernous warehouse. For as far as he could see, every inch of space contained an array of the horrible animal amalgamations that were kept in place behind metal bars as if a part of a bizarre alien zoo of some kind. The place smelled of raw meat and rotting flesh.

That's when Jimmy awoke, startled from the nightmare. Sweat poured from every inch of his skin and soaked his clothing. Blurry eyed, he felt nauseous. It took him a couple of minutes to wake up and realize where he was. In the feeble light inside the caboose, he could barely see the silhouette of his brother, lying on the mattress. He could hear the disturbing rattle of fluids in Sam's lungs as he labored with each breath.

Jimmy struggled, trying to go back to sleep. No matter how hard he tried, however, he could not. He was wide-awake when dawn finally broke on his third day together with Sam and Tony in the northern wilderness. At least they had survived the night, he thought, although another day trapped inside the caboose offered little hope or consolation from the danger that lurked outdoors. Somehow, he needed to figure a way to get them out of there...alive.

He longed for a cigarette as his stomach growled from hunger.

* * *

Bart Bakersfield found Frank Finnerdy in the Luce county maintenance garage office exactly as he always pictured him in his mind...sitting on his dead ass as usual with his legs propped on top of his desk. Patches of pale, milky-white skin picked out between the tops of his brown crew socks and the cuffs on his tan pants. Perched on a corner of the desk next to him in conversation was sheriff Ollie Svenson. The smell of freshly brewed coffee permeated the office.

The County road supervisor glanced up from their conversation and up at the clock on the wall as Bart walked in. The hands read seven-forty five. "Goddamn it Bakersfield, you're late," he barked. "Everybody else has already been here and left. They're out plowing the roads like they're supposed to be doing."

The sheriff bridled slightly. "Now, Frank, we don't need to use the Lord's name in vain. what would your lovely wife say if she heard you talking that way?"

Frank sighed. "Sorry sheriff, but ol' Bart here is always coming in late, ain't you Bart?"

The transplanted Tennessee hillbilly scuffed his shoes together like some naughty kid in grade school sent to the principal's office for a good whackin'. Still, he managed a feeble excuse for his lateness. "The old lady's car had a flat tire, so I had to change the dang thang before coming into work," he said.

"Flat tire…my ass," Frank said, rising up slightly out of his chair, obviously quite agitated with his plow driver. "Your wife going nowhere with all the roads in the county stacked up with three feet of snow, now is she?"

Bart thought about it for several seconds. "Suppose not," he said, scratching the side of his head.

Frank shook his head, exasperated, while the sheriff stifled a guffaw. "If I didn't need your help so bad I'd fire your ass right here on the spot," Frank said, exaggerating the point for the benefit of the sheriff. "As it is, I need you to go up in the northern part of the county and start clearing off some of them highways and secondary roads where we got hit the worst. Around Superior is where the snow was heaviest. Here's your route map. I marked the ones I want you to work on with red magic marker." He handed a photo static copy of the assignment to Bart.

Bart took the paper in hand and started studying the map like it was the Magna Charta.

"You was up that way yesterday, wern't you Bart?" the sheriff asked.

"Yeah, sheriff…I was."

"Did you happen to see anything out of the ordinary while you was working?"

It always seemed to take Bart's brain several seconds to work. "Naw, sheriff. Can't say as I did see anythang out of the ordinary. Should I be looking fer something?"

Ollie Svenson thought it best not to bring up the subject of the woman's dead body he and his deputy had found several days earlier up in that area. He purposely did not mention the strange animal tracks found at the site either. "No, Bart…just asking." Then he remembered, "By the way…I got a call early this morning from the State Patrol. Some woman down in Flint called, saying that her husband and three of his buddies was headed this way for some deer hunting. You might keep an eye out for them, Bart…just in case."

"Sure, sheriff."

"They're probably in a motel somewhere's safe, drinking up a storm, most likely."

"Yeah…okay." Bart said, anxious to get out of there and away from Frank. "Kin I go now?"

"Yeah. Get outa here," Frank waved him out the door with both hands. "Just be careful, and don't let anything bad happen to that equipment…and keep your radio on at all times," he ordered, as Bart hurried out the door and headed to the truck awaiting him in the parking lot.

Frank shook his head again and turned his conversation back toward the sheriff. "That dim-witted redneck will be the death of me yet, Ollie. One of these day he'll drive one of my trucks straight off a cliff into Lake Superior."

The sheriff nodded in agreement. "He ain't vorth blowing a gasket over, Frank." He grabbed his coat and Smokey Bear hat off the coat rack and sauntered toward the door himself. "See you later, Frank."

"So long, sheriff." Frank propped his fat legs back on the table and leaned way back in his chair. He nearly tipped the damn thing over in the process.

* * *

A shaft of bright sunlight streamed in the streaked window of the caboose. Morning had finally decided to arrive. The three survivors, groggy from an evening filled with terror, were in the process of deciding their options.

"You can't do it alone out there, Jimmy," Sam was saying. "You wouldn't make it very far before those things out there would jump you and you'd end up dead, just like the Polock." He could barely talk without coughing. So he left most of the planning to Tony and his brother.

Jimmy had suggested he try finding help on his own since Sam and Tony were injured and unable to travel.

"Besides, we're getting pretty low on ammo," Tony said. "Between the Winchester and the Colt forty-fives, we got less than a couple of dozen rounds left...not a lot, considering what we're facing."

"If we stay here, the only help that'll ever come along will be somebody coming down that road we followed to get here in the first place." Jimmy said. "Which means, we still gotta be prepared to let them know we're here. Anyone coming that way can't see the caboose from down there on the highway; we've got to make ourselves more visible somehow. If nothing shows up pretty soon, well...then we might have to do something else."

"Alright," Tony said.

Jimmy continued. "We need to finish up working on the signal fire. That'll take some time since the two of you are hurt and I'll have to do it mostly by myself. There's enough recycled oil in that fifty-five gallon drum outside that once we do get the thing burning it'll make one hell of a bonfire. Anyone coming down the highway should be able to see us real good…if they're lookin'."

"We don't have enough materials to keep the fire going all the time. We'll have to light it soon as we hear or see something," Tony said. "Besides, with those things still around, it's too dangerous for you to be alone outside, cutting down more trees."

"Yeah…so we'll go with lighting the fire when the time or opportunity seems right."

They agreed.

"Next thing we gotta do is put some kind of signal down closer to the road. That will get someone to stop, take a look, and give us some time to get down there."

"What'd you have in mind, Jimmy?"

"I dunno…a marker of some sort that's easy to see, that someone will notice and take the time to stop."

"How about this," Tony offered, drawing upon his former Boy Scout experience. "We can make a couple of flags out of some of the stuff we brought with us. If we attach them to some boards and put 'em in the middle of the goddamn road, that should get their attention."

"Good idea." Jimmy said.

Tony's face took on a serious look. "Only problem is…getting those flags down to the road. You're going to have to do it alone, pal."

"Yeah…I know," Jimmy nodded, mentally assessing the knotty problem facing him. "And we still don't know who or when the hell someone might ever come along."

* * *

Jimmy supported Tony as they ventured outside for the first time since the prior day. He arranged a place for the feisty Italian to sit on the platform in order to provide some cover for him while he worked on the signal fire.

First, however, Jimmy looked for any signs of the creatures both around the caboose and within close range of their location. He checked particularly well beneath the undercarriage of the railroad car from where the animals had mounted their night attack. Disappointed, he found no clues that they had ever been there. The howling winds of the previous night had wiped away all traces of their tracks with an additional half-foot of drifted snow.

Once Jimmy was sure of their relative security, he went to work cutting and stacking the wood for the signal fire in a spot ten or fifteen feet away from the caboose and most visible from the highway. He soaked each log with a liberal douse of oily sludge from a fifty-five gallon drum they had found outside the caboose that first night.

Tony, meanwhile, kept his eyes peeled for any signs of their enemy and held one of the pistols at the ready, while Jimmy cut and stacked wood for the fire. Although Tony couldn't fire the rifle effectively because of his injuries, he still had full use of his right side and would be able to shoot the handgun. Still, Jimmy never wandered very far from home base for fear of encountering the unknown. The entire time he worked, neither of the two men saw any of their dreaded killer pursuers. Every now and then, however, they heard the strange cries of wild animals and the horrible screams of what sounded like other animals being eaten alive.

While Jimmy was retrieving some old logs that had been stacked in a pile by someone prior to their arrival, a large rat, disturbed by the human's rude intrusion, came running out from under the logs in an attempt to break for freedom. Initially startled by the rat, Jimmy quickly regained his senses and grabbed the barrel of the Winchester and proceeded to clobber the unfortunate creature to death before it could escape.

Tony had watched the entire humorous confrontation between man and beast unfold before his eyes. When Jimmy was finished pounding the daylights out of the rat, he picked the dead rodent up by its long tail and carried it over to the platform where Tony was sitting. He handed the proud trophy over to his smiling chum.

"Lunch," is all Jimmy said.

"Lunch?" Tony replied, crinkling his nose while holding the dead rat in front of his big eyes.

"Yeah...Lunch." Jimmy reiterated, going back to work. "Unless you got any better ideas."

Tony didn't.

A couple of hours later, Jimmy put the finishing touches on the pile of wood, eventually reaching a height in excess of seven feet. Once lit, the pile, saturated with the smelly oil, should provide a considerable amount of smoke and fire and be visible for miles, Jimmy hoped. His ears, bare to the cold and already once bitten with frostbite, had turned fiery red, although feeling numb to him.

Finally, Jimmy scavenged a couple of old two-by-fours off the sides of the caboose, each over six feet in length, and tied long strips of bright cloth on the ends to act as signal flags. The mounds of snow down on the highway would provide enough support to hold them upright for easy visibility. The problem would be getting them down to the road. Although they had not seen any of the creatures, that didn't mean the beasts weren't lurking in the forest somewhere, waiting to unleash their murderous fury.

Before proceeding with the plan, they went inside the caboose to give Jimmy a little rest before embarking on his dangerous task and check on Sam's condition. They found Sam feverish, swooning in and out of delirium. They placed a cold compress of icy snow wrapped in moistened rags on his forehead, which seemed to make him a bit more comfortable.

Jimmy then went about the gory task of cleaning out the entrails of the dead rat in preparation for lunch. After cleaning and butchering the small carcass of the rodent, he filled a small pan with water and boiled the meat atop the cast iron stove. Despite the unappetizing notion of eating such a disgusting scavenger, the pungent aroma of the cooking made the men forget all about such niceties. They hadn't eaten anything for over two days and they were starved.

Jimmy served Tony his portion of the savory stew, saving some for Sam, and sat down at the table where the two men made quick work of their meager meal.

"I've had better," Tony remarked to the cook, who was chewing on the last sinewy part remaining. "But then, I've had worse too," he smiled.

* * *

A late autumn afternoon sun cast feeble rays of light through one of the windows on the caboose. Jimmy took notice. The colorful display reminded him of the little church his mother used to take him and Sam to back in Flint when they were kids, with light streaming through the stained glass windows onto the pews where they sat as a family. He remembered how Dad hated to go to church even more than his two sons and rarely did as a result.

"Getting towards mid-afternoon," Jimmy said, resting a bit after their meager meal.

Tony looked up and nodded in agreement.

Jimmy rose up from his chair. "I better get those signal flags down to the road before it gets too late."

Tony could tell that Jimmy was concerned by the task ahead. He started to get up himself, but Jimmy held him down with a strong arm applied on his friend's left shoulder.

"Hold it there, partner," Jimmy said. "Where do you think you're goin'?" He never expected Tony to answer. "You're not in any kind of shape to give me a hand on this one, buddy. I gotta do this myself. You just sit tight and look after my kid brother...just in case something happens."

Tony sat back more comfortably, resigned to Jimmy's admonition. "Be careful," he said. "Don't forget, take the Winchester with you."

"I plan to," Jimmy replied, already in the process of loading the remaining cartridges that were left, ten of them to be exact. That's all they had; that's all he could rely upon. He zipped up the front of his coat and screwed his union baseball cap snug on top of his head. "I'll be back in a jiffy," he said, as if he were going out to clear the snow from the driveway back home or conduct some other usual and mundane task. "Keep an eye on Sam."

"I will," Tony assured him.

The two men didn't have to say anything else to each other; their eyes said it all.

Jimmy exited the door of the caboose and made sure the rusted latch locked securely behind him. He grabbed the two signal flags under his left arm as best he could, while keeping the butt of the Winchester tucked under his right shoulder and the barrel balanced on his forearm. He surveyed the route down the formidable incline to the highway, perhaps a quarter mile distance away. He remembered the difficult walk up through the snow, at times hip deep, with Sam and Tony. This time he would have to do it alone, in both directions.

A couple of blurry, orange sun devils flanked either side of the sun, which now hung low in the southwest sky. Mammoth-sized drifts of snow covered all the trees and countryside as far as Jimmy could see. A crystal blue sky sparkled overhead. Soon enough, the bright early stars of dusk would make their stellar debut.

Before starting, his sharp eyes scoured the forest and surrounding open areas looking for any sign of the beasts. The air outdoors felt cold, still, and ominous. His breath hung in front of him in great billows of gray fog. Jimmy adjusted the load in his arms and proceeded toward the road with nervous caution.

Each step Jimmy took caused his legs to sink deep into the sugary mounds. Just keeping his balance proved a difficult task with all the cargo that he transported with him. His senses remained on full alert even though his mind wandered on to other thoughts. Those thoughts transported him back to just several days ago and the anticipation of the happy hunting trip he and Sam and Tom and Tony were about to enjoy. The bitter realization of their current situation, however, quickly brought him back to reality. Protected only by his own sharp wits and the Winchester in his arms, he proceeded forward, his stomach roiling at the task. An uncomfortable stillness lay across the area.

Jimmy struggled through the drifts pretending to be some pirate coming ashore in the deep surf. His progress was slow, his steps deliberate. The combination of the hip-deep snow and the load he carried made it difficult for him to maintain his balance. He toppled over several times in the process, but downy layers of soft snow cushioned his fall each time. After awhile, he got to looking like a well-armed snowman, gun and flags in hand, and glistening from head to toe with a thick coating of the powdery white substance.

It took Jimmy about twenty minutes to navigate his way down to the road. Once there, he dug down into the snow with the heel on his boot until he reached the asphalt surface just to make sure. He rammed the ends of the two-by-fours into a nearby drift and crisscrossed the flags against one another like a warning to an open mineshaft. Hopefully, anyone seeing the flags would stop long enough and thus give Jimmy time to make his way down from the caboose to get help.

Jimmy wished he had a cigarette to reward himself for his dangerous accomplishment, but unfortunately he had none left.

* * *

Jimmy started back up the hill. Wisps of tiny snowflakes twinkled like miniature sun catchers in the cobalt-blue sky. The sun had not yet set. The return path proved even slower and more slippery than on his trip down. He fell on numerous occasions, but his hands kept a secure grip on the Winchester at all times.

As Jimmy came around the last stand of white pines, marking the final obstacle on the way home, he suddenly encountered a large number of deer in an open expanse that separated him from the safety of the railroad car. The herd was about the same size as the one they had encountered the prior day, just before the violence which left Sam and Tony as casualties. The sight of the herd sent a cold chill down Jimmy's spine, as he remembered the resulting attack from the monstrous predators afterwards. The herd was milling about the area, foraging for food, and completely ignoring his presence. They used their sharp hooves to scratch down to the ground's surface in search of the tender grasses hidden beneath the snow.

He froze in his tracks and held his breath. He knew the hungry beasts had to be somewhere nearby and were not likely to abandon or ignore such a large conglomeration of game. The barrel on the Winchester swept the horizon. The strong scent of the herd accosted his nostrils. The musty odor smelled of feces and urine, reminding Jimmy of large feed lot, where cattle were often harbored for days to fatten them up prior to being slaughtered.

The deer were completely oblivious to him, as if he represented no threat to them even though he was armed with a rifle. Considering this was the height of deer hunting season throughout the entire state of Michigan, the herd's strange behavior seemed all the more bizarre to Jimmy. His mere presence, during the annual fall hunting season, should be enough to send them scurrying off back into the woods for safety. Perhaps they were much more afraid of something else in the forest.

Jimmy decided, however, that he would not make the same mistake Tony had unknowingly committed and attempt to harm the deer in any way. He gave them a wide berth, as he cautiously made his way toward the shelter of the caboose.

As he trudged through the snow, several of the larger does with fawns feeding beside them took notice of him, but more out of curiosity than a sense of fear. They studied at him with glassy eyes that reflected back the bright snow despite the ever-darkening sky. Something seemed unnatural about them, almost alien. Jimmy felt their gaze fall upon him.

About half way through his journey, one of the young males, with a rack of some five or six points, moved over to a position directly in front of Jimmy's intended path, as if blocking the way intentionally. The buck held his proud head high and stood in defiance at the human's coming. Jimmy tried to veer a little to the left, but he could only move over so far without encountering another deer, so closely were all the deer standing next to one another. He pulled the Winchester close to his chest so as not to alarm the animals in any way and appear less threatening.

As Jimmy passed, the young buck lowered his head and, with teeth flashing, nipped at the intruders leg. Jimmy felt a sudden sting on his right calf. The painful bite barely broke skin, but resulted in Jimmy taking a swat at the bothersome buck with an open hand. His knuckles rapped against the deer's furry snout.

The buck bleated an angry disapproval, while a dozen other deer heads bobbed up out of the snow to see what was happening. The buck emerged from their brief encounter with a piece of fabric from Jimmy's pant leg hanging loosely from his mouth.

Jimmy froze a second time, his senses on heightened alert.

Nothing happened.

The herd went back to their foraging and feeding, while the deer that had nipped Jimmy's leg acted as though the incident had never occurred.

A trickle of sweat ran down Jimmy's forehead and gathered on the bridge of his nose. The snow crunched and squeaked under his every footstep as he crept toward the safety of the caboose. He breathed sigh of relief upon reaching the steps leading up to the railroad car, but he couldn't help thinking that he was being watched the entire time by something other than the deer.

* * *

"Something strange is going on." Jimmy said, re-entering the warm and welcome confines of the caboose. He sat down next to Tony, the smell of rat stew still wafting in the air. It took him a minute to catch his breath. He related to the Dago what had happened when he came across the herd of deer on his way back from placing the signal flags down near the highway, and the young buck which had bitten him. He showed his pant leg with a little blood smeared through his jeans.

"I'm just glad you made it back safely," Tony said. "I feel like a piece of shit not being able to give you a hand, but I don't know if I could've been much help."

Jimmy appreciated his friend's concern, but realized that everything now depended on himself. "How's Sam?" he asked.

"Mostly been sleeping since you've been gone. He hasn't moved very much."

"Well...I'd better check on him," Jimmy said, muttering to himself. It's not that he didn't trust Tony to look after his brother during his brief absence. Jimmy just didn't know what else he could do. He was worried about both of his companions and frustrated he couldn't do anything more for either of them. And then there was the guilt, of course. The nagging feeling of responsibility came back to Jimmy...the trip to northern Michigan, the crash that followed, Tom Karrski's horrible death, and the perilous predicament in which they now found themselves...he blamed himself for everything that had happened.

Jimmy lifted himself from the wobbly chair and ventured over to his kid brother. Sam was still laying on the bed, exactly as Jimmy had left him, with his right hand clutching his chest. His diaphragm rose up and down like the bellows on an accordion, rattling with each breath. Jimmy couldn't tell whether Sam was asleep or unconscious, not that it mattered. His brother needed rest and medical attention even more. All Jimmy could do now was to sit around and wait. There was nothing more he or Tony could do. Patience was a virtue Jimmy sorely lacked.

Jimmy wondered about Sam's family back in Port Huron, his wife Martha, and the two kids, Lisa and Marc. What would he tell them if something happened to Sam? How could he excuse himself of responsibility for whatever happened? Jimmy longed for the safety and security of home.

He went back over to the table and buried his heavy head on his arms. He felt like crying, like he did when he was a little boy. He had to keep telling himself that he was a man, and that he needed to start acting like one.

It was going to be a long night.

* * *

"Base station, this is Bart. Do you copy? Over."

Ten or fifteen seconds of annoying electric static followed.

"Base station, this is Bart. Anyone home? Over." The hillbilly pulled over to the side of the road where he was working and turned off the engine so he could hear things better.

Five more seconds of static, then the familiar voice of Frank Finnerdy came over the radio clear as a bell. "Shit yes, we're still here…and we'll probably be here for at least the next twenty-four hours, until all them goddamned roads get plowed of snow. Where the hell've you been Bakersfield? We've been expecting to hear from you a couple of hours ago."

Same old shit, Bart thought to himself. Seemed like the harder he tried, the harder it got sometimes. Frank Finnerdy was constantly on his ass like a wart on a Tennessee toad. "Hell, took me all morning and most of this afternoon to clear all them roads you marked with your little red pen on the map. There's more snow on these here roads than there is stink on a skunk," Bart protested, barking back at his fat supervisor through the microphone.

"Hell, I gave you that map over eight hours ago. Sometimes you're slower than molasses in the wintertime." Frank's voice crackled through the speakers in the truck cabin.

Bart rolled his eyes as if searching for an acceptable excuse somewhere in his thick cranium. "Just trying my best, boss. Just trying my best," he offered.

"Yeah…well, you got lots more work to do," Frank answered. There were still a couple of hundred miles of streets, highways, and roads to clear in the county, and Bart was one of his main drivers. "Hold on a minute."

Frank went over to a detailed county road map, hanging on the far wall of the office, in order to determine which routes he wanted Bart to clear. He stuck two or three red pins on the locations he expected Bart to work. The map also contained an array of green pins and blue pins and yellow pins, representing other drivers and the roads they were in the process of plowing. Bright orange pins, covering about half the county, indicated routes that had already been cleared.

In the meantime, Bart slipped another disc into the C.D. player, waiting for Finnerdy to come back on the line.

The soothing voice of Chet Atkins singing a familiar melody soon joined him inside the chilly cab.

"Bart, you there?"

"Yeah, boss."

"I need you to head up on highway 221 and then shift over north to county 453. Matt Denkins cleared 221 a couple of hours ago, but no one's been up 453 yet. Take her clear on over to the Superior shoreline and then head back this way on a second pass. The further you go north, the deeper the shit seems to get. So be careful. I don't want to take any of my other drivers off the job if you get stuck somewhere. Understand?"

"Yep," Bart said, readjusting a plug of tobacco inside his cheek. "221 to 453, then back again."

"That's right. Keep the radio on in case I need to reach you. It's starting to get pretty dark out there so you'll need to be extra cautious. By the looks of things, you'll be working past ten or eleven tonight. I don't need you running into a tree or something and getting yourself killed," Finnerdy ordered.

"Okay, boss. Out."

Bart bit off a fresh chaw of chewing tobacco and added it to the plug in his left cheek. He looked like a chipmunk that had found an oversized chestnut. He flicked on the big truck's yellow headlamps and slipped the transmission into first gear and slowly pulled back on to the road. He was careful not to ram the plow blade accidentally into a nearby telephone poll as he pulled out. Despite having cleared tens of miles of roads, he hadn't encountered a single passenger car of truck for at least the past two hours.

Chapter Eight

"Bones and flesh, flesh and bones; these are the grist of monsters and hungry things. Insatiable appetites drive them forward without the slightest thought or remorse."
Anonymous

A pale moon peeked through a deck of broad early evening clouds over the snowy landscape, the frozen land falling fast asleep.

Jimmy's lips smacked together as he dozed fitfully inside the abandoned railroad car. A foul taste lingered in his mouth from the meager dinner of rat stew he had eaten earlier. His ears detected the subtle sound of distant machinery, the hum of an engine, and he thought that his nightmare from the night before had returned. He waited for the horrible dream of bloody animal parts passing by him on the assembly line to unfold, but it never did. Instead, the far off whirr of an engine persisted, his mind unwilling to believe what his senses heard. His eyelashes fluttered; the dim moonlight from a narrow window filtered into his sleepy eyes.

Jimmy's head lurched up from the table where he had fallen asleep, his ears alerted to the sound. He waited for more, a mental confirmation of what they so desperately needed.

He heard nothing at first, only the sound of the wind whistling through the cracks in the walls and the rattle of Sam breathing on the bed beside him. Then another sound, the unmistakable prattle of a vehicle's exhaust...a truck, perhaps a snowplow, he could only hope, coming down the highway.

Groggy, Tony awoke from his stupor as well. They glanced at one another in the dimness of the room.

"The signal fire," Tony said.

Jimmy leaped up from the chair and grabbed his coat in a rush, inserting his arms through uncooperative sleeves. He wrestled with the stubborn sleeves trying to put the thing on in almost complete darkness.

"The kerosene," Tony tried reminding him. "Don't forget the kerosene."

"Yeah...right." Jimmy fumbled in the darkness, looking for the kerosene they had previously set aside and that he would use to start the pile of wood outside on fire. He found the rusted tin can, which contained several precious ounces of the precious liquid right next to the door, exactly where he had put it the night before. It's all they had and would have to work.

"Don't forget your lighter," Tony reminded him.

"Yeah...yeah." Jimmy patted the outside of his coat pockets in an almost desperate attempt to find the thing. He found the elusive target buried down deep in one of the pockets. Despite the fact that he had run out of cigarettes, he had held on to the lighter. Unfortunately, it didn't have much fluid left, he feared. He'd have to make sure the thing worked on the first or second try.

The sound of the vehicle drew closer, no longer a figment of their imagination.

"I'll start the signal fire and then head down toward the road," Jimmy went over the plan aloud. "Hopefully, whoever's driving will be able to see the fire and stop. If not, maybe I can get down there in time."

Tony hoisted himself up from the floor to his feet, wobbling on his good right leg while trying to maintain his balance. He hobbled over toward the door.

"Stay here and watch Sam," Jimmy said.

"Sure thing." Tony rested a hand on Jimmy's shoulder. "Good luck."

Jimmy opened the door to the caboose and went out on to the small porch of the railroad car. Tony came to the doorway to watch but went no further.

"Hell...the rifle." Tony said it loud enough for Jimmy to hear. Jimmy waited for the Dago to retrieve the Winchester inside. Tony arrived several seconds later and tossed him the weapon. Jimmy made sure the safety was off and the weapon ready to fire before he descended the steep metal stairs off the caboose.

Low, streaming clouds rushed overhead and obscured the moon temporarily, plunging the area around them into an inky blackness despite the abundance of snow cover. Jimmy made his way along the side of the railroad car with his left arm extended, his hand and fingers touching the wooden frame of the caboose like a blind man trying to maintain his balance. About ten paces past the end of the caboose, he encountered the looming pile of carefully stacked wood.

After leaning the Winchester up against the pile, he poured the contents from the tin can on several of the central posts that held the massive stack upright. The sharp smell of the kerosene played in his nostrils. He could see the distant glow of headlights, moving in tandem, just off to his right on the other side of a large rise. Jimmy estimated the vehicle's distance to be less than a mile away.

He grabbed the rifle from the pile, placed the butt under his arm, and retrieved his lighter from his pocket. Only a light breeze was blowing, and a lifelong smoker of Jimmy's experience would have no trouble lighting the fire.

He flipped the metal top open and in one try sparks flew. The wick blazed to life instantly. Jimmy cupped the lighter in his hands, trying to protect the precious flame from becoming extinguished by the wind. He lifted the flame to the central posts saturated with the kerosene.

Fire leaped from the wick to the wood and spread up and over and around all the places Jimmy had poured the liquid kerosene. The blaze grew quickly as did the light from the burning conflagration. He felt as if he was standing in the middle of the spotlight in a dark auditorium about the give the performance of his life. Gradually, all the things around him became more visible.

At that exact moment, Jimmy suddenly realized...he was surrounded.

* * *

He counted at least a dozen of the huge killer animals, all with gaping maws of teeth on their monstrous heads, each more than two hundred pounds of flesh and muscle. Jimmy saw them for the first time, close up, and could hardly believe his eyes. So these were the things that had killed Tom Karrski and hurt Tony and his brother. Finally, he understood how they didn't stand a chance against monsters such as these.

There could be more of the beasts, lurking in the shadows beyond the glow of the growing bonfire, he couldn't tell for sure. The group surrounding him was no more then ten to twenty feet away, but their attention seemed clearly focused on the fire. Their wild eyes looked as if someone had taken hot coals from the signal fire and shoved the embers into the sockets on their monstrous heads. The warm, moist exhalations from their nostrils spewed out in vents of hot steam as if their bellies had been stoked with coal gotten from the fires of hell. One of the creatures began thrashing at the ground as if it were an angry bull ready to take on a helpless matador in some kind of strange and sinister bullfight. A gob of foamy spittle accumulated around its rubbery jowls. Several of the other beasts soon followed suit, until all of them participated in the aberrant behavior.

Jimmy raised the Winchester level with them, although if the monsters decided to charge him all at once he wouldn't stand a chance. He might succeed in shooting at two or three, but at this close of proximity, they would be on him in a flash. Quite unconsciously, he started walking slowly backwards toward the caboose.

By this time, the entire woodpile had caught fire. Flames leaped over ten feet high into the cold, November sky. A torrid funnel of sparks flew off the crackling wood, circling upward like a swarm summertime fireflies trying to escape earth's gravity. The brilliant conflagration bathed the weathered planks on the old caboose in blazing shades of red and orange and yellow. Off to his right, Jimmy could see the glow of headlights from vehicle still behind the rise but drawing ever closer.

He heard the door to the caboose squeak open behind him.

"What the fuck!" Astonished at the sight, Tony stood in the doorway.

Jimmy raised his arm up in stiff disapproval, like a policeman standing in the middle busy street intersection and directing traffic, a signal for Tony to shut up.

Tony understood immediately. For whatever reason, the animals appeared to be afraid of the fire, and for that reason, had not torn the puny human confronting them to shreds. Carefully, he closed the door and withdrew back inside.

Jimmy kept moving backwards in slow motion until his foot snagged on a long branch lying on the ground. The slippery surface on the hard rubber of his soles caused him to loose his balance and tumble backwards. He landed hard on his ass, the Winchester firing by accident harmlessly into the air.

At that very moment, Tony reappeared through the doorway. Thinking Jimmy had been attacked, he raised the pistol in his hand and began firing at the sinister congregation.

"Noooo…!" Jimmy yelled.

But Jimmy had been mistaken. Tony was not shooting at the animals. Instead, several of his well-aimed bullets were directed at the fifty-five gallon drum, still three quarters filled with the smelly oily brine, resting between the bonfire and the caboose. His second shot resulted in a massive explosion, which rocked the nighttime air and sent a huge orange ball of flame shooting upwards into the cloud-infested sky.

Jimmy shielded his face with raised arms from the intense heat of the explosion. The highly volatile liquid went spewing in all directions, coating some of the on-looking monsters in liquid flames. Those stunned creatures on fire took off running at a furious speed, heading back toward the forest line a quarter of a mile away. Jimmy thought they looked like gigantic Texas tumbleweeds set ablaze, hastened by a furious wind across the plains of snow. Their painful bellowing disappeared as the forest gradually gobbled them up

Everything happened so fast.

The rest of the animals scattered in various directions, fleeing from the growing conflagration. One of the beasts, however, darted out of the shadows and hurtled toward Tony, still standing on the railcar's wooden platform. Amazingly, the driven animal leaped the span of over ten yards and struck him full force in the small of his back. Jimmy heard his friend's spine crack the instant he was hit, like a sapling snapped apart by a whirlwind. Tony's lifeless body went flying through the air, tumbling head over heels, and then landed with a dull thud in the snow next to Jimmy. He was dead by the time his body landed, his neck broken. The beast jumped off the platform and then proceeded to disembowel the Dago's corpse to

Jimmy's horror. Pure anger coursed through Jimmy's veins at the horrible sight of his best friend being consumed by the monster.

"You goddamn, fucking bastard!" he yelled at the top of his lungs.

He reached for the broken branch lying beside him that had tripped him. Liquid flames from the burning oil had set one end on the wooden stake on fire. Jimmy grabbed it and charged toward Tony's attacker. The jagged point on the end of the branch struck the unsuspecting beast directly in one of its eyeballs. The burning tip plunged deep into the monster's socket while some of the flames scorched its ugly face. The thing let out a painful shriek as Jimmy rammed the branch deeper into the beast's skull.

With every ounce of his strength, he pushed the hairy attacker away from Tony's body. The beast kept up its painful howls, but Jimmy just kept pushing, driving his nemesis backwards with pure hatred. Eventually, he managed to shove the thing toward a pool of the burning sludge that had been created in the massive explosion. Somehow, Jimmy maneuvered the hindquarters of the beast into the oily inferno. Soon covered in a coating of the oil, the beast caught fire as well. It screamed in agony.

The monster shook the spear imbedded in its skull loose and charged forward in panic. Jimmy could do nothing to stop it. The animal ran passed Jimmy, knocking him down in the process, and disappeared behind the bonfire before Jimmy could react.

Crawling on his knees, Jimmy scrambled over to his fallen comrade. The glow of the fire reflected off Tony's pale face, as a tiny rivulet of blood trickled from the corner of his mouth. Tony's once bright eyes showed vacant and empty. A huge, gaping hole now showed just below his chest.

"Goddamned stupid Dago," he whispered, his fingers gently stroking the hair his dead friend's head. Tears mound in Jimmy's eyes.

Jimmy had no time to devote to such remorse, however. The incident sent a cloud of burning plasma in every direction and quickly spread the blaze to nearby evergreens and shrubbery. Some of the liquid fire flowed underneath the caboose and soon the dry outer shell of the railroad car became engulfed in flames. Jimmy could feel the intense heat of the growing blaze on his cold cheeks.

"Sam!" Jimmy said aloud to himself, suddenly remembering his helpless brother trapped inside the now burning railroad car.

Ignoring any risk to himself, Jimmy raced up the stairs through the open door into the caboose. He found Sam, sitting up on the bed and fully awake. Thick plumes of smoke billowed in one corner of the room where the fire raged outside. Choking fumes began to accumulate and made things all the more difficult to see.

"We gotta get outa here," Jimmy yelled.

"I don't know if I can make it." Sam winced in pain.

Jimmy had already lost two of his best friends; he was not about to sacrifice his younger brother. "C'mon, we can do it together." He grabbed Sam's right arm and threw it over his shoulder. "Just lean on me," he ordered, "until we get outside."

Flames erupted in the corner. The entire place would soon be on fire.

Sam shifted the bulk of his two hundred and sixty pound frame on to Jimmy's shoulder and tried to shuffle his feet forward as best he could. Jimmy sagged under the heavy load, while making slow progress toward the door. One of the kerosene lamps near the fire exploded and sent shards of glass and liquid flame skittering across the floor.

"Just a little bit further," Jimmy urged, struggling with Sam's dead weight attached to him.

They arrived at the doorway. The entire area outside glowed brightly as if dawn had broken with a vengeance, but the monsters had mysteriously disappeared. Jimmy had more important things to worry about.

He pulled his stout brother sideways through the narrow doorway. Negotiating the three steep stairs down from the porch provided the next challenge. He braced Sam against the rusty iron railing along the back of the railroad car and jumped to the ground.

"Sam," Jimmy instructed, "you've got to get down the first couple of steps by yourself. I'll try and break your fall if you slip."

Sam surveyed the fiery scene and the formidable task ahead with fear etched across his face. The wound in his chest ached.

"C'mon. Hurry!" Jimmy encouraged him.

Sam clutched the iron hand railing with both hands, knuckles white, and turned one hundred and eighty degrees in an attempt to hoist his large body down the steps backwards. He made the first step, but then his arms no longer hold the bulk of his own weight. He tumbled like a tree felled by a lumberjack. Fortunately, Jimmy managed to cushion his impact, although both of them landed in a sizable drift of snow.

"Are you all right?" Jimmy asked, concerned for his brother's very life.

Excruciating pain shot through him, but Sam put on his best face. "Yeah...I'm...I'm okay."

Jimmy stood up. He had a plan. "I'll be right back," he said. He scrambled up the stairs and darted back into the caboose where heavy clouds of black smoke rolled out from under a small eave leading inside. About a half a minute later he emerged with a sleeping bag in tow behind him. He tossed the smoldering piece of fabric into the snow and threw fresh snow on top of it in order to extinguish several parts that were smoking and ready to ignite.

Sam shot him a questioning look. "What's that for?" he asked.

"We've got to get down to the highway somehow. You can't stay here. If you get inside the sleeping bag, I'll try to drag you down toward the road with me. We heard a truck or some kind of vehicle coming before all this started.

"Where is Tony?"

Jimmy sighed, and looked over in the direction where the fifty-five gallon drum had been. There was too much smoke and fire to see anything clearly. "On the other side, over there...he's dead." Jimmy's head nodded toward the growing conflagration.

"Dead?"

"Yeah," Jimmy answered. "I don't have time to explain. Those things got him, just like they got Karrski and hurt you."

Flames now engulfed one entire half of the caboose and several stately pines nearby burned like huge cotton swabs set afire. They intense heat from the inferno was melting snow all around them.

"What the hell's going on?" Sam remarked, finally beginning to regain his senses for the first time in over a day.

Jimmy shook his head, wanting to explain more, but realizing the urgency of their situation. "Let's just get outta here."

He grabbed the sleeping bag, brushed off the snow he had just thrown on to extinguish the smoking patches, and told Sam, "Get in."

Sam wormed his way down into the folds of the sleeping bag, gingerly negotiating his way into the sack. Once inside, Jimmy zipped up the sides so that Sam would be safe inside the cocoon. Parts of the roof on the caboose began collapsing, sending a torrent of burning embers skyward and showering both of them with hot ashes.

"All set?"

"As good as I'll ever be," Sam answered.

"Hold on then." Jimmy wrapped some of the loose ends on the sleeping bag securely around his right arm, intending to pull Sam feet-first down toward the highway. He retrieved the rifle from the metal platform and handed the weapon to Sam. Considering they were almost out of ammunition, Jimmy didn't know how much good the gun would do anyway.

They entered deep snow right off, making the process most difficult. Jimmy's legs and back strained with the added weight of his brother. He wondered if sled dogs felt the same.

Once away from the brightness cast by the fire, Jimmy's eyes gradually grew accustomed to the early morning darkness. He had all but forgotten of the approaching vehicle. He glanced off toward the hill where he had last seen the approaching lights, but saw nothing at first. Then he saw the welcome flash from two headlamps, flickering in and out the trees about a half a mile away. Jimmy anxiously watched as the vehicle slowly made its way toward the small clearing at the bottom of the incline where he had placed the two flags.

It was a snowplow, and it was definitely headed in their direction.

A fresh shot of adrenalin helped Jimmy to pump his legs harder.

*   *   *

Bart Bakersfield had been plowing roads since seven forty-five that morning. He'd seen about all the snow he'd ever cared to see, except he saw all the white stuff in a different color than most people; green, the color of money. The unexpected November blizzard gave him the opportunity to make plenty of overtime pay. Little dollar signs danced in his dim head. "The more snow, the more money"; the simple mantra ran over and over in his mind. The ends of his mouth curled up in a big toothy smile, enhanced by an oversized pair of manmade choppers. With a little luck, he just might be able to parlay enough overtime pay from this storm to buy that new fangled washing machine for Doris that she'd had her eyes on down at in the local Sears store. He'd been wanting to buy himself a brand new bowling ball too.

He hadn't encountered a living soul for the past couple of hours. Hardly anybody lived in this part of the county, too many hills and forests and bad farmland to attract permanent residents of any sort, other than an occasional hunter or hiker or camper from downstate somewhere. Still, the highways needed plowing, more so for all the cars and trucks that regularly traveled back and forth between the city Marquette, about another hundred miles to the west, and Sioux St. Marie on east side of the peninsula.

"A lotta god forsaken nothin' in this goddamn Yankee state," Bart mumbled to himself, his eyes getting weary of the constant field of white snow in front of him.

It wasn't that easy trying to figure out where the goddamned road was either. Three feet of snow on a desolate two-lane highway, with hardly a straightaway longer than an eighth of a mile, made his task even more difficult. Steering a ten-ton truck and keeping the blasted thing on the roadway while he plowed required a certain amount of skill and experience. Occasionally, Bart found himself shoveling up huge swaths of gravel shoulder, in addition to the mounds of snow, when he thought he was driving in the middle of the highway. A couple of times, he missed the road entirely and almost ended up getting stranded in a massive ditch or deep culvert. On both occasions, he managed to stop the big rig just in time. Frank Finnerdy, his lazy ass boss down at the county garage, would have a cat fit if Bart somehow got the truck stuck. Another plow and driver would have to come and dig him out and probably waste a couple of hours in the process, at least. It was also embarrassing, if you were a regular driver, to admit you got stuck. The other drivers liked to tease each other when one of them messed up like that. Bart didn't appreciate the razzing he'd have to take from the other guys, if he ended getting stuck in a ditch or wound up wrecking the snowplow just because he got too careless.

So he eased up and took the job slow. Besides, he was getting paid lots of overtime. And the longer he took, the more overtime he got paid.

"More snow, more money. More snow, more money. What a great country," he chuckled to himself.

He eased the big truck down to about fifteen miles an hour. The fresh snow in front of the blade churned like an ocean wave encountering shallow surf. He imagined a swarm of miniature surfers with their tiny surfboards, coursing their way across the snowy wave just like he had seen on a southern California beach once on vacation.

A wide turn took him over a rise with a row of stately pine trees on both sides of the road.

"What the fuck is that?" Bart mumbled to himself through a mouth filled with a sticky gob of chewing tobacco.

A ball of light, glowing bright yellow, became visible on the horizon. From where he was, it looked like an explosion of some sort about a half-mile or so ahead of him, and a pretty big one from the looks of things.

Bart hunched over the steering wheel for a better look to see what was happening through the front windshield. It was hard for him to continue plowing at the same time, so he kept having to shift his attention between the road in front of him and the growing fire now off to his right side.

As he got closer, his view became even more difficult. Heavy forest lay between him and the blaze. Occasionally, he caught snatches of the fire through the narrow stands of hardwoods, but the impenetrable pines with their snow-laden boughs made it impossible to see anything further than a few yards off the roadway. Still, he could see the orange glow reflected in the night sky, so he knew he was headed in the right direction. If it was a fire, he might need to call in on the radio and report it to the authorities.

The truck took another broad turn, this time more in the direction of the fire. A small clearing came into view. Although dark outside, the combination of the snow and the radiance from the fire made things easy to see.

It looked like a building of some sort was burning, perhaps a barn or maybe even a house. It was hard to tell from as far as he was away. Several trees blazing along side the structure sent hot ashes spewing several hundred feet high into the crystal cold night sky. The heavens, sparkling with streamers of red, orange, and yellow cinders venting upward from the hot fire, reminded Bart of fireworks on the Forth of July.

Bart stomped on the brake pedal to avoid a collision with what appeared to be two flags suspended by a couple of boards, jutting out of the snow and stuck right in the middle of the highway. The big yellow truck skidded about ten feet and then came to an abrupt stop. He got out of the cab to take a better look at things. As he examined the flags, another tall evergreen near the building ignited like a pile of dry tender touched by a match. The tree blazed brilliantly as flames climbed to the top branches in red-hot licks of yellow and crimson.

"Damn,' he muttered under his breath. He stood transfixed, beholding both the beauty and horror unfolding in front of him. He spat a gooey gob of tobacco from his mouth, which landed on top the fresh snow, marring the pristine white surface with a swath of dark brown spittle.

Immediately, Bart considered either of two alternatives; reporting the fire on the radio or somehow driving the snowplow up toward the burning structure in case someone up there might need his help. He considered the two choices for a while, unable to make an easy decision, until he saw the silhouette a man, struggling in the shadows through the deep snow and headed down the slippery incline. Although still quite a distance away, the figure seemed to be dragging something quite heavy behind.

"Yo!" Bart yelled through cupped hands held to his lips. "Over here!" He raised his right arm up and waved, as if he was sitting in the indoor stadium at a Detroit Lions football game, trying to get the attention of a hot dog vendor. The engine of the snowplow sputtered behind him but kept right on idling.

The figure waved back. Bart stepped off the road into the deep snow and started walking up the slippery slope toward the fire.

* * *

Jimmy saw the driver of the snowplow signaling toward him. For the briefest of moments, he felt as if he and Sam had been saved. He waved back.

"Sammy, it's a snowplow," he announced between the puffs of his labored breathing. "Prettiest goddamn sight I've seen in a while." Pulling his precious two hundred and sixty pound payload through the heavy snowfall taxed Jimmy's stamina to the hilt.

Sam barely managed to respond. "Good, Jimmy. Good." Even speaking three short words hurt. He doubted if his brother could even hear him.

Jimmy slipped and fell for the tenth or fifteenth time; he wasn't keeping track. His legs just went out from under him. The textured soles on his boots were impacted with a thick layer of hardened snow and provided poor traction on the slippery surface. Immediately, he got up, regained a sure grip on the sleeping bag, and tugged the cargo along as hard as he could. Like a workhorse with blinders, pulling an oversized wagon, he trudged on valiantly. He managed to move Sam a few more yards down the incline until falling again. Covered in snow from the top of his union baseball cap down to his leather boots, Jimmy resembled a chubby snowman.

Jimmy saw the driver of the snowplow signaling toward him with his arms. Behind, the fire blazed. Thick black smoke and orange flames swallowed the caboose whole. Jimmy could still feel the heat on his back.

Then he saw them.

A neat row of beasts followed one another single file, running through some timber off to Jimmy's right side. The amazing creatures glided effortlessly over the snow, as if they could somehow magically fly around the natural barriers of trees and shrubs without the slightest impediment to their progress. There were more than a dozen of them, heading silently downhill toward the unsuspecting driver. Most likely, he hadn't seen them.

Jimmy froze a moment and watched the line of animals grow ever closer to the stranger. "Hey! Hey!" Yelling frantically, he waved both arms back and forth over his head. "Go back! Hey! Go back!"

Sam grumbled from behind him. "What's up, Jimmy? What's wrong?"

Jimmy didn't have any time to respond. He whirled around, grabbed the Winchester from Sam, and took a bead on the leader of the deadly pack.

* * *

Bart flinched at the sudden peel of gunfire. His shoulders jerked up automatically around his neck, as if someone had shot off a canon next to his ears. Bad memories of his own military experiences conjured in his dim mind. He stopped dead in his tracks.

"You crazy Yankee bastard," he yelled. Bart thought the figure in the snow some three hundreds yard in front of him was taking some pot shots at him. Out in the open with no way to defend himself, the big hillbilly felt vulnerable. His gun, which supposedly he wasn't allowed to carry with him on the job under strict orders directly from Frank Finnerdy, was back in the truck. Like most of the other county drivers, he always kept a weapon with him, tucked carefully away under the driver's seat, despite the foolish prohibition. No telling when a fella might need a gun to protect himself, and no two-bit, fat slob county supervisor would ever tell him different. A lot of good it did him now when he really needed the goddamned thing.

Several more shots rang out.

Bart winced, expecting bullets to rip through his flesh at any second, but nothing happened.

Just then, out of the corner of his eye, he saw the monsters charging toward him. They were huge beasts with massive heads and mouths dominated by row upon row of shark-like teeth...and they were coming toward him at a full speed. He realized that the bullets the stranger had fired had never been intended for him.

"Holy shit," he muttered, never having seen the likes of such monsters before in his life. Somehow, he realized the extreme danger he and the other two men faced.

The hillbilly raced back to the truck as fast as his fat legs would carry him. When he finally reached the passenger's side, he flung the door open with such vengeance it almost came loose from its hinges. His nervous hands grappled under the seat cushion, feverishly searching to free the weapon, which had managed to become wedged tightly under the springs. Finally, he pried the thing loose and pulled it out from under the seat. For just a moment, he examined his pride and joy; a fully loaded, semi-automatic M-16 military assault weapon, the same one he had stolen from the Tennessee National Guard in a brief and unsuccessful stint as a Spec Four grunt back some twenty years earlier. A small avalanche of metal-encased ammunition clips came tumbling out from under the seat as well. Bart grabbed several of the clips and shoved them into his coat pockets and then wheeled around quickly, his thumb flicking the switch on the side of the weapon to its fully automatic position.

He stepped back into the snow bank and raised the infantry assault weapon toward the approaching enemy.

For a moment, it felt like he was back home in the glorious south at a wild turkey hunt.

Two deadly bursts rattled forth from the muzzle in twelve-inch flames, hitting a couple of the lead monsters. The hapless beasts plummeted head first into a four-foot drift of powder and landed in a bloody explosion with snow and bits of flesh flying everywhere. The animals following could do nothing but collide with their fallen leaders and soon many of them were flaying madly about on the ground in the slippery snow, trying to regain their balance.

"Sons o' bitches!" Bart yelled. He spit a long stream of tobacco juice out the side of his stained lips, John Wayne style. "That'll teach you no-good, fuckin' Yankee varmints to mess with a good ol' boy from the hills of Tennessee."

Bart fired off a series of measured bursts toward the marauders. Even though dark, at his close range, he could see the effects of the .223 caliber bullets tearing through the flesh and bone and muscle of the creatures. Some of them bawled like cattle entering a slaughterhouse, while others managed to regain their footing and attempted to run off into the forest in apparent retreat. Bart, however, just kept shooting until the clip was emptied, which he soon replaced with another.

* * *

Jimmy and Sam watched the snowplow driver inflict a rain of lethal steel on the killer beasts from their location, about midway down the incline from the burning caboose. As if acting in prearranged tandem with their unintended savior who was armed with an automatic weapon, Jimmy kept shooting the Winchester in between the M-16's noisy bursts of fire until he finally ran out of ammunition. Soon, all that was left were the stinging clouds of blue smoke from their guns along with the downed and scattered remains of their beastly pursuers, lying bloody in the pristine snow. The rest had retreated back into the shelter of the forest.

Jimmy handed the Winchester to his brother, strengthened his hold on the sleeping bag, and started down the incline toward the driver.

The brothers reached Bart a few minutes later. "Damn, it's good to see you," Jimmy said, his eyes burning from the smoke, but glad to see another human being.

The huge hillbilly surveyed the dirty and tattered clothing on the pale man standing in front of him and the injured human cargo he carried with him cocooned in the middle of the sleeping bag. "What the hell's going on? What are those goddamn things?"

Another tree ignited near the caboose. As it did, the pupils of a hundred or so more killer creatures lurking in the far off timber reflected the brilliant yellow light of the blaze. The men did not fail to take notice.

"No time to explain, buddy." Jimmy grabbed the end of the sleeping bag and rolled it firmly around his forearm. "Those…things killed two of my buddies and damn near killed my brother. We gotta get outa here…fast."

Just then, two more groups of the monsters emerged from opposite corners of the forest. One of the beasts trumpeted an ear-shattering wail, which must have been a signal of some sort for the rest to attack. The two herds took up the chase and thundered toward the men.

"Help me," Jimmy pleaded, struggling to pull his brother in the waist-deep frozen snow to the idling snowplow still some thirty or forty yards away.

Rather than give Jimmy a hand, the huge snowplow driver simply reached down, picked Sam up and threw his two hundred and sixty pound frame over his left shoulder fireman style. Immediately, Bart started walking with long, certain strides back to the idling snowplow with Sam in one arm and the M-16 in the other. Jimmy tried his best just to stay even with the big man.

When they got to the truck, Bart carefully placed Sam inside the cab. With the beasts but seconds away, he grabbed hold of the material on Jimmy's coat in his massive hands, lifted him off the ground, threw him on the seat next to his ailing brother, and slammed the door closed.

"Now you boys just stay put in thar whilst I tend to things," he said to Jimmy through the closed window. Bart had a wry little smile etched across his unshaven face, the kind Jimmy recognized on a few of his old union buddies back in Flint, the ones who enjoyed an occasional bar fight every now and then.

Immediately, Bart turned and began firing at the beasts charging at him from both directions. He rattled off a series of short volleys every couple of seconds. He mowed the bloodthirsty creatures down one by one, the bullets from the automatic weapon blowing their limbs out from under them. At the same time, he went over to a large metal toolbox attached to the undercarriage of the plow. Among the tools, the burly fighter retrieved a double bladed ax with a long wooden handle. Armed with the ax and the M-16, he waded into the deep snow to confront his attackers head on. He looked like an angry marine yearning to scrap in hand-to-hand combat with his opponents.

The beasts kept coming, and Bart kept shooting. The ground in front of him became slick with blood and littered with the dead and squirming remains of those creatures unlucky enough to be still alive. Eventually, however, Bart inserted his last clip of ammunition. In a matter of seconds, the M-16 sputtered a loud but final rapport. Bart threw the useless weapon aside and grabbed the ax handle with both hands.

"You boys done picked on the wrong fella to mess with this morning," he yelled at the twenty or so creatures now circling around him. He wielded the ax high over his head, waiting for them to attack.

They came at him all at once.

Bart swung the ax with all his might and in the process managed to disable three of the creatures in one fell swoop. The ax blade lodged in the thick skull of a fourth. He yanked on the handle and managed to pry it loose, the brains on the creature spilled onto the cold snow. Bart kept swinging the ax at his relentless opponents like some crazed lumberjack gone crazy. Streaks of blood and guts were splattered across his front; sweat poured down from his forehead.

"Yeehaaa!" he yelled at the top of his lungs, his eyes bulging from their sockets. The blade came down again and again, as parts went flying in all directions.

* * *

Sam and Jimmy watched the bloody battle through the frosted windshield of the plow. Eventually, however, the valiant driver of the snowplow was overcome not by his lack of strength or courage, but by the sheer numbers of his opponents.

"Holy mother of God..." Jimmy whispered under his breath.

The hard skull on one of the creatures struck Bart dead center in the chest. The blow sent him tumbling in the air, head over heels, like a discarded toy rag doll thrown out of a moving train. The moment his body landed, the ravenous monsters were on him in a flash. Their sharp talons slit the man's throat cleanly from ear to ear, while other gaping mouths with gigantic teeth grabbed onto his limbs and literally tore him apart in mere seconds. So quickly did the killers butcher the man, that he never had time to emit a single scream.

Jimmy watched the bloody carnage unveil right before his own eyes. The Polock and the Dago had been torn apart in the same gory way.

Sam also witnessed the terrible tragedy. "Oh, my God," he kept saying under his breath over and over again, while clutching his aching chest. "Oh, my God."

After the brutal attack, the murderous creatures returned back to the woods as quickly and just as mysteriously had they first appeared, leaving the lifeless hump of the driver behind. Within seconds, they were gone. The eerie headlights on the truck shined on the motionless body of the fallen Samaritan.

"Maybe he's still alive," Sam said in the sudden stillness of the cab.

Jimmy knew no one could have survived such an attack, but he nodded just the same. "Yeah…maybe," his frosty breath billowed from his open mouth. He looked around, searching for any sign of the beasts. Seeing nothing, he twisted the handle to get out. The door popped open, letting some cold, fresh air tumble into the cab.

Jimmy grabbed the Winchester, knowing he had fired all the remaining rounds of ammunition, and opened the door wide. "Stay here, Sam. I'll check on…our friend."

Sam wheezed in pain but nodded to his brother to go ahead.

Jimmy stepped off the floorboard onto the snow. More than a quarter of a mile away, the fire still raged. He could hear the occasional popping of glass and other objects exploding, as the caboose succumbed finally to the flames. Several nearby white pines blossomed in fiery red as the blaze continued to spread.

Reluctantly, he walked over toward the body, which had landed some twenty feet or so in front of the plow. The remains consisted of a contorted heap of flesh with gaping wounds and massive bite marks scattered across what little was left of the man. Blood saturated the ground underneath and most of his limbs were missing, viciously torn from their sockets. The poor man's head hung limp off to one side where his throat had been slashed clear down to the vertebrae.

"Poor bastard...never had a chance," Jimmy remarked to himself. He had no doubt the driver of the snowplow was dead.

Along side the body, Jimmy noticed the man's wallet trampled into the ground. He reached down and flipped it open. A tattered Michigan's driver's license peeked out from one of the inside plastic flaps.

"Bart...Bart Bakersfield," Jimmy read aloud from the license by the glow of the truck's headlights. He sighed heavily as a sign of grief for the innocent stranger.

"Sorry...Bart," Jimmy said sincerely, looking directly into the vacant eyes.

Right next to the license was an old, faded photograph of the same man, standing beside a woman, most likely his wife. The picture might have been taken during some past holiday, with a Christmas tree and brightly wrapped presents in the background. Jimmy had a hard time looking at the happy couple.

Jimmy felt an urgency to get out of there. He glanced back at his brother who was slumped over in the seat of the snowplow. It was then, however, that Jimmy saw a large congregation of deer on the other side of the highway from where the truck was parked. He estimated that there had to be several hundred of them already gathered. Like locusts, they appeared to be emerging in droves from the out of the thick forest. The eyes of the entire herd seemed to be focused on him, as if he was being watched. For the time being, he forgot all about Bart Bakersfield.

He rose up and headed straight for the shining headlights on the truck, leaving the Winchester and the wallet on the ground behind him.

* * *

The ears on all the nervous deer flickered in the frigid night and then, suddenly, the stampede started. A cloud of white frozen powder lifted in their wake, a tidal wave of snow and ice. The frenzy began with the deep rumble of hooves pounding on the frozen ground that increased in intensity as hundreds of crazed deer charged toward Jimmy and the snowplow.

Jimmy's sore and tired leg muscles strained to carry himself the few remaining yards back to the relative safety of the plow. He could smell the welcome odor of exhaust fumes as he drew closer to the truck. Jimmy knew the predator beasts would soon follow in the wake of the frenzied deer. Visually, he scoured the wood line, searching for any sign of bloodthirsty hunters.

Finally, he reached the truck with only seconds before the first line of the deer swarmed the area. He flung the door open and jumped in, pulling the heavy door closed just as the initial wave of deer arrived. The center console contained an array of gearshifts and plow controls, which Jimmy had hardly any time to study before the first deer collided with the left front fender of the truck.

The creature's bony skull hit the hard metal surface.
Clunk!

It sounded as if huge chunk of cement had had been thrown from an overhead expressway overpass into the side of the truck. The collision left a sizable dent above the wheel-well about the size of a bowling ball. The impact left the animal a bit dazed at first, but after two or three seconds, the crazed animal recovered and scampered off toward the rest of the rampaging herd.

Soon, more deer collided with the truck. The terrified animals were running helter-skelter in absolute fear for their lives. Some of them rammed full speed into the vehicle, seemingly without regard for their lives or their own safety. The herd left scores of bumps and dents and gashes in the metal exterior of the bright yellow truck along with marks of their own bloody passage. Several of them took flight, trying to avoid a collision by soaring over the top, their hoofs rattling noisily across the hood and roof.

They came wave after wave, like armed soldiers assaulting enemy trenches. The glass in the window nearest Jimmy and the windshield soon shattered under the constant onslaught. A thick mat of spider webs formed across all the windows, making it almost impossible to see what was going on outside.

Frantically, Jimmy reached for the ignition. Forgetting the engine was already idling, he turned the key. The engine protested like a noisy coffee grinder and made such a terrible sound it caused his teeth to clinch together. He grabbed the gearshift knob, trying to find the correct gear, as his foot pounded feverishly on the floor, searching for the elusive clutch.

The cab lurched forward and then stopped dead, apparently flooded. Jimmy cranked the ignition again. The engine coughed and protested. Sam moaned beside him, slumped forward in the seat. Several more deer clambered over the roof of the cab, their noisy passage sounding like golf-ball hail plummeting down from the sky.

Then Jimmy heard something pop, soon followed by a slow hissing sound.

He managed to roll down the window far enough to see a large buck with its huge antlers entangled in the front tire. He realized that all the tires were in danger of being punctured unless they got out of there fast.

Just then, a number of the killer monsters came running out of the woods at full bore. They acted in perfect concert with one another, like a school of ravenous sharks, hunting in the depths of the deep blue ocean, herding the frightened deer in the direction toward the snowplow. Several of the creatures would circle around the outside perimeter of the fleeing herd of deer, squeezing them toward the center, where others of their kind would then pick off the stragglers or those unfortunate animals lagging behind. A bloody carnage would then ensue, as the beasts would make quick work of the prey in a gory feast that sickened Jimmy in the watching. The screams of hunters and the hunted grew louder as the line of killing approached.

Jimmy ratcheted the ignition key again. The engine sputtered back to life, coughing like a sick old man. Jimmy threw the transmission into first gear, popped the clutch, and pounced on the accelerator.

The tires on the truck spun against the slick pavement. The truck began moving slowly forward, mere inches at first, at only two or three miles per hour as deer by the hundreds continued to rush by. A young doe bashed into Jimmy's driver side window, shattering the thick pane and sending a cascade of glass all over Jimmy and the front seat. Jimmy looked out the gaping hole. Another whole wave of deer charged from the left. Abruptly, he spun the steering wheel so that the massive blade on the front of the plow would face the assault. Although he could not see them crashing into the blade, he could hear their fleshy collisions against the immovable metal object. The tattered, but still intact windshield became spattered with thickened gobs of blood and slather.

Jimmy manhandled the steering wheel as if he was at the helm of a huge ocean liner. The truck gradually turned back around toward the direction from which it had come. Jimmy worried about getting stuck in the snow off the road, but somehow the truck made it through and returned to the original path on the narrow highway, which Bart Bakersfield had plowed just minutes earlier.

The deer had smashed both headlights on the truck early on in the attack, so Jimmy had to navigate the big rig in complete darkness through a shattered windshield. Wave upon wave of the marauding creatures continued to crash into them. Jimmy's eyes strained trying to determine the actual course of the road. On several occasions, the fat waffle tires on the truck ventured off the road and further slowed their progress. Jimmy fought with the steering wheel, trying to keep the vehicle on course. Besides the constant collisions with the deer, the plow blade managed to take out a fair number of trees and saplings along the way.

One of the monsters managed to catch up to the fleeing vehicle. The fleet-footed creature ran along side the truck, easily outmatching it in speed and maneuverability. Jimmy watched the beast through the smashed window on his side of the truck so that he could see the monster quite clearly. The thing was all teeth and claws, built purely to hunt and to kill. He pulled the pistol from his belt and began shooting at the agile creature. Jimmy felt a little like he was in some sort of weird Hollywood movie scene, taking pot shots out the window while being chased by some cowboy bad guys. Jimmy's aim, however, proved to be quite poor, considering he barely could drive the truck let alone point the gun with any sort of accuracy. After a half dozen unsuccessful shots, Jimmy had expended all the ammunition and his intended target continued on it murderous path unharmed.

In the meantime, a strong wind had suddenly come up as well, hurtling icy plumes of powder across the roadway and making it even more difficult to see. To his left, out through the broken driver's side window, a blinding wall of windswept snow obscured the burning caboose on the receding horizon. In a matter of seconds, the sea of brown and tan deer was engulfed by the blizzard blowing all around them.

Jimmy looked over to the beast running along side of the truck that was in the process of tearing into the flanks of a frightened fawn. He watched the poor creature succumb to the ravenous bites of its pursuer through the shattered rearview mirror mounted on the side of the truck.

And then they were gone.

Jimmy couldn't see a thing outside any of the windows. The total whiteout erased everything within eyesight. He had no idea where or in what direction the truck was headed. It seemed as if the truck and everything inside had been sucked up into the swirling vortex of a tornado filled with millions upon millions of tiny white bits of confetti.

Chapter Nine

Bury your dead
For enough has been said
And look to tomorrow for better days ahead
Old English Poem

The black box squawked mostly with static inside the cab of the snowplow as the swirling snow gradually tapered off outside. The engine whined in second gear, the needle on the R.P.M gauge on the instrument panel pushed into the red zone. The lights on the panel cast a soft orange glow in the interior cab of the truck.

Jimmy shifted gears and took his foot off the gas pedal. Knuckles white, his fingers loosed their grip on the steering wheel. He listened for the electric static again, letting his ears lead his eyes. A braided black cord swayed gently to and fro on the dashboard from a black box with several dials and switches to a small handheld microphone the shape of a hockey puck, hanging along the side. Jimmy's right hand fumbled for the object as he tried to steer the vehicle down the center of the highway. A visible line of dark asphalt marked the way.

He depressed the little button along side the microphone with his index finger and brought the thing up to his lips.

"Hey…is anyone there?"

He released the button and looked toward the small black box, as if waiting for the thing to talk back to him.

He tried again. "Hello…can anybody hear me?"

Jimmy shifted into fourth gear. The orange needle on the speedometer inched toward the number thirty. A thin swath of clouds marked the night horizon directly to Jimmy's front. He wondered which direction they were headed.

"Anybody! Is anybody there?"

A jolt of static blasted out the speaker as if hit by a bolt of lightening, and then a voice. "Bakersfield, you lazy turd, is that you?" Where the hell've you been?"

The sound of another human's voice brought a feeling of hope to Jimmy.

"No…no. This is…my name's Roland…Jimmy Roland!"

There followed a brief pause as Jimmy waited for another response.

"Say, Roland, or whatever the hell your name is, you are transmitting on a restricted channel reserved for county road emergencies only. You have no business using it for normal communications. Now get off, pronto, or you'll be in violation of the law."

Jimmy shook his head as if the person talking could see him. "No, you don't understand," he said, trying to gather his thoughts and speak as clearly as possible. "There's been…an accident. People are hurt. We need help." He glanced over toward the passenger's seat next to him at Sam who looked pale and still. Then he said, "Over," to indicate that he had finished speaking. Jimmy had used walkie-talkies a couple of times in the service, but he was by no means an expert.

"Repeat. Say that again. Over." The voice on the other end of the line crackled with more static as the snowplow drove through a narrow draw with hills and thick forestation on both sides.

Jimmy waited a few seconds for the truck to clear the low spot. "I'm driving a snowplow…headed east, as best I can tell. I have a man who is seriously injured. We need help. Over."

"Okay, Roland. This is Frank Finnerdy, county road supervisor in Newberry. Some kind of accident you say? Where are you at exactly, your location…and where's my driver?"

Jimmy thought quickly. For some reason, he didn't think now was the right time to tell about the dead driver. There would be too much to explain. Besides, he was afraid the monster creatures might return and more concerned about Sam right then.

He keyed the mike. "I'm not sure where the hell we are. We're on a narrow, two-lane highway out in the middle of nowhere. We were up here deer hunting from downstate and got lost in the snowstorm. My brother's hurt real bad. He's got a chest wound, bleeding like hell. Your driver," Jimmy tried remembering his name, "Bart…something or other…stopped to help us, but he got hurt too. We had to leave him back where he found us. We need help! Over."

"Roland, you hold on. I'll be right back to you. I gotta figure out where the fuck you are. But stay on the line. Out."

Jimmy replaced the microphone back onto the dashboard. The near blizzard conditions, which they experienced just several miles earlier, had vanished mysteriously. The sky had cleared. Despite the shattered windshield, he could see well enough to steer the truck down the narrow corridor Bart Bakersfield had plowed earlier. At least six to seven feet of snow was mound up along either side of the highway. Jimmy glanced to the front and sides and then in the rearview mirror, looking for any signs of the stampeding herd of deer and their hunters. He saw nothing.

He turned his attention to his brother. "Sam…Sam. Are you alright?"

Sam grimaced a smile.

"Hold on, buddy," Jimmy said. "Hold on."

He nudged the speed up another notch. Any faster and he worried they would slid off the slippery road. Jimmy patted his coat pockets, quite unconsciously searching for a cigarette. He fingers found an empty box in one of the pockets. He sighed in resignation.

"Roland, are you there? Over." The box squawked again.

Jimmy grabbed the mike. "Yeah, we're still here. Over."

"If you're where I think you are, you're about twenty miles north of Newberry on Highway 453. You should be looping down in our general direction some time soon."

Jimmy noticed the road had been gradually turning in a different direction for some time.

Frank Finnerdy continued. "I called the sheriff's office too. He said they'd send a car out right away to see if they can find you and give some assistance. Now that highway you're on is gonna dead end into another road some ten miles west of here. Keep a sharp look out cause the turn's kinda sharp and tricky. Should be a sign pointing toward the middle of town somewhere there. Most of them roads should be plowed by now, especially if Bakersfield done what he was supposed to. We'll have an ambulance waiting for you when you get here. No use sending them out to meet you in case I have you spotted on the wrong highway. How's that injured man doing?"

"He's okay," Jimmy replied, but worried. "He needs a doctor real bad."

Frank had more questions, but Jimmy held off answering them directly. He knew there was too much to explain, and so much he could not. After signing off from his radio conversation with the county road supervisor, Jimmy drove as fast as he could towards town.

Thirty minutes later on the outskirts of Newberry, they encountered flashing lights on what appeared to be a county pickup truck with a snowmobile loaded in the back end. The sheriff along with his young deputy were standing in the middle of the road, waving their arms, as Jimmy pulled the snowplow to a complete stop.

Sheriff Svenson as wearing winter jacket made out of a slippery green material with a warm fleece collar pulled tightly around his neck. On top of his gray head, he had one of those world war two bombardier hats on with floppy earmuffs jutting out the sides and a shiny silver sheriff's badge pinned on the front. The combination of his hat and grizzled face gave him the look of a forlorn schnauzer with newly clipped ears. The sheriff immediately noticed the extensive damage on the county snowplow. It reminded him of the Pearson's abandoned Ford they had found a few days ago. He came over to the driver's side window and spoke to Jimmy through the plate of fractured glass.

"Vat the hell happened to the truck, by golly?" he asked.

Jimmy failed to notice the sheriff's Norwegian accent. "Sheriff, I don't have time to explain," he said, out of breath. "It's my brother. He's needs a doctor right away."

The sheriff jumped up on the floorboard and poked his head through the broken window, examining the injured passenger on the other side of Jimmy. White as a ghost, Sam was sitting upright and holding his chest. Blood dribbled down both his hands and dripped on his lap. It was obvious the man needed medical attention immediately

"Freddy!" the sheriff yelled down to his deputy, Freddy Haizer.

"Yeah, sheriff."

"Get over on the other side and get in. You need to help these two fellas get into town right avay."

Freddy hustled over as the sheriff instructed. He opened the door and squeezed beside Sam. His horrified facial expression betrayed his youthful inexperience. He couldn't take his eyes off of Sam's bloody wound.

The sheriff turned his attention briefly back to Jimmy. "Vat happened to your buddy over there?" he asked. "And vhere's the driver of this here truck?"

Jimmy knew the sheriff deserved an explanation, so he tried offering one as briefly as possible. "Sheriff, some kind of...animals attacked us. Got my brother there and a couple of my buddies, too."

A light went off in the Ollie's head. "Say, are you that fella from Flint up here hunting with three of your buddies?"

Jimmy looked surprised. "Yeah. How'd you know about us?"

"Your vife reported you fellas missing. Ve sorta been on the lookout for you," the sheriff said. "You say some kinda animals attacked you fellas?" Ollie asked, his curiosity suddenly perked.

"Yeah," Jimmy said, anxious to get on their way. "About twenty miles north of here. We got stranded in an old railroad caboose when," he hesitated again, "...these animals attacked us. They got the driver of the snowplow, too. He's still up there. I think he's dead though." Jimmy was afraid the sheriff would arrest him on the spot, considering the unbelievable tale he had just related.

"Yah, I know the place you're talking about. Miners and lumberjacks used to stay there thirty, forty years ago. Been abandoned mostly since then." Sheriff Svenson mulled over Jimmy's explanation. "Now there, Freddy. Take these fellas up ahead a couple more miles. There's an ambulance vaiting over by Frank Finnerdy's office. They'll know vat to do," the sheriff instructed. He looked at the driver a little closer and noticed the blackened skin on Jimmy's ears and the tip of his nose caused by frostbite. "Looks like you could use a little help over there too, Mister."

"Where're you goin', sheriff?" Freddy asked with a pair of wide eyes.

"I'll go see if can find old Bart Bakersfield," the sheriff announced.

Jimmy grabbed hold of his arm. "You can't do that, sheriff! Them…animals are still up there. They killed three people already and a mess of deer too."

Ollie saw the fear in Jimmy's eyes. At the same time, he thought about the remains of the dead woman from Kalamazoo they found just days ago in the same vicinity and all the other missing people he had been investigating.

"That's okay, Mister…Roland, ain't it?"

Jimmy nodded.

"You and your brother go get patched up. Freddy there will help you. Right, Freddy?"

The young deputy nodded, but obviously very unsure of himself.

Ollie turned his attention back to Jimmy one more time. "Yah, thanks for the varning," he said. "But stuff like this comes vith the job."

Jimmy understood.

"Now get on your vay, fellas." He jumped off the floorboard into the freshly plowed street.

Jimmy put the truck in gear and started to pull forward. "Thanks sheriff," he said, as the back wheels to the truck spun before finally taking hold.

The taillights on the snowplow with the three men inside disappeared around the corner as sheriff Svenson opened the door on the pickup. He pulled two double barrel shotguns off the gun rack on the back window, threw them on the passenger seat next to him, and then headed north on highway 453 in the direction that the snowplow had just come from.

* * *

The Ford heavy-duty pickup had no trouble negotiating its way up Highway 453. Even when sheriff Svenson encountered the area where tornado winds swirled in a blinding blizzard around Jimmy in the snowplow only an hour or so earlier, the huge snow tires on the Luce County pickup truck made short work of the half foot of fresh snow. Ollie knew he was close to the area that Jimmy had briefly described when he saw the unmistakable orange glow of a fire on the horizon. A quarter of a mile later, he encountered some rags tacked on to the ends of a couple of two-by-fours, blocking the center of the road. The highway had not been plowed past that point. He suspected Bart Bakersfield had never gotten any further than right there.

He stopped the pickup and got out. A quarter of a mile on top of a steep hill, a fire still smoldered. Otherwise the countryside and the surrounding forest rested peacefully, covered in a blanket of deep snow. There was a faint odor of burnt wood wafting in the air.

Ollie was anxious to investigate. He didn't know exactly what he was looking for, but there were several men reputed to be dead or seriously injured and a fire he knew nothing about. There was also the matter of the dead woman he and Freddy had found not more then six or seven miles from this very location, and all those people who had been reported missing over the course of the past twenty-five years. The way Ollie figured, all these things might somehow be related to one another.

He went over to the back of the pickup, lowered the tailgate, and pulled out two long runners in order to remove the snowmobile loaded in the backend. The loud prattle of the engine on the snowmobile disturbed the quiet solitude of the whole place the minute Ollie turned the key. Carefully, he backed down the steep ramp. Before heading out toward the fire, he made sure to retrieve both shotguns from the passenger side of the pickup. He placed the guns in a rack along side of the snowmobile, lowered his earmuffs tightly over his ears, and mounted himself comfortably on the cold leather seat. The fiberglass frontrunners on the machine lurched forward into the deep snow the minute he engaged the gears.

On his way toward the crest of the hill, he looked around, as best he could, considering the darkness, for any signs of the missing men or the struggle that Jimmy had briefly described to him. Everything appeared quite ordinary, other than the flags in the middle of the roadway he had first encountered and the fire burning to his front. On his brief journey up toward the fire, Ollie saw nothing of the missing Bart Bakersfield or anything resembling large wild animals Jimmy Roland had talked about. Quite the contrary, the area around him appeared undisturbed and completely void of a single living thing.

He reached the dying flames of what little remained of the caboose a couple of minutes later. The place had been completely destroyed and whatever trees or bushes grew within a fifty-foot radius of the structure lay in charred ruins. The intense heat had melted all the snow, so the area looked like a huge black scab on an otherwise pristine landscape. What was left of the fire posed no danger of spreading to other areas and would extinguish itself eventually in a matter of hours on its own.

With shotgun in hand, Ollie got off the snowmobile and examined the location on foot. A large foot long aluminum flashlight lit his way around the smoky remnants of the now destroyed railroad car. The steel undercarriage and rusted wheels appeared to be about all that had survived. A coating of thick, black soot covered the ground and the stumps of burnt trees, some of them still slowly being eaten by small fires at their base. Nothing else was recognizable and probably wouldn't be until a full inspection of the place could be made during daylight hours.

The sheriff poked around the area for ten or fifteen minutes but found nothing; no evidence of any bodies or any indication that anyone had even been there recently. The place seemed completely deserted. He began to get the impression that the fellow whom he had met driving Bakersfield's snowplow was some kind of crazy nut or had been drinking too much. That, however, didn't explain why Bart Bakersfield was missing or how the man's brother got injured so badly.

Ollie shook his head, frustrated and in dire need of answers. He got back on the snowmobile and headed back toward the pickup.

As the sheriff came around the front end of the pickup, the bobbing headlight on the snowmobile fell upon an object gleaming brightly in the snow. Drawn to his attention, Ollie drove along side the object and scooped it up out of the deep drift of snow in one crisp motion. It was a Winchester rifle. Lying next to it was a leather wallet.

He had no idea where the weapon had come from or how it got there. The gun had no ammunition in it as well, although the fresh smell of gunpowder coming from the barrel indicated it had been fired recently. He opened the wallet and soon discovered pictures of Bart Bakersfield and his wife, Doris, along with the usual other pieces of identification inside.

Ollie placed the wallet safely in the inside pocket of his coat and brought the Winchester with him. After securing the snowmobile in the back end of the truck, he took one last look around the area on foot. Seeing nothing, he climbed back into the pickup and started the engine.

Just as he did, Ollie caught the flash of something very large and covered in thick brown fur out of the corner of his left eye. A huge paw studded with long claws scraped against the side window right next to his face while almost breaking the glass in the process. A huge mouth filled with an array of sharp teeth gave out a deep roar, shattering the quiet solitude.

"Holy smokes!" Startled, Ollie applied his full weight to the accelerator pedal.

The pickup with its big snow tires and deep treads jumped ahead, immediately knocking down the makeshift barrier of flags and the would-be intruder aside in the process. A couple of seconds later, Ollie then brought the truck to a quick stop. He grabbed one of the shotguns, threw the door open, jumped out, and aimed both barrels at the furry mound laying some twenty-five feet in the middle of the road behind him. His finger pressed against the trigger ready to fire.

The creature rose up on its hind legs and protested what had happened to it with another loud roar, while waving its big furry front paws up in the air. Ollie lowered the shotgun. It had been at least fifteen years since he had seen a black bear in Luce County the size of the one that stood in front of him.

* * *

Jimmy ended up in a small hospital right on Main Street Newberry for a brief stay. He suffered a slight concussion, a couple of minor cuts and bruises, and frostbite on his toes, ears, and parts of his face. Brenda drove up from Flint the day after he called her on the telephone to explain what happened.

Sam had to be transported to the big regional hospital down in Escanaba, his injuries being more serious. Besides having several broken bones and multiple contusions, he had received a life-threatening chest injury that had penetrated his ribcage and narrowly missed severing his aorta. He required an emergency operation to sew him back together and four transfusions of blood. A day or so after his surgery, Jimmy kept the promise he made to his brother back in the caboose. He sent him over a big, juicy sixteen-ounce sirloin steak with mashed potatoes, corn, and a slice of apple pie from a local restaurant. Unfortunately,

Sam was in no condition to eat such a grand dinner. Nevertheless, the meal made him smile for the first time in at least a week.

"At least he'll live," Jimmy remarked to Brenda, tending to his care that first couple of days in the hospital. "Can't say the same for Tom or Tony or that poor bastard in the snowplow." Tears welled in his eyes.

The questions for Jimmy began almost immediately. The authorities, the county sheriff and the state patrol, were most interested in the fate of the three missing men, Bart Bakersfield, Tony Gianinni, and Tom Karrski. Even before Jimmy recovered, a search party was sent out to reconnoiter the area where Jimmy claimed everything happened. After the first day, they found the crashed wreckage of the WindStar and conducted a more detailed search of the smoldering ruins around the railroad caboose. They found nothing of the three missing men. Because of limited manpower and the deep snow, which made overland travel almost impossible, further investigation was delayed until Jimmy could accompany the authorities and lead them to the exact location where the men had died.

Several days later found Jimmy sitting in the back seat of sheriff Ollie Svenson's tan Buick cruiser, traveling north on Highway 453. "So you were meaning to go deer hunting with your buddies?" he asked, laced with his Norwegian accent.

"Yeah," Jimmy answered, nervous. "Four of us, up from Flint." He didn't bother to mention his brother lived in Port Huron. "Mind if I have a smoke?" One of the first things Jimmy did upon he return to civilization was to buy a pack of cigarettes.

Ollie shook his head. "Nah, you better not. Smokin's not allowed in public places here in the county, including in the car. Besides, the missus don't like the smoky smell on me neither."

Jimmy huffed in frustration.

They were driving on the last stretch of highway Bart Bakersfield had plowed in his life. Since that time, additional county road crews had cleared both lanes along the narrow roadway. For the first time, Jimmy could actually see the countryside without darkness or a blizzard interfering with the view passing outside the windows. Ten miles outside of town, they hit sheer forest for the most part, with little or no signs of civilization. The blizzard of four or five days ago had left a mantle of heavy snow ranging from three to four feet in depth in every direction.

They rounded a sharp turn and came to a stop.

"Down there's is where we found your motor home you fellas was driving in." The sheriff pointed down a long ravine that stretched for over a quarter of a mile before disappearing in a row of twenty-foot white pines.

Jimmy stretched his neck, trying to see.

"You can't see it much from here," the sheriff added. "It's further around the bend down there, a couple of hundred yards. Yah, one of the state troopers saw the vehicle from up top, searching from the helicopter. Be next spring, until the snow good and melts, before we can really get at her and do a complete search. Then we'll get down there soon as we can, that's for sure."

"How far is it from here to the railroad car where we were hold up?" Jimmy asked.

"Well, if you're meaning that old burned out caboose…close to nine, ten miles, as the crow flies. That's where we're headed." The sheriff started to back the patrol car up. He looked at Jimmy through the spaces between the mesh of the wire cage separating them. A pair of dark green sunglasses hid the officer's eyes.

Jimmy felt like he was being watched. He realized how bizarre his explanation of the incidents must have sounded to everyone he had told. And he had related the fantastic story to many people including the sheriff, his deputies, several state patrol troopers, Frank Finnerdy and a couple of his drivers from the county garage, Brenda,

Sam's wife, Doris, and several doctors and nurses at the hospital in Newberry. As they drove along, Jimmy looked for anything familiar along the way. He tried finding the location where they had left Tom Karrski's body, cocooned in the limbs of a large tree, but he recognized nothing.

"So you and the others did this on foot, did you?"

"Yeah," Jimmy nodded. "During the blizzard...at night, most of the time."

"Near as we can figure, you must've got lost somehow from the main road here. You might accidentally have got off on Harper's Road. It jigs off about a half mile up here, just as the highway turns. Easy to do, especially if you don't know your way around these parts."

"Harper's Road? Where does it go?"

The sheriff grinned. "Basically, both roads end up in the same place. Harper's Road is an old logging road when this area got lumbered out over fifty years ago. Now, most everybody uses the main highway. Harper's road swings back to the highway eventually, just takes you twice as long and double the distance. Yah, if you fellas went that way, you pretty darn near walked fifteen or twenty extra miles before finding that caboose. Lucky you did. You and your brother could've froze to death otherwise."

A flood of memories flashed through Jimmy's mind; the terrible accident in the blinding snowstorm, days of trudging through waist deep drifts, the bloodied bodies of Tom and Tony. He could still hardly believe what happened.

They drove for about fifteen minutes more with few words spoken between them; the sheriff driving in front, with Jimmy seated in the back seat, and a security cage separating the two men from one another. Pretty soon, Jimmy saw a dark smudge on the bleak snowy horizon that marked the ruins of the caboose. The patrol car glided to a stop exactly where Bart Bakersfield's snowplow had parked that fateful night. Jimmy noticed the two signal flags that he had managed to place in the middle of the road were gone. The two men got out of the car.

Immediately, Jimmy noticed numerous footprints in the snow, but they were likely those belonging to the sheriff or state patrol's investigative team who had examined the site earlier, looking for clues. There were no signs of the stampeding herds of deer that had trampled across the area or the beasts that hunted them in their murderous rampage. The slate had been wiped clean. The strong winds that Jimmy had encountered as he fled the site in the snowplow had erased any memory or signs of what had happened there. The place looked unusually peaceful and utterly quiet.

"So this is where everything happened you suppose?" Sheriff Svenson squinted in the bright morning sunlight through his sunglasses, causing the crow's feet on both sides of his eyes to bulge out prominently on his reddened face.

Jimmy surveyed the scene. "Yeah," he said, not really hearing the sheriff's question and hesitating as if unsure of himself. "You didn't find anything around here, sheriff?" he asked.

Ollie arched his eyebrows. "No…was we supposed to, Mister Roland?"

Again, Jimmy looked confused. When he answered, it was more like he was muttering to himself. "I don't understand. There were…hundreds of deer…right here. Then those things came out of the forest, across the road over there, and killed at least twenty or thirty deer. I saw it with my own eyes."

"Like I said, Mister Roland, we didn't see nothing like that." Ollie was more anxious to get Jimmy to talk about the men who were missing. "Tell me a little more about what happened that night."

"Well…that's the caboose where we holed up a couple of nights, up that-a-ways." He pointed toward the charred area about a quarter-mile across a snowy incline from where they were standing. "At least what used to be the caboose. After the fire started and Tony, my friend, got killed, I hauled my brother down through that draw over there...toward the highway here. That's when we saw the snowplow driver coming up toward us. He helped me get Sam down the rest of the way and then he went after those things with an M-16 until he ran out of ammunition and they killed him. Me my brother barely got away after that."

The sheriff listened with obvious skepticism scrawled across his face. He knew Bart Bakersfield for years and had never seen him with an M-16. But then Bart wouldn't be the first man to hide a weapon from the law.

Jimmy shook his head in disbelief. "I don't see a goddamn thing though. It's almost like nothing happened here by the looks of things. This place was a mess the last time I seen it. I don't understand."

Ollie scratched an itch on his neck. "Think you can point out where the driver and your buddy got..., he struggled for the appropriate word, "... got killed maybe? Me and my deputies been looking all around here quite a bit over the last couple of days and we haven't come up with much."

"You haven't been able to find...them yet?" Jimmy found it difficult to accept the fact of their deaths.

"Yah. Nope, can't say as we have," sheriff Svenson replied.

"Hell," Jimmy said, in growing disbelief. "The driver got whacked no more than ten or fifteen yards from here...just a little way up from where we're parked." He indicated an unmarked location in the snowfield stretching before them.

"Well, Mister Roland, why don't you show me exactly where this so-called attack took place?"

Jimmy didn't miss the sarcasm in the sheriff's voice. "Sure. Follow me." He waded into the deep snow, anxious to prove himself.

They stopped at the general location where Bart Bakersfield had been attacked. Jimmy tramped around the area looking for some sign of the man's massacre. After several frustrating minutes of flattening out the snow and digging around by hand, Jimmy came up empty handed. He stopped, confounded. "It...it was right around here...I'm sure..." Jimmy's voice trailed off. He searched the ground looking for deer prints or blood or something, anything.

"Maybe it happened a little further up...or more to the left of here. With all this snow, everything looks the same you know."

"No," Jimmy insisted. "I'm positive it was right around here. There was a lot of blood and stuff...and his wallet. When I left, I forgot to pick up your driver's wallet. That's how I knew your driver's name, cause I seen it on his drivers license in his wallet. Your deputies found nothing?"

"Yah, I found the driver's wallet. It was sitting right next to that rifle of yours, laying in the snow. I found it the first night I seen you, but there was nothing else around here. No sign of Bakersfield though...or anything else for that matter. Oh, we found the caboose, just like you said, destroyed by the fire. Only thing left now is a pile of burned wood and stuff. We didn't see anything else, not the body of your Italian friend you say got killed either."

"Tony Gianinni."

"Yah, him. Tony...whatever. We found the flags you put up on the highway just like you say you did, but we haven't found anything else, that's for sure."

Jimmy glanced around the ground and surrounding forest looking for answers.

"So where's old Bart Bakersfield's dead body and your friend's, do you suppose?" the sheriff asked.

Jimmy considered his question briefly. "I don't know," he said. "I don't know."

Just then a doe emerged from behind some white pines off to their right side. The small female took notice of them, hesitated a moment, and then hustled back into the forest with its brown and white tail flicking in nervous gesture.

"Think that's one of them super animals you been talking about, Mister Roland?" Sheriff Svenson remarked his head cocked slightly. "If that ain't one of the craziest things I done ever heard."

The expression stretched across the sheriff's face made Jimmy question his own sanity and what, if anything, had really happened. It also mad him angry. He couldn't help but think about Tom Karrski, Tony Gianinni, and the Good Samaritan snowplow driver…all of them dead, lying somewhere in the snow. If only he knew where.

Jimmy had just about had it. "I'm not crazy," he said. "There are three men missing. Just what do you think might have happened? Are you accusing me of killing them or something?"

Ollie suddenly realized he gotten a little too rough on a man who had been through quite a bit of adversity himself. He was just interested in finding plausible answers to many of the strange things that had been happening in his neck of the woods. He wanted some answers too, and he wasn't finding any.

"No, Mister Roland, I don't think you killed nobody. Maybe you fellas got to drinking too much and don't remember so good. We also been seeing a lot of black bears in this area, something we haven't seen around these parts for a good many years."

"Bears?" Jimmy had an incredulous expression on his face.

"Yah. Over the past two days we seen three or four of them. One tried to attack me that night when I come over here. Them bears can be mighty dangerous. They can kill a man real easy if they feel threatened or they got cubs. They're fast too; they can out run a man real easy. Maybe that's what happened to those three fellas. You know in the dark when it's snowing, it's kinda hard to see things clearly. Likewise, you was hungry and cold. Maybe you just thought you saw something else. A mind can play tricks on a fella, especially if you're hurt or starving for food."

"I don't know sheriff," Jimmy said, still unconvinced. "I know what I saw and what happened to those men and it wasn't a bear that killed 'em."

Jimmy put his cold hands into his coat pockets to warm them up. The frostbitten fingers on his right hand brushed against something smooth and hard. He pulled the object out and examined it carefully. It was the six-inch long talon that Tony had carved off the animal they had collided with in the WindStar mobile home that first fateful night.

Jimmy handed the talon to Ollie.

"What the hell is this?"

"You tell me," Jimmy answered. "But whatever kind of animal that came from is what killed my two friends and your snowplow driver."

Sheriff Svenson didn't know what to say, the wheels in his head were spinning around too fast. The talon looked exactly like it might match some of the holes in the tracks he had observed at the site where he and his deputy Freddy had examined just days earlier, the site where the remains of Valerie Pearson had been discovered. He was anxious to get back to his office and see if the strange artifact might fit in with any of the other cases he had been investigating as well. Still, he would have preferred finding at least one of the bodies of the missing men. He had no doubts they were all dead, but he hadn't a clue as to their exact fates.

* * *

A fat row of lilac bushes, growing inside the mile long fence in Woodlawn Cemetery, was in full bloom, awash in deep purple and lavender. Spring had come late to Flint, it being the middle of May and the weather just beginning to warm up. The morning sun streamed in through Jimmy's rear truck window as he made his way westward on Bristol Road toward work. The usual clutter of traffic didn't bother Jimmy like it used to. He drove the speed limit, staying in the right hand lane most of the time, while faster drivers more in a hurry whizzed past him on the left.

He was on schedule this morning, like he had been every day for the past four months. He took his time, feeling no need to rush. He hadn't smoked a cigarette since before New Years, nor had he had a beer for the past two or three months. Those things just didn't seem as important as they used to be.

When he punched in at the G.M. Powertrain Assembly Plant, Jimmy was ten minutes early. He went straight to the pop machine, as usual, and deposited eighty-five cents in exact change. The price of his morning Coca Cola had gone up by ten cents since last March, despite the threat of a plant wide strike by union representatives who opposed such an increase imposed on their membership. He grabbed his windbreaker and his dented lunch pail, with a banana and a baloney sandwich Brenda had made inside, and headed toward the fuel injector assembly line. A variety of machines and robots coughed and spat and sputtered as he passed along the noisy corridor, Jimmy not really paying attention to them at all.

"Mornin' Jimmy boy."

"Hey, Rodman."

"Not like you to be early, Roland."

The usual chorus of morning greetings followed him down the line. Jimmy didn't answer to them like he used to; he just kept heading down the line, lost in his own thoughts, minding his own business.

He walked straight to his locker, put his things inside, and gathered up his tool belt. He started toward the two large workbenches where about a dozen fuel injector assemblies awaited his final inspection. On his way there, he glanced over toward the empty spot on the moving assembly line where the Dago, Tony Gianinni, used to work. Jimmy bit down on his lower lip, looking at the empty hole. They still hadn't hire a replacement for him and probably wouldn't, just another way for the company to save money.

Just as he put the tool belt down on one of the workbenches, Jimmy noticed a crude picture scrawled all across the top. The hand drawing, done in bright white chalk, depicted the head of a deer with its big eyes crossed like some dopey cartoon character. The silly looking beast had a pair of long fangs sticking out of its mouth with what looked like blood dripping from the sharp tips. Shreds of torn clothing were hanging from its long antlers.

"Obviously, some idiot's idea of a sick joke," Jimmy thought.

He took an oily rag out from one of the drawers and proceeded to erase the ill attempt at humor that he considered in the poorest of taste.

"Asshole!" he muttered to himself, wondering which one of his stupid union buddies was responsible for such cruel gesture. He looked around to see if he could identify the culprit, perhaps some jerk off snickering to the side or just someone with a silly smirk on their face. All of his coworkers along the noisy assembly line, however, seemed totally occupied with their normal work. It could have been any one of them.

Jimmy had just about had his fill with all the usual antics on the assembly line. For the first time in his life, he began to ask questions he had never thought about before. He even considered leaving his job at General Motors. He had heard through the grapevine that one of the new grocery store chains in town was looking for new people. And except for the fact they were a non-union shop, Jimmy would not have hesitated. Jimmy had always been a union man, just like his dad and granddad before him.

It was going to be a long, ordinary day on the assembly line.

THE END